between the lines

(between the lines #1)

by

tammara webber

Cover Image used under license from Shutterstock.com
Copyright © Milos Stojanovic, 2011
Cover design by Stephanie Mooney
Additional cover design by David Creagh

ISBN: 978-0-9835931-6-4

Dedicated to Paul:
fearless romantic boy turned loving husband,
dream-catcher, hand-holder, coffee-bringer,
partner in crime and punishment and domestic bliss
both real and imagined.

Chapter 1

REID

"You live with your *parents?*"

If you're a celebrity and over twelve, people don't expect you to live with your parents, if they even imagine that you *have* parents. Movie stars are believed to spring fully formed into apartment-acquiring adulthood. Older girls are the worst offenders when it comes to these expectations of independence, and the one leaning against me now is no different.

Her question is whispered in response to me shushing her as I'm trying to fit the key in the lock and get the two of us into the house and into my room without any interference. Now she's giggling, both hands over her mouth, muffling the sound—though maybe I can't hear her because my ears are still ringing from the concert in which she was on stage with an electric bass in her skilled hands while I watched from the VIP section.

I squint at her, because I'm swaying and she's swaying and our movements are not synchronized. "I said I was turning eighteen tonight, not thirty. Where do you *expect* me to live?" There's no rancor behind the slurred words, and luckily she seems to deduce as much from my tone.

"Okay, okay, God. I forgot what a baby you are."

I arch a brow at her as the key slips into the dead bolt with a metallic scrape. "Nope. Tonight, I'm a man. Remember?" I won't bother to tell her that other girls her age didn't wait until I was a legal adult; I prefer to let her assume she has something to teach me. Who knows, maybe she does. I turn the key until the lock clacks, depress the lever and push a shoulder against the door. We're in. Putting a finger to my puckered lips, I repeat, "Shhh," while I wrestle the key from the door.

This time, she nods, swaying closer with a wicked smile, inclining against me while I grab the door frame for support. Her makeup is smeared and she smells like stale cigarettes and beer—but so do I. "I remember." Her voice is raspy, like the teeth of the key against the lock.

Alcohol-induced dreams are always weird and crude—and I mean that in the best possible way. Then comes the unfortunate act of waking up. By that point, the buzz is long gone, inhibitions are flooding back, and the only thing hammered is the inside of my skull. Add an outside stimulus like, say, a ringing cell set on level wake-the-hell-up, and I'm propelled to the opposite of a pleasant stage of inebriation. Suddenly a brain-rototilling free-for-all is taking place in an enclosed space, right behind my eyeballs. Welcome to hangoverland.

I click *talk* to make the screaming stop (I like this song? Really?), but don't bother trying to answer, because my mouth is a desert and speech is improbable. There's a water bottle on the bedside table, but when I stretch to grab it, I drop the phone, which emits the barely audible voice of my manager, George. "Hello? Reid? Hell-o-o?"

"Shit." Swiping the phone from the floor, I nearly fall off the bed. "'Lo?" My voice sounds and tastes like it's flowing through gravel.

"Rough night?" George is sarcastic, but not callously so. He's my manager, not my parent. I assume he's grateful to the universe, fate, God, whatever/whoever's in charge for that. I'm a better client than I am a son. Just ask my dad.

I lift my head a fraction, to see if that hot little bass guitarist from the band John and I saw last night is still here. I vaguely remember her stumbling around my room with me, giggling like she was thirteen instead of the twenty-whatever she said she was. She's nowhere, but a barely legible note is under my water bottle, the ring around the bottom splotching the ink. I take a generous gulp from the bottle and check it out: *Reid—awesome night. More please? I put my number in your phone—Cassandra*

Cassandra. Did she ever say her name last night? I can't remember.

"Reid?" George's voice. Crap.

"Yeah." I lurch to a seated position on the side of the bed, my head in one hand and the phone in the other, trying to decide if I need to throw up or not. Verdict: possibly.

"Richter just called—you got the part in *School Pride*. He said he's looking forward to working with you." Adam Richter is one of Hollywood's leading directors. The man is a legend with an eye for teen dramas. "You're scheduled to do a two-minute spot on *ET* tomorrow, by the way, so rest up. Also, Richter wants you in on auditions for the Lizbeth role. Those will start in a couple of weeks. We'll discuss all of this on Friday."

"Sure." God, my head feels like it's going to fall off. "What's the location?"

"They've decided to film in Austin."

"*Texas?*"

"Last time I checked, yes, that's where Austin is located."

"Yeehaw."

School Pride, *ET*, auditions, Austin. Jesus, my head is splitting. Why don't I ever remember that mornings like this are the predictable conclusion of nights like last night?

Emma

My father ladles Alfredo sauce over bowls of linguini while I set the table for three. "Dan called this afternoon," he says. Dan is my agent, and this is my cue to brace for a new audition. What this time—a tampon commercial? Another side role in a Lifetime movie? "He got you an audition for the *lead role* in a wide-release film. How would you like to play—" his hands move into frame-the-shot mode "—Elizabeth Bennet?"

I frown. "Another remake? But they just did a *Pride and Prejudice* adaptation a few years ago." Then there's my rusty (and honestly, sort of abysmal) British accent.

"That's the thing—this isn't nineteenth century England. It's a modern version, set in a suburban American high school." He waits for my enthusiasm, but all I can think is: *Yay! A cute role in a corrupted version of one of my favorite novels ever.*

Before I can stop myself, I go one better than a simple lack of enthusiasm. "*Pride and Prejudice*. Set in a high school. Seriously?"

He sighs and tosses the script packet on the kitchen table, and we don't discuss it further. This is our standard resolution to this sort of conflict: we both pretend I'm all good with what he wants. In this particular instance, I'll take the packet to my room and start memorizing lines, and he'll tell Dan how psyched I am about the audition.

Landing this role would be career-altering, no doubt about it. All the bit parts, the commercials for department stores and bacon and grape juice have led up to this moment… where I try to win another (more prominent than anything before) girl-next-door role. Truth is, I'm not just tired of one-dimensional roles. I'm sick of doing films, period.

When I was thirteen, I was one of the fairies in a local stage production of *A Midsummer Night's Dream*. I loved the live performance, the thrill of the audience reaction. I've pleaded to do more live theatre in the four years since, but it's never going to happen, because Dan and my manager-father consider my role in *Midsummer* a one-time community service project. They want Emma Pierce to be a household name, so there's no time for silly local theatre roles.

As a compromise, I've tried suggesting quirky, edgy independent film scripts. Every time, they shoot me down. "I don't think this is what we want for your career," one of them says, and I fold up and cave, because when it comes to running my own life, I'm a yellow-bellied coward.

Just this morning, I felt like a regular girl—scanning my computer and phone for overnight messages, planning a trip to the mall with Emily. A day of typical spring break activities with my best friend was exactly what I needed to make me feel *normal*. We rolled down the windows, sang along to our favorite songs, talked about boys we know, and speculated about the ones we haven't met.

I'm not a regular girl, though. I'm a working actress. I don't attend school; I have tutors. I don't hang in the commons at lunch with my friends; I grab something from the caterer on set if I'm filming, or make myself something in the kitchen at home if not. I read scripts and review lines while exercising, do homework on set.

In the past year, my relationship with my father has grown more strained than ever, but it hasn't been great for years. I inherited little from him apart from his gray-green eyes and a passion for running. In every other respect, we're polar opposites. He doesn't get me. I don't get him. End of story.

Chapter 2

REID

"Your father says he'll be home tonight. Please, Reid?"

Shit. "Yeah, sure, Mom."

Dinner with Mark and Lucy—always entertaining. I avoid it when possible, but Mom's got me cornered before I leave for my meeting with Larry, my PR guy. She's so persistently anxious that it's hard for me to say no to her. Dad doesn't seem to have the same struggle. She's got this idealistic vision of the three of us as a happy little family: if we sit down together at the dinner table, domestic bliss will magically occur. Why this doesn't strike her as wishful thinking given the fact that it's never worked before, I don't know. I'll be gone soon anyway. I refuse to contemplate how far she'll sink then.

I haven't decided when I'll actually move out. My room has a separate entrance and is more like an apartment attached to my parents' house than a room within it. My grandmother lived with us until she died a few years ago, and this was her suite. Not long after she was gone, I talked Mom into letting me switch rooms. Dad was pissed because I was like fifteen and could then come and go without their knowledge, but it was a done deal by the time he noticed, and I just entrenched and ignored him until he quit blustering.

"Congrats on getting *School Pride*, man." Larry's toadying, as usual. We're at a sushi place on Ventura, and he's annoying the crap out of me. He can't even use chopsticks correctly—it's like his hands are retarded. That may sound like a pretentious prick thing to say, but *he* chose the place. Plus, my gut says he's bitter about what I make compared to him. There's a lot of envy in this business. The more successful you are, the larger the target.

"Thanks." I pop a piece of salmon sashimi into my mouth.

He clears his throat. "Okay, so, well…" Shit, man, spit it out already. "We're thinking that you should, uh, align yourself with some charitable efforts, now that you're an adult." He has this look like I'm going to have a problem with that, which makes me wonder if I *should* have a problem with it.

I eye him, still chewing. "Like what?"

I swear to God he squirms in his seat like a kid on the verge of peeing his pants. "Well, lots of options. Telethons, or, uh, a day or two of something like Habitat for Humanity, or you could endorse adult literacy or childhood vaccinations with a television spot."

I forgot about Larry's tendency to *well* and *uh* when nervous. It makes me want to shovel sushi into his mouth until he can't speak at all.

"I'm not doing some telethon, or manual labor. And childhood vaccinations?" I quirk an eyebrow. "Shouldn't that be left to people with kids?"

He mops his face with his napkin. "Well…"

This is going to take all damned day. "Anything else?"

He pokes at his tuna slices. "You could visit schools, participate in drug and alcohol awareness presentations—"

"Um, *no*." The irony would be too hilarious, but I'm not doing it. It would be like those teen celebs who pretend virginity, wearing chastity rings and preaching abstinence to other teens, only to get caught with their pants down at some point. Literally. I get enough close scrutiny from the press without daring them to catch me plastered or high.

"Well… uh, you could just donate cash—"

"Let's go with that. Check with my dad, he'll handle it."

"Do you have a cause in mind?"

I look at him blankly. The only cause I believe in is my own. Chicks like animals, right? "Something with animals." Stipulation: the cuter the better. "But no crazy activist groups. And domesticated animals—not some endangered salamander or shit like that."

"Oh-okay, well...domesticated animals—like the SPCA?"

"Sure." SPCA: something-something-something-animals.

Emma

I'm removing my dinner of reheated leftovers from the microwave when my cell plays Emily's ringtone. She doesn't wait for hello. "Turn on channel ten!"

"Okay, just a minute—"

"No! *Now*!"

I head obediently for the television. "Keep your shorts on, I'm going. What's on?"

"*Who's* on, you mean."

I key in the channel on the remote and the screen erupts in flashing images and the familiar theme music of *Entertainment Tonight*. "…and he's here tonight to talk to us about a new project in the works," the host says as the 52-inch screen catches up with the surround sound system.

The camera cuts to Reid Alexander, the hottest guy on film. "Yeah, I'm really psyched about it." He swings his dark blond hair out of his eyes and smiles that trademark smile: a little shy, sorta humble, totally hot.

"Oh. My. God," Emily breathes.

Reid Alexander is flat out eye candy: dark blue eyes and facial features bordering on pretty—long, dark eyelashes, almost pouty mouth—but the lines of his face are all male. His hair is perpetually disheveled, but it's a flawless sort of mess. He doesn't seem real; he's like an artist's interpretation of an eighteen-year old sex god.

"We hear the film is going to be an adaptation of Jane Austen's classic novel, *Pride and Prejudice*?" The host holds the microphone under his chin.

"Um, yeah. It's set in an American high school, so it'll be different. Fresh, you know? I'll be working with Adam Richter, which I'm really excited about."

"Emma!" I feel Emily's elation through the phone. "This is your movie, right? I saw the blurb and I thought *holy shit that's Emma's movie*!"

"Uh-huh." I can't reply coherently yet. Reid Alexander is playing Will Darcy in a film adaptation I wasn't all that jazzed about auditioning for twenty-four hours ago.

"The question everyone wants answered: *who* is your leading lady going to be?"

"We're running auditions in a couple of weeks, so hopefully I'll know the answer to that real soon." Another killer smile.

The host turns to the camera. "You heard it here, folks. Reid Alexander to play Will Darcy opposite a lucky as-yet-unnamed costar as Lizbeth Bennet. Who will it be? We'll keep you posted! Filming should start late summer."

I click the TV off and slump onto the sofa.

"Emma, this is destiny. It's going to be *you*. Reid Alexander is *Darcy* and you're going to be *Elizabeth Bennet*."

"It's Lizbeth," I say. "They changed the names."

"Whatever." Emily is full of her usual confidence on my behalf. "You're going to be *her*."

I'm exhausted from poring over audition sides until 2 a.m. Coffee aroma drifts up from the kitchen, and I shuffle towards it single-mindedly, a zombie who craves caffeine instead of brains, until I hear Chloe, my stepmother, talking to my father in the kitchen. Reluctant to encounter either of them this early, especially if they're feeling slighted over my lukewarm reaction to the audition news, I hesitate at the top of the staircase.

"She'll come around. She always does. What's she going to do? Manage her own career?" I stiffen at Chloe's sarcastic tone.

My father is less mocking, more exasperated. "This could be her ticket out of bit parts and commercials. They've already cast *Reid Alexander* for the lead. Dan says that kid hardly has to audition. If he wants a particular role, he's almost guaranteed to get it."

"Plus he's yummy hot." How can Chloe say things like this when Reid Alexander is disgustingly close to the age of the geography students she teaches? You'd think she'd draw a personal line. Gross.

"I have no idea what she wants," he says. If I rent a billboard or hire a freaking skywriter, might he comprehend what I say I want?

"She'll come around," Chloe says. "When she's rich and famous, she'll get decent work instead of chasing down whatever crappy roles she can get. Though it would be a stretch to call what she does *working*." I grip the banister, waiting for him to say something in my defense.

"Humph," he says, marching out the door to work. Chloe parks it in front of *Good Morning America*, because unfortunately spring break applies to teachers, too. Usually, I couldn't care less about her opinion, as annoying as it is to listen to it at early-o'clock in the morning. Not even coffee can induce me to go down there now.

My father was there when I did my first commercial—nineteen takes to get the precise sip of juice that wouldn't inhibit my two lines about how delicious and wholesome it was. I still can't look at grape juice without gagging. He was there when the maniacal director of a low-budget made-for-tv movie screamed in my face because I dropped a prop phone. He watched as I sweltered through Arizona desert heat with a parka zipped to my chin, portraying the daughter of an intergalactic explorer who'd been exiled to a dry, frozen planet.

I thought he was clear on how hard I work, at least.

Don't misunderstand—I love what I do. And I'm good at it. Some people assume acting is just putting on someone else's clothes or accent, but that's not enough. You have to unzip the character's skin, step into her completely, allow yourself to meld with her. You have to *become* the character. Even if the character is a kid who *really* likes juice.

I should be grateful, I should feel lucky, and I am, I do. But even if you have what everyone else wants—if it isn't what you want, it isn't what you want. A high school film version of one of the greatest novels of all time? Really? Unless Jane Austen is a Reid Alexander fan, she's probably spinning in her grave.

Chapter 3

REID

These auditions are killing me. They did screen tests on I don't even know how many girls, and narrowed it down to twenty. Richter wants her to be attractive, but not exceptionally hot, which blows, but he's right. Lizbeth Bennet is someone Will Darcy falls for against his normal inclinations.

I'd like to think I'm capable of having onscreen chemistry with anyone, but sadly, that isn't the case. Before each girl comes in, we go over her headshots, clips of past film work, and her screen test. I've done auditions with eleven of them so far, and I'm thinking *these are the ones we narrowed down to?* We've spent varying amounts of time on each one, and I'm trying to figure out how Richter operates, because we're spending longer with the ones I want to cut. Not that I'm complaining to Adam *Richter* about whatever method he uses or who he chooses.

"Daria," Richter calls to his assistant, his finger on the clipboard of information in his hand. "We're ready for the next girl. Belinda, is it?"

"Yes, sir," Daria says. "I'll bring her right in."

"I'm going to kiss this one, aren't I?" I say.

Richter barks a laugh and his bright blue eyes regard me over his glasses. "What makes you say that?"

Oops. "Um. It just seems the less jazzed I am about one, the more likely we are to do the kiss."

His eyebrows—equal parts black and silver—rise slightly. "Good observation. I don't want to miss out on possible physical chemistry, so the ones who aren't passing the test on script audition get one final chance before we reject them."

"That makes sense."

"Thanks, I appreciate your support." His mouth twists, and he laughs again when I color slightly, which I *never* do.

"Adam, this is Belinda Jarvis." Daria leaves the girl standing in the center of the camera equipment.

I can tell right away that Belinda isn't the one. Her face is too sensual, her expression too calculating. She could, perhaps, be Caroline Bingley. Reciting lines I know so well that I could deliver them while juggling, I read her body language and the way her half-lidded eyes gaze at me and decide that Belinda would be fun to have on set. We get to the kiss, and not two seconds into it, her tongue is in my mouth. Entertaining, yeah. Lizbeth Bennet, no. When she's dismissed, I mention what I think to Richter, about using her for Caroline.

"We've already chosen Caroline and Charlie," he says. "We ran their auditions concurrently, since their sibling chemistry and appearances must be convincing."

"Can you tell me who?"

"I hope to be able to let you know Charlie by tomorrow. I'm calling him tonight. As for Caroline, she'll be played by Brooke Cameron."

Brooke Cameron. I try not to react, but Richter's eyes miss nothing and I'm too knocked off center to hide my reaction. "You two worked on something together before, I think?"

"Yeah." I do *not* want to go into detail. "A few years ago." Almost four years ago, in fact.

He looks as though he has a follow-up question, but Daria pushes the door open and leans in. "Emma Pierce is here, Adam."

Emma

I'm as intimidated auditioning for Adam Richter as I am auditioning with Reid Alexander. Dan warned me that Richter wouldn't waste time on small talk, so I have to swallow my anxiety and convince him that I'm his ideal Lizbeth Bennet. (I called Emily for moral support but wasn't helped by, "Oh. My. God. The thought of being that close to him. I can't *breathe*.")

"All right Reid, Emma, begin with 'There you are,'" Richter says. "And… action."

```
INT. School hallway - Day
WILL walks up to LIZBETH at her
locker, touches her shoulder.

                  WILL
    There you are.

LIZBETH pushes books into locker,
turns to WILL, scowling.
                 LIZBETH
    Yes?
```

(Scowling at Reid Alexander for any reason seems all wrong, but it's *in the script*.)

WILL

I can't take this. Obviously we're on different levels socially and you're a complete one-eighty from my usual type, but I can't get you out of my head. Go to Charlie's party with me on Saturday. I'll pick you up at eight.

LIZBETH looks up at him, tilting head as if confused:

LIZBETH

Usually if I'm not interested in going out with someone, I try to be nice about it. But I'm sort of in shock right now.

WILL

(incredulous)

Are you saying no?

LIZBETH

I'm saying you couldn't pay me.

(Again, this feels dead *wrong*, but it's *in the script*.)

WILL glares at LIZBETH, steps closer to her:

WILL

What the hell? You're actually saying no?

LIZBETH, squaring shoulders:

LIZBETH

So you think you can ask me out and I'll trot after you like every other idiotic girl in this school? I won't. Even if you weren't so rude every time I'm around you, do you think I want anything to do with you after what you did to Jane? And to George?

WILL

What happened between George Wickham and me is none of your business. This is ridiculous. I only wanted to take you to a party, even if you aren't exactly in my league. Would you rather I just lied about that, to save your precious ego?

LIZBETH

I couldn't care less how you asked.

(We're inches apart. Reid waits for my one-word line—his cue to kiss me. Up close, Reid Alexander is the most beautiful guy I've ever seen, though it's hardly the best time to appreciate this fact, as Lizbeth is currently livid.)

What?

WILL grabs LIZBETH'S shoulders.

"Cut!" Richter calls. "Good, good. Thank you, Emma. We'll be in touch." He dismisses me with a smile.

Good smile or bad smile? The audition felt good, but he stopped us right before the kiss, which seems not good. "Reid, let's take a look at the next to last line…" he says, and Reid jogs over to consult with him after giving me a mesmerizing smile of his own.

"Ms. Pierce?" The scene attendant breaks my trance, her expression telling me that she witnesses the stupefied look on my face all too often. "Right this way," she says, showing me to the exit.

Chapter 4

REID

Lucky number thirteen—Emma Pierce. We'll see two more girls today and five tomorrow, but I already know it's her. That spark, the chemistry—we've got it. The source of it is inexplicable; it's more than and many times separate from simple attraction. There are couples who have it onscreen but can't stand the sight of each other in real life, and couples where sexual orientation should negate it, but there it is, on film. Like magic.

I've never heard of this girl before. If chosen, she'll be a virtual unknown, and I wonder if Richter will have problems convincing production to take a chance on her. We auditioned two prominent actresses for Lizbeth on the first day. Either of them would work... but not like Emma. Richter knows it, too. After her audition, he asked me what I thought.

"Yeah," I said, smiling.

He smiled back. "I think 'yeah' sums it up nicely. Let's see these last... seven, is it? But I'll go ahead and give Emma's agent a call tomorrow, and get her set up for a callback. Let's see what you two can do with the entire scene."

He wants to see the kiss.

So do I.

Emma

My father and Chloe keep eyeing each other with sideways glances; he sighs noisily every couple of minutes while she chews her lip. Neither has asked me anything since their initial *How'd it go?* probes, which I answered briefly and with no specifics. They deserve the silent treatment for that speech over the breakfast table a couple of weeks ago, even if they don't know I was listening.

"So… Reid was there?" Chloe prompts, following a full five-minute silence in the taxi after dinner.

"Yeah." I hope they'll take my attitude as typical seventeen-year-old reticence.

She waits another minute for me to elaborate, then realizes I'm not going to. "So, is he gorgeous in person? Was the scene with him or was he just, you know, there?"

"With him." The hotel finally comes into sight, thank God. Soon we'll go to our separate, adjoining rooms and I'll have my thoughts to myself.

My father heaves another perturbed sigh. "Do you think you'll get a callback?"

"I don't know."

Chloe rolls her eyes and pulls out a compact mirror and lipstick, as though her exit at the curb of the hotel is a red-carpet event. Hopefully that ends the interrogation for tonight, though I'm positive it will start up again over breakfast.

In my bag are the *School Pride* sides I was expected to memorize for the audition, and the copy of *Pride and Prejudice* that belonged to my mother, who died when I was six. What my mother bequeathed to me: cloudy memories of our lives before she was gone, a handful of photos, her wedding band, and dog-eared copy of her favorite novel. On page 100, there's a faint coffee ring. On page 237, a smudged fingerprint, undoubtedly pressed to the page while she was simultaneously cooking and reading to me, something I vaguely recall her doing. When I feel the absence of her the most, when I crave her arms around me and can't bear the knowledge that she's never coming back no matter what I do or how much I need her, I open her book to these pages, touch my fingers to the fingerprint and the coffee ring, and feel comforted.

I don't want to discuss the audition with anyone but Emily. We've been known as Em and Em since kindergarten, when we became best friends, and attended school together until sixth grade, when my father put me into tutoring, citing my erratic schedule. Thanks to my grandmother and Emily's mom taxiing us back and forth, we stayed close. I don't know what my life would have been like without her. Lonely, I think.

With Emily, I got my ears pierced and spied on cute neighborhood boys (armed with her dad's binoculars), learned to skateboard (sort of) and took driver's ed. With Emily, I have sleepovers, get pedicures and talk about everything. With Emily, I feel normal.

I call her as soon as I'm in my room, and she answers on the first ring. "So which scene did you do? Was it a *good* one? Did you nail it?"

"The scene where he asks me out."

"The one where he kisses you at the end? Aaaaaand?"

"When we got to the part where he grabs me, which by the way isn't something Darcy would *ever* do, because he's fully in charge of his emotions at all times—it's his *defining characteristic*! I don't think the screenwriter even *read* the novel..."

"Emma, you're killing me. I'm dying. *Spill.*"

"No kiss. The director stopped us right before, and I guess they brought the next hopeful contender in."

"Aw, crap. No fair." She sighs, taking the loss personally.

"Yeah, kissing him would've been a nice consolation prize."

"Emma, I told you, you're getting this part. Are you ready to handle all the screwed up stuff in the script? Movies are *never* as good as the book, no offense. You can't let it drive you insane." Emily knows me so well.

"I can do it. I'm just worried that if I do this movie, I'll be stereotyped as insubstantial and *cute*. I'll never end up doing something significant."

"At some point *you'll* be in charge of your career, and you can do whatever you want."

"When will that be?" I can't help the whine that seeps into my voice.

"When you're like forty," she answers. "No doubt about it—by forty, you'll be in complete control."

I smile. "Night, Em."

"Night, Em."

Chapter 5

REID

After the last two auditions, I'm waiting for my car to be brought around and pulling my phone from my pocket to call my friend John when I get a text from Mom reminding me about dinner at 8:00. My first thought is how the hell to get out of it, but then I remember how she looked this morning when I said yes. I hit reply and type: Yep.

The valet zooms up in my Lotus, which I convinced Dad to let me buy a few months ago by telling him I would just get it when I turned eighteen if he said no. He hates the car, from the engine roar when I gun it to the stereo vibrating everything in the house as I pull into the garage, but above all, he hates the color—lemon yellow. He calls it a douche taxi. Last week I pulled into the drive when he was getting the mail, and as I walked up to the house he stared at the car and said, no inflection, "You're keeping that thing at least a year."

As he knew it would, that remark made me want to sell the stupid-ass car immediately.

Dinner in two hours should be all kinds of enjoyable.

I might as well do some shopping—no sense in being home early. Rodeo Drive is closing down for the day, but I head over to Robertson and hand over the keys to another valet, wondering if valets actually drive my car as much or more than I do. Paul & Joe is open and nearly deserted, the sales clerks (both hot—gay guy, wispy blonde chick) hovering, waiting to be helpful. They exchange a look as I browse. Between the two of them, they probably generate interest from anyone between fifteen and fifty who walks through the door.

I grab a few funky shirts and a pair of jeans and request a dressing room from the girl. "Yes, of course, Mr. Alexander," she says. Maybe someday I'll hate it, but for now, I love being recognized. I've just pulled on the jeans when she comes into the dressing room with another pair in a different shade. Without a trace of apprehension at walking in on me half-undressed, she holds them out. "This is the newer wash. I thought you might want to try them, too." I toss them onto the pile as her eyes rake over my chest. Turning to the mirror like I don't notice, I button the jeans and pull on one of the vintage t-shirts.

"What do you think? Too dug-it-outta-Dad's-closet?"

Her mouth turns up on one side and she shrugs. "If your dad was cool, then that's in." She bites her lip, lightly. "Let me see the other one."

I pull the shirt off and step closer. "Hold it for me?" I can almost hear the porn soundtrack starting up in my head, until my phone beeps—another reminder text from Mom about dinner. I reply that I'm on my way.

"So, Kaci," I touch the nametag just over her breast, "I'll take both shirts, and the jeans I'm wearing. I don't have time to take them off right now." My meaning is clear as I rip the tag off and hand it to her. "I'll just wear them out, if that's okay."

When I leave, the discarded tag, her phone number written on the back in red ink, is in the bag with the new shirts and the jeans I was wearing when I came in.

I park next to Dad's empty spot in the garage. Not a good sign; I hope he's just late. As much as I'd prefer to pass on sitting across the table from him, I live in constant dread of having to watch the effect on Mom whenever he bails on her—which is often. Immaculada is perched on a stool in the kitchen, chin propped in her hand, watching reality TV. Everything on the stove is set to low. Waiting.

I'm afraid to ask, but I do. "Mom in her room?"

Her head inclines towards the master suite. "Sí, in her room." *Damn*. I can tell by her tone what that means.

The sitting room off the master bedroom gives the impression of a cozy personal library, which is accurate, I suppose. Mom loves to read, or did at one time. The floor-to-ceiling shelves house an enviable selection of books and very few knickknacks or framed photos. I drop into one of two plush leather chairs; she sits in the other, an open book on her lap, an empty martini glass in her hand, her eyes unfocused on the darkened window.

"Mom?" I don't have to actually ask the question.

She looks at me, blinks likes she's waking up. "He's not coming." The tears are in her voice, even if they aren't on her face.

"Got held up with a case, I guess." The words are sour in my mouth and I don't even know why I said them. If his absences and last-minute cancellations were infrequent, his recurrent justifications would work. But they aren't, and they don't. "Come on—Immaculada has everything ready. We can enjoy it without him." I try to keep the bitterness out of my tone, but fail.

"I don't really… I'm not really hungry," she says, and I want to shake her. How can his behavior possibly surprise her now? This is his demeanor towards both of us, and has been forever. I don't *get* it, but I don't give a shit anymore, and she shouldn't, either.

"Okay." I stand up, hands in pockets, unable to fix this for the millionth time. "I guess I'll go ahead and meet John. I'll tell Immaculada to pack up the food; maybe you'll be hungry later." She won't.

"Yes. That's a good idea. Thank you, Reid."

I breathe a sigh. When she says my name, it drains the anger—at her, anyway—like she's pulled a plug. I lean down and kiss her before I leave, pretending not to hear when I get into the hallway and she says, "I love you."

Emma

When Chloe tags along for auditions, she insists on a five-star hotel, as though I'm already a big star. No penthouse suite, yet, but I'm sure she has plans.

I'm the first one down to breakfast. The waitress brings my coffee with cream in a tiny crystal pitcher and little straws of raw sugar in a matching crystal box. My omelet is created to order and served on toile-embossed china. If I land this part and achieve the fame and fortune my father wants for me, this could be my life. All the time.

Just outside the restaurant window, a blonde celebrity walks by, surrounded by her entourage. Dark sunglasses obscure her face. She ducks her head and slides into the back seat of a waiting black Mercedes SUV with black tinted windows just as the paparazzi catch up, at least a dozen photographers calling to her.

I've only been approached by someone in public twice. The first was several years ago, here in LA. As my father and I had lunch after an audition, a woman with a toddler in tow approached the table. She told me that my role as the daughter of a bipolar woman in a television ad for antidepressant meds prompted her to seek help for her depression. My father beamed and said, "Would you like an autograph? Emma, sign your napkin."

The second time was a couple of months ago, the result of a minor role in a periodically re-aired Lifetime movie. Emily had a choir competition in San Francisco, about ninety miles south of Sacramento, and I tagged along for the weekend. While exploring a tiny indie bookstore, we were approached by a girl.

"Hey, were you in that movie about the Civil War? You were the sister of that guy who deserted the Rebs to join the Union?" I nodded guardedly, and she continued. "Well my dad went to Notre Dame, and my brother decided to go to Michigan State, and it's like he defected to the dark side!" She laid a hand on my forearm and I resisted the urge to jerk away. "My whole family's *pissed*! I totally identified with your character, you know?" I nodded, but I didn't know.

Emily offered to take a photo of me with my fan, this stranger who eagerly slung her arm around me and pressed her face to mine. I'm pretty sure I looked beyond freaked.

"Okay, we've gotta go now, thanks for watching," Emily said, thrusting the phone into the girl's hand, linking my arm through hers and propelling me out the door.

While I was reviewing lines in my room last night, my father and Chloe went out. When Chloe knocked on my door to tell me, I could see her to-the-shoulder earrings and full-throttle eyeliner through the peephole. Her outfit was more like a couple of wide belts than a legitimate top and bottom. They returned at 3 a.m., obviously wasted. I heard them trying to get their key card to open a neighboring door, then mine, and finally their own.

At the table this morning, my father is mute and Chloe wears sunglasses and nurses black coffee. She's not thrilled about my table choice, adjacent to the floor-to-ceiling wall of windows with a view of the sunny blue sky on this rare non-hazy day; but it's the perfect spot to people watch. Until Dan arrives to interrogate me about my audition for the enviable role of Lizbeth Bennet opposite Reid Alexander.

"In his last film, he all but named his costar." Dan gestures animatedly with both hands, his elbows on the table. "The director was on the fence between two or three, and I heard that he said 'I want Allyson' and she was *in*." I seriously doubt that even Reid Alexander has *that* sort of power, but I keep this thought to myself.

Dan eyes me closely, as he always does when he is about to make an Important Statement. "They're looking for chemistry. This is 'Darcy and Elizabeth,' for chrissake." All three of them stare at me. Chemistry between the romantic leads. What a novel concept.

"Um, okay, I know." I only just refrain from rolling my eyes. "I think it went well, but we're either going to have chemistry or we aren't, right? I assume they'll do callbacks on several—"

"Richter has been directing for two decades. Big names, big films. He knows chemistry, and if the two of you have it, he'll see it." Is that not what I just said? "What—*specifically*—did he say when he stopped the scene?" He asked me this exact question five minutes ago. I don't know if he thinks I'm lying or just carelessly omitting something significant.

My jaw clenches and I repeat, verbatim, the answer I gave five minutes ago. "He said, 'Good, good,' then thanked me, then said they'd be in touch."

Dan pinches his chin between his perfectly manicured fingers, the face of his TAG Heuer watch peeking out from the cuff of his impeccable azure blue dress shirt. "He stopped you before the kiss was started, then," he reiterates, "But he said, 'Good, good,' right after."

Oh. My. God. "Yes."

"This could work, this could be fine, possibly he wants to see buildup—I mean anyone can kiss." If Dan actually believes *that*, I feel sorry for him. Even with my somewhat limited experience, I know that not everyone can kiss. If rumors are reliable, Reid Alexander will leave me in a puddle at his feet. I doubt the likelihood of this, though, because the best-looking guys aren't always the best kissers, as backwards as that notion seems.

My first kiss was with a costar in the intergalactic explorer movie. We engaged in hours of private rehearsals after that while on location. But Justin lived in New Jersey, and once filming ended, we were too young to cross the distance between Newark and Sacramento. At the time, I thought I would die from heartbreak. Later, I was more depressed to discover that Justin had been a bright kissing light in a sea of dim bulbs.

Dan's cell phone begins playing a late-80s rap song, and he unclips it from his belt and punches it, holding up one finger to shush the three of us, though no one is talking. "Dan Walters here. Yes, of course. Fabulous. Three o'clock, no prob. Thanks much, Daria."

His expression is almost manic as he turns to me. "We're on, baby. You and Reid are having another go, tomorrow."

"Yay!" Chloe claps her fingers as though Dan is speaking to her. This is a fundamental Chloe move. She's like a wind-up monkey that winds itself.

Dan shakes his head slightly (I know the feeling) and addresses my father. "Connor, have her there tomorrow by 2:50. Early enough to look interested, but not overly eager. I'll start working on what we're going to push for in terms of salary. I'll be in touch, hopefully soon." He lays a hand on my forearm. "Knock 'em dead." One more gulp of coffee (no way Dan actually *needs* any sort of stimulant) and he's gliding back through the restaurant and out the entrance.

Me: Got a callback. 3pm tomorrow. Probably kissing reid alexander. Wish me luck.

Em: Do you NEED LUCK?!? Sounds like you already HAVE IT, lol.

Chapter 6

REID

Emma Pierce is the fourth of five callbacks. In an attempt to be professional, I've focused on each of the three before her while we were running scenes, but all day I'm crackling with energy, humming with it, waiting for her.

When Daria shows her in, I feel as though I've been plugged into a socket. I study the sides though I could recite all of my lines *and* hers, delaying the moment when our eyes meet, knowing it will trigger a power surge between us when we speak the lines. We're doing the same scene we did two days ago, but this time there will be no interruption from Richter.

He calls us to our places and she turns away, a shadow of confusion on her face, but ready. Richter calls action, and as I touch her shoulder, she turns to me, scowling, perfectly in character, and I wish we were filming on set right now because this will be as good as it gets. We run through the lines as though we've rehearsed this scene a dozen times, and when she says the last line, "What?" I grip her shoulders per the script direction and kiss her.

I know when I touch her that my hold on her isn't going to be right and will seem antagonistic, but I'm following script direction. We'll have to redo it, but that's fine. The chemistry is undeniable. She sways a bit when I release her, the green in her gray eyes sparking. She feels it, too.

"Cut." Richter is out of his chair, his lips pursed in thought. One hand taps against the side of his leg as he stares at us. He didn't budge from his seated position during the last three callbacks. "Too aggressive, I think, Reid." More lip-pursing and thigh-tapping. "Let's go again from the beginning. More passion, less dominance on the kiss." He's letting me guide the scene physically—precisely how I work best. "Emma, a little more reaction—you're starting to respond just before he pulls away."

As the cameras are realigned, I smile down at her, whispering, "Don't worry."

She smiles back, still nervous, which is fine. All she has to do is follow my lead, which she's doing flawlessly so far. This time, I pull her towards me, one hand cradling the back of her head, the other sliding down her arm, tugging her forward onto her toes, unbalancing her so that she leans into me as I kiss her. Hands curled into my chest, she's a perfect illustration of Lizbeth Bennet's surrender to Will Darcy's passion.

"Excellent, spot on," Richter says. He rubs his hands together.

Hell, *yeah.*

Daria shows Emma to the exit after we run another couple of scenes and Richter tells her he'll be in touch. She nods and thanks him, glancing at me. My relaxed expression gives nothing away, but there's no doubt in my mind—she's Lizbeth.

Emma

When I come home from the gym a week after the audition, my father and Chloe are popping a bottle of champagne. "You got the part!" he says as Chloe squeals and offers me a glass. I've been chosen to play Lizbeth Bennet in *School Pride*. The financial details were settled for more than I've earned in the past several years combined. Filming will start in mid-August, on location in Austin.

Dazed by the news, the salary, and the thought of working with Reid Alexander for three solid months, I do what any other girl would do. I grab my phone and text my best friend. Emily is at choir practice, but I'm hoping the threat of choir director ire won't keep her from answering.

Me: I GOT IT
Em: OHMYGOD!!!
Me: I know! Holy CRAP.
Em: I have never been jealous of you before, but OMG REID ALEXANDER!?!!!!
Me: I'll call you after the champagne celebration and chloe's dance of glee. UGH.
Em: Ignore her. This is about YOU <3
Me: Will try, idk if ignoring her is possible, you have no idea.
Em: Oh trust me, i have an idea.

"I guess we might not be able to do this forever, huh?" Emily says, glancing around the mall food court, the straw of her smoothie never leaving her mouth. It's late July. In less than a month, I'll be departing for Austin to film my first wide-release movie.

"What, go out in public?" I recall the paparazzi-mobbed celeb I'd watched from the hotel restaurant in LA. "I don't think I'll be *that* well-known."

"Well, we don't know how famous you'll be, do we? Don't forget," she leans closer and lowers her voice, "you'll be kissing *Reid Alexander*, making you the object of loathing and hate mail for half the preteen girls from here to Canada."

Any time I think of that kiss, I still feel it. What I said about hot guys not being the best kissers? Scratch. That.

"Crap."

"Totally. Except the *kissing Reid Alexander* part." Emily leers, waggling her eyebrows.

"Em," I shake my head, "you have a one-track mind."

"Whatev, babe. I've tried to warn you regarding the underbelly of the lives of the rich and famous—it isn't pretty. Drugs, drinking, accidental porn…" She slurps the last of her smoothie.

"Emily, you know I don't—okay wait, what is *accidental* porn?"

"You know, the kind where you have no idea your innocently lascivious weekend was filmed through a teeny camera in the ceiling, until it's too late and people are downloading it off the Internet like, well, online porn." She swirls a fry through the pool of ketchup we're sharing.

"Innocently lascivious?" I'm not sure if I should be insulted or jealous of this version of myself that Emily is painting.

"Hey, I'm not judging your sex life here, I'm just saying it like it is."

"Emily Watson, you know better than anyone that I don't *have* a sex life."

"Hollywood changes things like that. It's like a giant vortex of hedonism." Clearly, Emily needs a break from her SAT prep books.

"And you're the expert on all things Hollywood."

"*Duh*. I read the *Globe, Sun, Star* and of course *The National Enquirer*. The facts are all there. It's a seamy little business you've gotten yourself into." Emily has inherited the online form of her mother's inability to pass a juicy tabloid cover in the grocery line without buying it. On many occasions we've grabbed stacks of them on the way to the pool, where we challenge each other to unearth the wackiest story.

"I wish I could take you with me," I tell her, meaning it. "You keep me sane."

"Yeah, well, I'll just have to keep doing it from afar. One of us is obligated to actually *attend* high school, while the other stars in a *movie* in which she attends high school. Irony. Gotta love it."

Chapter 7

REID

No matter how rich or famous you are, you still have to pack when you go somewhere, and packing for a three-month absence is a pain in the ass.

Tadd Wyler is playing my character's best friend, Charlie. We were introduced at a Grammy's after-party a couple of years ago and have been friends since then, so this was uber cool news. He's meeting me on the flight, and production is sending a bodyguard along with us, which is a first. Usually one delivers me to the flight and another meets me when I land. My last film came out two months ago and the recognition factor has gone through the roof since then. You haven't lived until just standing near a pack of girls makes them *cry*. Insanity.

Bob the bodyguard arrives right on time, sweeping three months of luggage into his beefy paws and ferrying it out to the waiting limo in two trips. He's a brick building shaped like a man. I can't imagine anyone getting past this guy—not that I'm afraid of my fan base, but en masse, they can get a little out of hand. "I'll be back for the rest of your luggage, and then I'll wait in the car. We'll leave in about fifteen minutes, if that's good with you, Mr. Alexander."

I need to get over the strangeness of grown men calling me Mr. Alexander. I feel like they can't be talking to me. "Thanks, man. And call me Reid."

"Sure thing, Mr. Reid." He disappears into the dusk as Mom sidles up behind me.

"I'll miss you." Her voice is wobbly. She has a drink in her hand, so I don't know if she's overcome by emotion or she's already sloshed. A little of both, perhaps.

"I've got a few minutes. Let's sit." I take her hand and lead her into the front parlor, sinking onto the sofa with her. She leans into me, still holding my hand, finishing her drink and setting the glass lopsidedly onto a coaster. This must be her third, at least. She doesn't miss the coaster before that.

"I'll be back for a weekend or two during filming. You'll hardly notice I'm gone." This isn't quite true. Even if we don't interact much, Mom and I are aware of each other in the house. I'll be in Austin, working, playing… I think of Emma and my pulse spikes for a moment. Mom will be here, wandering the house like a ghost. "Don't you have that breast cancer benefit to work on? That should keep you busy until I'm home, right?" I hate to think of her with nothing to do but drink. Alone.

She brightens. "Yes. Melinda and I are organizing a fundraiser for that."

"See? You'll be so busy you won't miss me at all." I put my arm around her.

"That's not true."

"I'll miss you, too, Mom." The words feel insincere. I'll think of her occasionally, worry about her here and there. But we won't miss each other the same way. I glance at my watch. "Time for me to go. The flight's in a couple of hours—gotta get checked in and stuff."

We stand, and she puts her arms around me, tears in her eyes. I kiss her cheek and hug her back gently. "I love you," she says into my chest, and I feel myself tense. I don't know why it's so hard for me to say those three words. Most guys throw it around like breath, like bait.

I give her another hug, and then release her, steadying her by the shoulders. Kissing her cheek one last time, I force the words out. "Love you." And then I'm in the limo, staring out at the house that Mark and Lucy Alexander built, the house where I've lived most of my life. We circle the turn-around and out onto the street, and the tension begins to seep out of me.

Emma

I find myself on a flight to Austin—first class—with three *School Pride* cast members, all of whom are nice, and none of whom are Reid. Dammit.

Meredith Reynolds will be Lizbeth's older sister, Jane. We did a commercial for peanut butter when we were five, and small roles in a Lifetime movie together two years ago. MiShaun Grant recently left her comedic role on a Disney channel sitcom that never quite hit expected ratings. She'll play Lizbeth Bennet's best friend, Charlotte. The most famous person on our flight is Jenna Black, who'll play the youngest Bennet sister, Lydia.

Cast as the daughter of the main character in an Oscar-nominated film two years ago, Jenna collected rave reviews for her performance. She's rumored to be incredibly smart and planning to attend Princeton. I will earn my high school diploma in a few months, and have never considered going to college. Jenna, fifteen with her whole life mapped out, is insistent.

"You should go! You might want to do something else someday. And if you do continue your acting career, you'll want to cultivate your intellect to get better roles."

Cultivate my intellect?

Her logic may make perfect sense, but I'm not sure. I've always thought of myself as an average student, but when school is a tutor in a hotel room and you're turning in assignments over the Internet, there's no comparison or competition. I have no idea how I measure up to others my age, academically speaking.

We discuss the script and do some informal rehearsing during the flight. According to the film schedule Richter's assistant emailed, filming begins at 8:00 a.m. tomorrow at an Austin high school. We have two weeks until school begins there, at which point filming during the week is out, so we're doing the school sequences first.

At the hotel, girls mill around the entrance, which seems odd for this hour on a Sunday. "Fabulous," Jenna says. "The 'I heart Reid Alexander' fan club lost no time on the stalking stakeout."

The concierge, after apologizing profusely for giving the four of us the stink-eye when we walked in, confirms her assumption. "We keep escorting them out, and they keep sneaking back in, bless their hearts." His set jaw doesn't say *bless their hearts* as much as it says *I'm getting a migraine*.

Most of the fourth floor rooms are cordoned off for *School Pride* actors and crew, the studio's beefy bodyguards in place to protect Reid from his more zealous fans. As I locate my room and slide my key card into the lock mechanism, a door opens two doors down and a cute guy comes into the hallway wearing drawstring pajama bottoms and a white t-shirt. He glances back as if he's merging into traffic, nods once in my direction with a smile and a soft, "Hey," and raps twice on another door. I'm not sure if he's production staff or another one of the actors, but I'm way too tired to think about it for long.

Reid isn't shooting any scenes the first day, so he's not on set. I'm apprehensive about seeing him, nervous about what we'll be doing on film, in front of everyone. I've never worried about this sort of thing before, but then I've never been the star of anything before. I'm glad to have a day or two to get familiar with the rest of the cast.

We finish our first day of filming around five. Some days will be much longer, and some will require night filming, so we should enjoy this reprieve; but we lost two hours between California and Texas, which made eight a.m. feel like six a.m. Exhausted, Meredith and I climb into one of the cars that will transport us back to the hotel, and Brooke collapses onto the seat next to me. She's basically a life-sized Barbie doll: perfect build (thin, but curvy where it counts, long dancer's legs), perfect bone structure, clear blue eyes, blonde hair. Everything is pretty and flawless. Ninety-five percent of what people notice or talk about is her appearance, despite her acting skill. "Are you guys hungry? Because I'm star-*ving*."

My stomach, activated by the thought of food, reminds me that I skipped lunch. Craft services served gourmet pizzas and salads, but I had first-day jitters and couldn't eat.

"*Yes*," Meredith and I chorus.

Thanks to celery stick lunches, no-bread dinners and lots of cardio, Meredith and I are both slim, with physical features unlikely to inspire either resentment or adoration, but I'll take a favorable acting review over someone gushing about the shape of my ass any day. My hair color (and Meredith's) would be termed *pecan* or *tweed* according to Chloe, fake hair color expert, who's been trying to get me to highlight my hair for years by declaring things like, "It's so freaking *dull*," for motivation.

Brooke gives the driver directions to a corner bar and grill a few blocks from the hotel, where we sit by the window and watch as people leave their downtown offices. I ask if she's been to Austin before, and she says, "I grew up here," smiling as a group of college boys stroll by, all three slowing when they spot her, one waving with a shy grin. Laughing, she crosses her arms over her chest loosely, sighing, "I would chew him up and spit him out." The boy who'd waved glances back twice, disappointed and earning a punch in the arm from one of his friends.

How does Brooke find the time for enough life experience to cause this level of sexual ennui when I don't have time to go to a regular school or on a regular date? My moments of free time are erratic; granted, I'm more likely to spend them with Emily than with a boy. Boyfriends have been rare—only three. Two were fellow actors and the other was a friend of Emily's. We broke up because I literally never saw him.

Brooke scans the place after we've eaten, her eyes settling on two young professionals sitting at the bar. "I want an older guy," she says. As if she's called his name, one of them glances at Brooke, right in the middle of a sentence, his mouth slightly ajar. She smiles, holding the eye contact for a beat too long to be mistaken for anything but interest. His friend, noting his reaction, looks over as well.

If either of them watched *Life's a Beach*, the teen series Brooke spent the last two years doing, she'd look familiar. Doubtful, at their ages. I watched the show with Emily a few times. Brooke seems shockingly similar to her boy-crazed beach-girl character. Is this an act, or was her character so convincing because she was essentially playing herself?

She turns back to us, silky hair tossed over her shoulders, and the guy at the bar can't tear his eyes away from the back of her head. "It's been a while since I was in Texas. Maybe it's time to find out if *everything* is bigger here."

"Ohmigod," Meredith says. "You are *so* bad."

"I try." Brooke laughs and flashes a quick smile over her shoulder to the guy who's debating whether or not to walk over. "Let's get out of here."

Chapter 8

REID

I spot Emma the moment I get to the set, watch her glancing around—looking for me, I think. When our gazes connect, she smiles shyly. I return her smile and then shift my attention back to Tadd, who's got a running commentary going about the disappointing lack of boots and cowboy hats he's seen since landing in Austin.

"I get the whole 'keep Austin weird' and 'we're an artsy, freethinking town,' but you'd think they could at least *nod* towards the conventional Marlboro man look enough to give the place an authentic Texas feel." He huffs a sigh and twitches his head, his hair lifting and falling right back where it was.

Occasionally someone in the media or the public sees my blond hair and blue eyes, adds 'lives in California,' and concludes *surfer dude*. Standing next to Tadd, though, I could be from Canada. His platinum blond hair, straight as a razor, has two options: feathered straight down around his face, as it is now, or spiked straight up. That, coupled with clear blue eyes, a perpetual tan and his propensity to actually say things like *dude*, edge me out.

"You do realize *Brokeback* was set in Wyoming, not Texas, right?"

He peers at me through his bangs before pushing them back. "And your point is?"

"Maybe you should go look for your personal Marlboro man there."

"Unfortunately, we're filming just over a thousand miles south of Wyoming right now," he retorts.

"How do you *know* that?" I ask. Tadd has a memory bank full of trivia, apparently including an innate knowledge of US geography.

"That is not the point!" He pretends exasperation, and I laugh as conversations fade and eyes widen near us. "The point is where the hell are the *cowboys*?"

"Dallas?"

"Har-de-har," he deadpans.

That's when I spot Brooke coming onto the set. I haven't seen her, in person anyway, in years. She's even more beautiful than she was at sixteen. Staggeringly so. A morbid curiosity settles over me concerning how this is going to proceed. She's talking to Meredith Reynolds when she sees me. My role in *School Pride* has been well publicized—it can't be a surprise that I'm here. Even still, she appears taken aback. I stare at her with just a hint of a smile. I don't want her to know that her face still has the power to take my breath away. Her eyes narrow for the length of one heartbeat, and then her face goes passive. She never wavers in her conversation, turns away, doesn't look at me again.

We'll have to interact at some point. Her character is the sister of my character's best friend. We have scenes together, speaking parts with each other. Plus, in a group this small, there will be interaction between all of us, socially. If we're wishing each other dead, even silently, it won't go unnoticed.

When I walk up to the craft services table during lunch break,

I end up just behind Emma and MiShaun. Perusing the spread of sandwiches, fruit, cookies and drinks, MiShaun touches Emma's arm lightly, saying, "Don't fall asleep standing up. That wouldn't end well."

"Huh?" Emma blinks, stares into the steaming cup in her hand, and yawns. "I would kill for a double shot latté. This coffee is awful, but I need the caffeine."

MiShaun selects a turkey sandwich and a bottle of raspberry iced tea. "The time change can feel like mini jet lag. Why don't you get one of the set assistants to run to the nearest coffee house and grab a latté for you?"

"Can I do that? I mean would that be an asshole thing to ask?"

Wow, she's got a lot to learn about being a movie star.

MiShaun laughs. "No, *crazy*, they don't want the stars running off set to get their own drug of choice."

"What's funny?" I ask, stepping up between them, grabbing a sandwich from the top of one pyramid and taking a bite. Tuna. Not my favorite, but Olaf, my trainer, would approve of the protein content.

MiShaun cocks an eyebrow at me. "*You're* funny. Don't you two have a kissing scene in a few minutes? And there you go eating tuna fish, no care at all for poor Emma."

I stop chewing. "Shit. I forgot." I want to kick myself—*I forgot we're about to kiss* isn't the most flattering thing to say.

"Um, that's okay." Emma takes the smallest wedge of tuna sandwich on the platter. "I'll eat a bite, and then I won't really notice you, uh, having eaten any." She nibbles it, grimacing almost imperceptibly. "See. Problem solved."

She just ate something she hates to make me feel better. This bodes well on multiple levels. "So both of us eating it counteracts the effect? Clever. I was about to find a potted plant to spit it into."

She laughs, thank God. "Nuh-uh."

"Yuh-huh!"

MiShaun shakes her head as though we're both unbalanced.

"So, some of us are heading down to the strip tonight. Are you tagging along?" I invite her as part of the group, rather than disclosing that I want her there for myself. I take another sandwich and MiShaun gives me a horrified look.

"Reid Alexander, what would your legions of faithful fans think if I told them you eat smelly tuna sandwiches non-stop?"

"My trainer says I need to eat! Can't a guy get some protein without seeking approval from everyone? God!" Smiling, I snatch a third sandwich and start to walk away, turning without stopping and pointing at Emma. Like an afterthought. "So yes for tonight?"

"Yeah, sure. Sounds cool."

"Awesome. See you in a few."

Emma

We're filming the scene of the audition.

When Reid pulls me into his arms and brushes his mouth over mine, he tastes like spearmint. There's no trace of tuna anywhere, which means we've both brushed our teeth since our earlier conversation at the craft services table. (I also flossed and gargled. Twice.) No one but me would know or care whether he tastes like fish or candy when we kiss; his minty fresh breath is for me alone. This knowledge sends a silly spark of euphoria through me.

And then Richter pulls me back to earth. "Cut! Perfect. Unfortunately, we have to film it again." *Unfortunately* is not the word I would use for a required retake. He swivels around, looking for someone. "Scott—the lighting is much too ambient. It's a high school hallway for chrissake, it's going to be *bright*."

I steal a glance at Reid as he stands next to me, the ends of his hair being tweaked to best show the streaks of light blond highlights through the natural dark blond. His eyes are closed as our hair girl, all five foot zero of her, circles him, pulling and spraying. Someone brushes powder on my forehead and refreshes my lip color. Before I have the sense to look away, his eyes open and he's staring back. He smiles then, and my mouth goes dry. I lick my lips lightly and his gaze darts to my mouth. When his gaze drifts back to mine, his smile both devious and breathtaking.

Oh, yeah. I'm in trouble.

We have an outdoor scene to film this afternoon. Meredith and I rehearse lines as we near the exit, until we hear screams from the street-side end of the parking lot. Brooke and Jenna come up behind us and we all peek out.

Jenna sighs. "Looks like afternoon filming is about to hit a snag."

"I think every mindless girl in Texas between twelve and twenty is at the other end of that lot," Brooke says.

"More I heart Reid Alexander fans?" I ask needlessly, and she nods. I'm relieved to see our cast bodyguards and two local police officers on our side of the temporary three-foot barrier. Meredith and I exit cautiously while Jenna and Brooke stride out ahead, unconcerned.

"Don't worry, if any of them get over that blockade, they'll make a beeline straight for Reid," Jenna tells Meredith and me. "Maybe Quinton, but he shouldn't hold his breath."

"He'd want *that*?" Meredith points at the screaming crowd.

"Guys always want it." Brooke answers. "They assume every girl on the planet thinks they're hot as hell and they'll get laid any time they want. Which is, for the most part, true."

A piercing scream for Reid rings across the lot. "God, how will we get any filming done?" Meredith mumbles.

"Depends what Richter does about it." Jenna shrugs. "Fans aren't inherently evil, and they don't want to ruin the film. They're just a little irrational."

Jenna's Oscar-nominated film starred a couple of red-hot thirty-somethings, and the experience left her with an undaunted perception of celebrity groupies. I suspect she'll need that aloofness. Her dark hair, huge gray eyes and full lips inspired a *Vogue* photographer to dub her face a work of art last spring, and the cover featuring her not-quite-grown version of Brooke's build kicked off a few *countdown-to-18* calculations (yet another reason I'm satisfied with my non-bombshell body).

Reid's exit from the building causes pandemonium like nothing I've ever witnessed, with the possible exception of a bad call during a game my father and I attended at Yankee Stadium years ago. He ducks his head shyly before raising one hand in the direction of the uproar, which only increases the clamor.

The fans are eventually persuaded to settle down with the promise of an up-close visit from Reid for photos and autographs when we're done. He's either exceptionally dedicated or just reckless; nothing will entice *me* to venture near that insanity. The crowd remains hushed every time Richter turns towards them and holds his hands up, right up until he yells, "Cut!" at which point they lose it again.

By the time the light is too muted to film outside, the fans have been waiting for hours. "Come with me," Reid says, smiling and holding his hand out for mine.

"Er…" I eye the crowd, remembering my earlier intention to never get anywhere near *that*.

"Come on, they'll want to meet Lizbeth Bennet." His voice is warm, coaxing. I take a deep breath and reach for his hand against all of my natural inclination.

Well. Maybe not *all* of my natural inclination.

Me: Reid dragged me over to meet his rabid fans when we were done.

Em: OMG! Will there be pictures on the internet??

Me: Ha, i'm sure. Going out with everyone tonight. A club i think. Not sure i can get in?

Em: You're a celebrity now, they'll let you in everywhere!

Me: Idk

Em: If you make out with reid take pictures on your phone and SEND THEM TO ME

Me: EMILY you know i don't kiss and sext

Em: Oh fine just forget the little people now that you're a big star

Me: Em. You know you'll never be little people to me

Em: Miss you toooo

Chapter 9

REID

"Look at this suite—holy shit, dude, do girls even get all the way into the room before their panties hit the floor?" Tadd's come up to my room with me to borrow my laptop.

"Jealous?"

"Of the girls? I think not. Of your room? Hell, yeah." He plops onto the king-sized bed, hands behind his head. "Corner balcony. Elevated bed. Fresh flowers. Dude. *Sweet.*" I hand him the laptop and he brings up his email. "Hey man, is Quinton a go for tonight?"

I pull out my phone and tap a text. Quinton texts back a yes a minute later. "Of course he is—Quinton's always a go. Who else? MiShaun and Emma said yes earlier."

"I talked to some of the extras about where the best spots are, so a bunch of them might show. And I told Meredith, Jenna and Brooke… and Graham, who, by the way, is *hot* and I was hoping also gay, because he appears to be close friends with Brooke, but no such luck."

I process this for a moment. "Graham and Brooke are close—and he's straight? How do you know they aren't screwing each other? Maybe they're a thing. Or a friends-with-benefits thing."

Tadd shrugs. "Maybe. I didn't get that vibe, but hey, you people make everything more complicated."

"What's complicated about friends-with-benefits?"

He shakes his head, his eyes still on the screen. "Dude, that's something my people perfected long ago. You guys can't get away with it because girls are more likely to want emotion, attachment, *love*." The latter is punctuated with an exaggerated shudder.

"You obviously don't know Brooke very well. She's like a guy with boobs."

He laughs. "Sorry, Reid, but in my world, the primary aspect being a guy is *not* the having or not having of boobs. I've seen Brooke's *Life's a Beach* promos—her swimsuits are a couple of ribbons tied together. If she has underlying physical features of which I'm unaware, I'd like to know where she's hiding them."

"Aaaand thanks for that mental picture," I say. "What I mean is, she thinks like a guy. She's detached. Calculating."

He closes the laptop and puts it aside. "So you screwed her and she didn't love you back? Aww, that's so sad."

"Piss off, man." Laughing, I shove him and he rolls off the bed.

"What I mean is, she sounds perfect! You can screw each other's brains out and just walk away." He sits back down on the bed, his eyes on mine. "Or is that pretty much what already happened…"

I forgot how good Tadd is at digging deep fast. "Something like that. I really don't care." And I don't.

"Then who cares what she and Graham are doing?" he says, making all sorts of sense.

I think about Emma. "You're right. I've got better ways to spend my time."

Emma

I raise my voice above the music so MiShaun can hear me. "I can't believe we all got in."

"Get used to celebrity, baby!" She clinks her glass to mine. Once the guy at the door got a look at Reid, we were all escorted inside without an eye-bat at anyone's ID.

Our group takes up a corner near the bar plus half of the tiny dance floor, and our brawny bodyguards look like they're standing inside a child's playhouse. While I sip my drink, we examine the rest of the cast. Jenna, Meredith, Tadd and Reid are dancing. Brooke is seated on a velvet sofa with the guy I'd seen leaving his hotel room in his pajamas two nights ago.

I lean to MiShaun. "Who's the guy sitting next to Brooke?"

"That's Graham Douglas." Though he's twenty feet from us and can't possibly hear, his eyes snap up. He smiles and tips his chin back like guys do to indicate a sort of non-verbal *hey*, and MiShaun raises her drink in his direction. When Brooke turns to see who's taken Graham's attention from her, I develop a sudden and intense interest in the dance floor.

Running through the cast names in my head, I realize Graham is playing the part of Bill Collins, one of the nerdiest guys in literature. I slide my eyes back to him. In close conversation with Brooke, he leans in as she speaks, one arm draped across the back of the low sofa. "Do you know him?" His dark hair is on the longish side, swept back except for errant sections that fall forward. Unlike the other guys in our group, who are fashionably disheveled in t-shirts and jeans, Graham wears black slacks and a blue button-down, top buttons undone, sleeves rolled up.

"I've never worked with him. He's done mostly indie

stuff. He was in something that did well in Sundance this year…"

Graham Douglas is nothing like I would picture Elizabeth Bennet's ridiculous cousin. "He's sort of, I don't know—too good-looking to play Collins?"

"A fellow Jane Austen fan!" MiShaun puts a hand up for a high-five. "Don't worry, once he gets into makeup, they'll do ghastly things to that handsome mug."

I can't help thinking that will be a shame.

Dragging my gaze from Graham, I notice that Reid has gathered a small harem of locals on the dance floor. The bodyguards hover, not interfering, but ready to at a second's notice. MiShaun follows the direction of my gaze and shakes her head. "That boy is such a player."

In everything I've ever heard about Reid Alexander, one thing he hasn't done is sustained a relationship past a matter of weeks. *Player* is right, and I shouldn't expect anything more from him, chemistry or no chemistry. Even still, I don't think he's looked at me once since we arrived.

Quinton Beauvier, whose role is the notoriously charming George Wickham, steps up behind us then, placing a hand on each of our shoulders. "Ladies," he says. Tall and dark-skinned, hair cropped short, he's boyishly handsome and easily the most muscled guy in the cast. An article in Emily's favorite gossip magazine claimed he was as the hottest young actor to watch, and included a pull-out poster—now prominently taped on her closet door—in which he leans against a rickety rail fence wearing an introspective look, hands hooked in the front pockets of his low-slung jeans, biceps bulging out of a skin-tight white t-shirt.

"Mr. Beauvier," MiShaun says, smiling.

"Would either of you like to dance? Reid and his cult followers are monopolizing the floor, and that boy can't even dance. Look at him, just swaying around. Pitiful."

"In his defense, he doesn't have room to do much else," I say, and Quinton laughs.

"Yeah, yeah. So it's the principle of the thing."

"Go dance, Emma. I'm gonna head back to the bar for another one of these," MiShaun holds up her disappearing cosmopolitan, "and then I'm going to go ask that blond guy who's been staring at me for the last fifteen minutes to dance. Or something…" She gestures over her shoulder, where a guy in a white starched shirt and loose tie leans against the bar within a group of friends. Any time he looks away from MiShaun, his eyes wander back to her within seconds.

Quinton takes my hand and flashes a brilliant smile. "Let's show that boy how it's *done*." I don't know if Reid's watching or not, but for a few minutes, I forget about him.

Ten minutes later, I tell Quinton, "You're an awesome dancer."

He smiles, revealing small dimples and utterly perfect teeth. Emily will *die* when I tell her. "I love to dance. It was my backup plan, in case the acting thing didn't work out." I look out over the crowd, most of whom are watching our group. Reid sips a beer near the bar, girls surrounding him. He glances up then and smiles at me, but doesn't make any move to break from his groupies.

I turn away, ask Quinton if he's seen MiShaun.

"She's still talking to that scruffy white guy." He gestures towards a dark corner, where the two are seated at a tiny table in close proximity, talking animatedly. Quinton shrugs and we both smile.

After a couple of hours, another drink, and several dances with numerous cast members (none of whom are Reid, dammit), the physical exertion reminds me how much I need to get back into my daily running routine. There's no way I can stay out later and get up at the crack of dawn to run. I tell Quinton and Meredith I'm going back to the hotel.

Quinton sways closer, a beer in one hand, the other outstretched. "You can't give out now. It's early!"

"It's 1 a.m.!" I laugh. "That's early?"

"We're just getting started!" Meredith says.

"I have to get up tomorrow morning and run."

They both look horrified. "What, before shooting?"

I wave to Jenna, who's dancing nearby, but I *don't* look for Reid. "Yeah, it's a million degrees by noon. See you guys tomorrow!"

The valet calls a taxi while I wait in the shadow of the building, watching the mixture of young professionals and college students pass. I've never told anyone except Emily, but I know I owe my acting ability to compulsive people-watching. I could never express the emotions of so many various people, some of whom I can't stand even if they *are* fictional, if I didn't constantly watch people interact.

"They'll have a taxi over in a couple minutes," the valet tells me with a slight drawl.

"Thanks," I answer, handing him a tip.

"No problem." He smiles back and stuffs the bill in the front pocket of his vest.

As I peel a breath mint from its wrapper, Graham Douglas exits the club alone and moves to the opposite side of the entrance, lighting a cigarette. Something about a well-dressed guy lighting up is curiously attractive. This allure can probably be traced to the old black and white movies Mom and I used to watch, where everyone smoked: Cary Grant and Clark Gable and Bette Davis, men in tuxedos, women in glittering gowns, cigarettes loosely held like insidious little props.

Lighter back in his pocket, Graham takes a deep draw, exhaling as though every muscle in his body is releasing the stress of the day with the hazy stream. Passing girls glance at him with sidelong gazes, checking to see if he's noticed them while he leans against the brick wall, running a hand through his dark hair and tapping on his cell. He seems oblivious until with no warning he lifts his gaze and I'm caught staring at him for the second time tonight. Smiling and pushing away from the wall, he crosses to me.

"Hey, you caught me," he says, echoing my thoughts.

"Taking a break from the club scene, or are you just that addicted?" I ask, teasing.

He glances at the cigarette in his hand like he has no idea how it got there. "Er… both?"

"Ma'am, your taxi's here," the valet interrupts.

"Going back to the hotel?" he asks, and I nod. "Mind if I tag along?"

"Sure, no problem," I say. He crams the cigarette into an ashtray atop a trash can and follows me into the cab as I give the name of the hotel to the driver.

"I'm Graham, by the way." He holds his hand out and I take it. His grip is firm but not crushing.

"Emma." The cab driver makes a *humph* sound and I realize that we've just gotten into a cab bound for a hotel, and we're exchanging *names*. My face flames in the darkness.

Graham's eyes narrow, flashing momentarily to the cabbie. He clears his throat. "So how did filming go today? I meant to go along to observe, but decided I could use a day to go over the script and, you know, oversleep."

"It went really well. Some interesting off-camera action, too—Reid had a devoted crowd of groupies just off set."

He shrugs, smiling. "Yeah, if fans discover his location, he's mobbed wherever he goes."

"Huh," I say.

His phone buzzes and he checks the screen, types a reply and returns it to his pocket. When we arrive at the hotel, he brushes off my effort to pay half. We're both silent as we walk to the elevator. I think about him leaving his room in his pajamas to play sleepover with someone, probably Brooke, from their postures in the club… But he left the club, and Brooke, and came back to the hotel with me. Maybe it was her he was just texting.

The elevator's low-key ding announces the fourth floor, and I nearly stop breathing as I realize what he might expect—having come back to the hotel *with me*. What if he thinks *I* want to play sleepover? Heart pounding as we walk down the carpeted hallway, I hear nothing beyond the *swish, swish, swish* of the blood racing through my ears. I recall Emily's tales of Hollywood hedonism. *Crap*. I didn't plan to stand out as the cast prude quite so soon, but there's no way I'm sleeping with some guy I just met, I don't care how hot he is.

As we approach his door, he pulls out his wallet, retrieves his key card and turns to me as he sticks it into the lock. "Thanks for sharing your cab."

"No problem." *Swish, swish, swish.*

The lock on his door blinks green and he opens the door. "Well, goodnight," he says, while I stand there like a moron.

"Goodnight." I turn quickly, rummaging in my bag for my key card as I walk away. Unlocking my door, I glance back, and I'm alone in the hallway, muttering, "Idiot," to myself.

Chapter 10

REID

A quarter after one, and I haven't seen Emma in a few minutes. I've been keeping track of where she is all night, covertly. The one time we made eye contact, she was dancing with Quinton. They moved perfectly together, and she looked so hot I almost ditched the mindless pack of girls clustered around and asked her to dance right then. I opted to wait a little longer. Now I'm rethinking that dimwitted decision, because she's nowhere.

Did she leave with some guy? Disappointing, but not impossible. She may be better at this game than I've given her credit for. Time for inventory. Quinton's here, dancing with Jenna. Tadd's chatting with Brooke—which gives me a moment's pause, but he's too loyal to tell her anything I've said. He also won't tell *me* anything *she* says, but I don't care to know what she thinks or says anyway.

Looking at Brooke, though, reminds me of Graham. And I don't see Graham anywhere.

"God, I'm so drunk!" one of the girls near me says, making sure I'm listening. "I feel completely crazy tonight, like I could get talked into doing practically *anything*."

Wow. Subtle. "Oh, yeah?" I say.

"Absolutely. Try me." She leans against me, breasts all but escaping from the plunging neckline of her sundress.

"Okay." I glance around the circle, take the hand of another awestruck girl. I pull her forward gently and say to Miss I'm-So-Drunk, "Take my friend here, and go out there and dance together."

A flash of disappointment darts across each of their faces before they size each other up. Sharing is better than not having at all. With a wicked smile, girl number one takes girl number two by the hand and they proceed to make a spectacle of themselves, just because I said to.

Meanwhile, Meredith comes to the bar for a drink and I pull her aside. "Have you seen Emma?" My voice is as casual as can be.

"Oh, yeah, she left a while back. She said something about running in the morning?"

"What, before filming?"

"Yeah—crazy, huh?" She takes two drinks from the bartender.

"Definitely." I get another beer and pay attention to Thing One and Thing Two, who are learning the value of sharing.

Emma

My phone alarm sounds at six. I'm momentarily disoriented, then sorry that I made a pact with myself to run. As I pull on shorts and brush my hair into a ponytail, I avoid looking towards the unmade bed, all soft sheets and downy pillows. Perusing the map of running routes around Town Lake that the hotel provided, I lace up my shoes, determined to escape this room before the bed convinces me to ditch the run and sleep.

As I cross the lobby, I hear my name. Turning, I'm surprised to see Graham in a t-shirt, shorts and Pumas. "Hey, going for a run?" he asks, and then he stops, noting my confused expression. "Listen, I don't want to impose if you like to run alone—"

"Oh… no, I was just going to look for one of the trails on this map."

"Come on, then," he says as we exit the hotel. "I have a vast one day of experience in finding the trails, so I sort of know where to go. If nothing else, I can promise we won't end up in Dallas. Or Mexico."

I note a few girls standing in a cluster off to the side, coffees in hand. They're watching as Graham and I walk down the steps, disappointment clear on their faces. I wonder if they're part of Jenna's "I heart Reid" fanclub.

"Do you run every day?"

He shrugs one shoulder. "I do all kinds of stuff—running, rock-climbing, biking, spin class, weights, yoga. Gets boring otherwise."

"Huh," I say. "I mostly run. I have a hard time remembering to do a sit up or a crunch every now and then. I can't do aerobics because I'm a horrible dancer. I *won't* do a spin class. If I want someone to abuse me verbally during exercise, I'll just get my agent to drive alongside me and yell obscenities while I run."

"I don't believe you're a horrible dancer, since I know better from personal, well, not experience, exactly, but maybe personal *observation*." He's studying the map and street signs, and I wonder if he actually meant to tell me he'd watched me dance last night. A warm hum shoots through me, especially in light of Reid's brush-off, which doesn't sting any less this morning than it had last night.

"Dancing in a class is different, especially if they have equipment like portable steps or those ginormous rubber bands? Disaster."

He laughs. "Seriously, who thought up those rubber bands?"

We run the couple of blocks to the trail as the sun emerges fully behind us, the sky transforming to a lighter and lighter shade of blue, no clouds in sight. Austin is having an unseasonable "cool spell." According to the local weather update the temps will *only* be in the mid-nineties by five p.m. I wonder if they understand the definition of the word *cool* here.

"Thanks for inviting me along," Graham says, and when I look up at him with the same confused look I had in the lobby, he smiles.

I can't help but smile back as he matches his pace to mine.

We're far enough from the hotel now that when I glance back, I can't see it. "Did you see those girls in front of the hotel?"

"Wondering if they were some of Reid's followers?" he asks, and I nod. "Probably so."

"Crazy."

"You may want to prepare for your *own* groupies, you know."

"Pshhh." I wave him off, unconvinced that I'm about to become famous, though he's only echoing what Emily said just before I left home.

"When you're playing opposite someone with his fan base, everything the two of you do will be scrutinized. For instance, if there's on-screen chemistry, people will assume you have it off-screen."

"Huh," I say, remembering my foolish thoughts about Reid and chemistry. Before last night. When he blew me off.

"You say that a lot, you know." As we find the trail, the cityscape gives way to gravel paths surrounded by faded, end-of-summer green.

I frown. "I say what a lot?"

"Huh."

A light bulb goes on in my head. "I say 'huh' a lot?"

"Maybe we should start counting." He grins down at me as I'm estimating exactly how embarrassed I should be. "By the time I get to twenty or so, you'll have broken the habit if for nothing else than sheer annoyance's sake. We'll call that last time *one*."

I frown at him good-naturedly and he laughs softly again. Is this an old habit, or a newly ingrained one? *Why* would Emily not point this out? I make a mental note to grill her during our next conversation.

"Maybe we won't be that convincing onscreen," I say, returning to the previous subject, which is not, I realize belatedly, grounds for non-self-conscious discussion.

"I doubt that. This is an adaptation of one of the most romantic novels ever written. There *has* to be chemistry."

I give him a narrow-eyed look. "If this is your idea of 'no pressure,' it's not working."

"They wouldn't have chosen you if the chemistry wasn't there. I'm just pointing out what being a romantic lead opposite him might do to your private life. Such as, there's no *way* Reid could do what we're doing right now without bodyguards." He moves behind me briefly so the elderly couple walking towards us on the pathway don't have to squish together.

"I hadn't thought about it like that," I say as he falls in beside me. I think of Emily, who isn't a crazed fangirl, but would still freak out if she saw Reid in person.

"Well. No reason to panic. Yet."

"Yeah. Yet," I echo.

Chapter 11

REID

Most of the cast is going to Kenichi for sushi. So far, Austin hasn't been as backwater as I assumed it might be, though most of the city is more laid-back and casual than the parts of LA I'm used to.

One glance at Emma tells me she's still adapting to the commotion caused when we all go anywhere. Tonight, Richter and Leslie Neale are joining us, which adds to the crazy. Leslie, cast as Mrs. Bennet, boasts an impressive film career spanning nearly forty years. Even still, she's undeniably hot, and as famous for her romantic exploits (often with men decades younger) as she is for her professional capability. The tabloids love her.

The restaurant staff is either used to celebrities popping in, or they've been cautioned to remain composed. The effect on the patrons is a different story. Cell phones angle towards us as we're ushered to the table, voices whispering from person to person alongside us, like waving grain. Typical crowd reaction to celebrity in their midst.

Graham and Brooke are behind Quinton, Tadd and me on

the way in, Emma and the other girls ahead of us. I haven't seen Graham with Emma, so I'm not sure if they're acquainted. If Emma left the club with Graham, or someone else, she did so damned discreetly, because no one appears to have any idea. I step up to her now, say quietly, "Hey beautiful," my hand at the small of her back. She glances up, the faintest blush spreading across her cheeks. The room instantly begins to speculate about us. I can feel it.

We're led through the restaurant to a long table, offset from the others, set parallel to the back wall, which is covered in shoji screens. Semi-private, conversationally speaking, we're visually conspicuous. I take Emma's elbow and lead her to the center of the side facing out, and MiShaun files in next to her. Richter takes one of the ends with Leslie Neale to his left, and Quinton takes the other end, everyone else filling in. Graham sits next to Brooke, directly across from us. He smiles at Emma, which tells me they're definitely acquainted.

The staff hovers, cordial and professional greetings are spoken, menus handed over shoulders, drink orders taken and filled. While Richter and Leslie are ordering, Quinton leans up and asks the rest of us, "We going out after?"

"I heard there's a cool blues place around here somewhere," Tadd answers.

MiShaun regards him skeptically. "You like blues?"

"I like *music*, especially live music."

"Do you play anything?" She sips her sake.

"I play guitar," he answers. "Just enough to be dangerous."

"Graham plays guitar," Brooke says then, and from my viewpoint it looks as though she follows this announcement up with a hand on his leg under the table. "He's *amazing*."

"Uh-oh," I say quietly, leaning close to Emma's ear, "looks like Brooke has decided on this film's prey." She looks confused, so I elaborate. "You know—one guy from every film. I'm not sure what the policy was on her little cable series." This is gossip, not fact, but hey, I didn't originate it.

Her voice is equally hushed. "That's, um, kind of sleazy."

I laugh. "You think?"

"What?" Brooke sips a Japanese beer, her eyes narrowed at me. Emma tenses while Graham watches our tête-à-tête from across the table, his expression guarded.

"Nothing, nothing, keep your shirt on," I say. "We were just wondering who'd be more dangerous with a guitar—Tadd or Graham."

Brooke arches one brow and narrows her eyes even more. "What's the verdict?"

"Well, I've never heard Graham play, so it's hardly something I can decide here."

"Maybe we should stage a little competition in my room later," Brooke suggests. "They can both play for all of us."

"Sounds cool," Tadd says. "Alas, I didn't bring my guitar this trip. I forgot my laptop, extra contact lenses, hell, I barely remembered pants." Emma laughs softly next to me. She's so damned cute I can barely stand it.

"You can borrow Graham's," Brooke says, turning to ask Graham after the fact, "Is that okay?"

"Sure, no problem." He couldn't be more compliant. She *must* be sleeping with him. "Let's call it a jam session, though, rather than a competition."

"You know, if there's no competition, you can't *win*," she adds, and I hear this comment with the gossip I just passed to Emma in mind.

"Winning is overrated," he answers.

"Huh," Emma says, and Graham's eyes snap to hers.

Four? he mouths, and she shakes her head once, glaring but looking more like she's trying not to smile. *Three*, he mouths, and she rolls her eyes and mouths back *fine*.

Um, *what*? I glance at Brooke and see her thoughts are similar to mine, her eyes darting back and forth between them.

Emma and Graham don't look at each other again the rest of the meal.

Emma

Brooke suggests that we all raid our mini-bars of tiny liquor bottles so we can pool our resources. Her room, predictably, is the one I saw Graham enter my first night in Austin, less than a week ago, when I didn't know who he was. Now we're becoming friends, but he hasn't said a thing to me about Brooke.

I call Emily when I'm changing in my room a couple of hours later. "He seems like a nice guy… and she seems like a junior Chloe."

"You don't know him well enough to point out *that* kind of hazard. If they're just screwing around, and you guys are just friends—you *are* just friends, right?"

"*Yes.*"

"He's a guy, Em. They think differently than we do. You can bet a *guy* invented the whole friends-with-benefits thing. Though if Quinton Beauvier showed up at my door and said, 'Which way to your bedroom?' I'd be like, 'Right this way!' But, you know, we wouldn't be friends. We'd just be benefits."

I shake my head. For all of her talk, Emily's the most guarded person I know when it comes to actually getting involved with a guy. Smart of her, because once she's involved, she's in all the way. She's had her heart shattered twice, and standing on the sidelines was the hardest thing ever for me. "Well, at least you have your standards. I'm putting you on speakerphone while I get dressed for the guitar hero challenge."

"What are you wearing to this little soiree?"

"Brooke suggested PJs." I toss the phone on the bed after

hitting speakerphone and adjusting the volume.

"What are you guys gonna do? And moreover, if all these hot guys are going to be there *why was I not invited?*"

I groan. "Emily, *focus*. I have no idea what the agenda is, beyond the guitar playing. I've never been on a set with so many people in my age group. I've always been pointedly excluded from cast get-togethers, what with me being a decade or several younger than everyone else." I stand in front of the mirror holding up a pink t-shirt and then a black tank top, back and forth. "Plus you *know* if you were here, I'd share."

"Fine, you're forgiven. Got capri pj pants?"

"Yeah." I pull a pair out of a drawer and shake the creases out. "They're pink with black polka dots. Too babyish?"

"No, perfect. Pink and black are so retro lingerie, very chic. Slap your black tank on and you're ready to go." I pull the pants on, tie the drawstring loosely, and then pull the black tank over my head. Mirror check. Cute.

"Emily, you're a genius."

"Yeah, yeah. Text me when you get back in your room, I want to know *everything*."

"You are such a gossip whore, Emily."

"Hey, just be glad I'm not asking you to set up a webcam… wait a minute, that's an idea…"

"Bye, Emily!" I laugh, shaking my head.

"Text me, text me, text me." Her disembodied voice comes from the bed. "Do *not* forget!"

"I won't forget! You know I tell you everything. Miss you."

"Miss you, too."

As I pass Graham's room, he exits with his guitar in one hand and a standard-sized bottle of tequila in the other, which reminds me that my hands are empty. "Oh, I forgot—" I say, turning back.

"Carry this." He hands me the tequila. "Should be enough

entry fee for both of us." He's wearing a different pair of drawstring pajama bottoms than the other night, paired with a heather gray t-shirt.

I'm about to go into a room full of people near my age, all wearing pajamas and drinking. Cue a hearty dose of panic. "What exactly are we doing?"

He shrugs. "I assume Tadd and I are going to provide some musical entertainment. And then, I don't know. Sit around and talk, I guess."

Talk. Right.

Thanks to Emily, I didn't miss *all* of my high school experiences. I tagged along to enough parties with Em and her friends where there was a keg, or someone's parents didn't lock the liquor cabinet, or a fake ID was good enough to score a case of beer or a bottle of vodka. Talking isn't what people end up doing when they're young and plastered. But this is a small group, and we still have most of the film to shoot. Things can't get too out of hand or it will be insanely awkward.

We stop at Brooke's door and I take a deep breath. Graham touches my arm. "Hey, don't stress. I'll make sure you get to your room safe and sound. Well, safe and as sound as you can be if you have any of *that*." He points to the bottle in my hand.

"All right." I'm just hoping that me plus alcohol plus Reid Alexander in the same room won't equal potential humiliating candor.

"Ready?" At my nod, Graham knocks, *thunk-thunk*, just as he did a few nights ago. Tadd opens the door, and Graham stands back, smiling down at me. "Ladies first."

Chapter 12

REID

I got to Brooke's room first. When she opened the door, it was déjà vu for about two seconds. And then not. Four years ago we would have been all over each other before I got five feet inside her room. Tonight, she just glared and backed up enough for me to enter. "Reid," she said.

"Brooke." I set several small bottles down on a table, keeping a couple and opening one, which I downed immediately. Tossing the bottle into her trash, I opened the second. "So how long has it been?" I said, knowing this was a reckless path to navigate.

Her jaw tightened and she plopped onto the loveseat, trying to look indifferent and fearless at the same time, raising her chin and looking me in the eye. "I have no idea."

A knock sounded then and I turned, relieved, to admit MiShaun, Quinton and Jenna. A moment later, Tadd arrived.

Brooke holds court from the loveseat while MiShaun flips through the most recent *Cosmo* from the only chair. The rest of us lounge across the floor, chatting, while I wonder how disturbed I should be that Emma and Graham are the only two who haven't shown yet. Five minutes pass before they show up, together.

"The prima donnas arrive," MiShaun teases.

"Seriously, what took you guys so long?" Brooke's eyes dart back and forth between the two of them.

Emma picks up on her territorial vibe and bristles visibly, her shoulders stiffening. "I had a phone call to make." She holds out the bottle in her hand. "Um, where—?"

"Put it with the other stuff." Brooke indicates a side table boasting a dozen miniature bottles. Emma hands the tequila to Quinton while Tadd lines up gift shop shot glasses with college emblems stamped on the sides. Smiling up at Graham, Brooke pats the cushion next to her, while Emma sits on the floor in the space between Jenna and me, exactly where I want her.

"What's first, children?" Brooke asks.

Tadd stands, places one hand over his heart and enunciates as though delivering a line from Hamlet. "I require a dose of liquid courage for the challenge before me."

"I second that." Quinton pries the wrapper from the neck of the bottle Emma brought, which I suspect came via Graham, twists off the lid and begins pouring tequila shots.

Grabbing a bottle of rum from the stash and pouring it directly into her Diet Coke bottle, Brooke suggests we toast the success of the film, "before we're all too hammered to remember what we're doing." Everyone obediently clinks glasses and bottles, murmuring *to the film*.

"Where's Meredith?" Jenna asks.

"The *boyfriend* was waiting for her in the lobby when we got back from dinner." Brooke shrugs. "Looks like splitsville to me."

"Okay, wait." Tadd is incredulous. "The guy showed up *on set* to break up with her? What a douche."

"I don't know who's breaking up with who, just that it looked imminent. So, Mr. Wyler, what are you performing for our listening pleasure?" she asks as Graham hands him the guitar.

"Either *Stairway to Heaven* or some John Mayer," Tadd proposes, standing and picking out a few chords, testing the instrument.

"If that's all you've got, then definitely John Mayer. What are we, fifty?" Brooke says.

"Zeppelin is classic!" he insists, which earns him a steady *boo* from the girls.

"The queen has spoken," I say, handing him a second shot of tequila, catching Brooke's eye and grinning as she seethes. She's determined to be pissed at anything I say or do; might as well enjoy it.

Tadd downs the shot, plunks the glass on a table and starts strumming, singing lines of *Your Body is a Wonderland* to each of the girls, strolling around the room and ending the performance perched on MiShaun's lap. As everyone applauds, he bows and passes the guitar to Graham.

"Graham, no Zeppelin, as I believe we've already established," Brooke says.

"I thought I'd do something I've been working on."

"Something you wrote yourself?"

"Still a work in progress, but, yeah."

"Cool." She touches his arm lightly, and I bump Emma lightly and raise both eyebrows in the universal gesture of *do you see that?*

Graham slides to the edge of the loveseat and starts playing, the chords complicated, his fingers moving over the neck of the guitar like he's caressing it. The vocals are definitely good. Unlike Tadd, he doesn't look at anyone while performing, except once, towards the end of the last chorus, when his eyes meet Emma's for a split second. I move from *guarded dislike* to *I hate this guy.*

When he finishes, everyone erupts into applause. He and Tadd trade sets while the rest of us sip whatever poison we've decided to utilize, and Quinton suggests a drinking game.

Brooke explains the rules to Jenna, who's never played. "This game has two objects: we learn stupid stuff about each other, and everyone gets wasted." She scoots off the loveseat, taking Graham's hand and pulling him down. "Tadd will start by saying, 'Never have I ever,' followed by something he's never done. Anyone who *has* done whatever it is has to take a drink. Girls, we can handicap ourselves by taking half-shots."

The first Never Have I Ever that pops into my head involves Emma, and isn't one I can say aloud. Besides, I intend for it to be invalid by the end of the week, if not the end of the night.

Emma

Quinton pours out shots as Tadd supplies the first never-done thing. "Never have I ever… been an only child."

Reid and I each down our glasses, and as the tequila blazes a path down my throat, I gasp. I've never been much of a drinker. During the parties I attended with Emily, we pretended to drink more than we actually drank.

"This isn't a good start for us." He grins as my eyes tear. "That, or it's an *awesome* start." He leans the length of his arm against mine for a moment, his skin a couple of shades darker, his forearm chiseled, the fine blond hairs raising goosebumps where we touch. "Are you cold?" He runs a finger along my arm, multiplying them.

"I guess so." I don't want to admit that I have goosebumps all over my body, that my stomach has just gone end-over-end due to his proximity and attention. He moves closer until our sides are pressing together. Oh yeah. *That's* gonna help.

"Never have I ever bungee-jumped," Jenna says.

"Well, crap." MiShaun throws back her half-shot, along

with Tadd.

"Far be it from me to suggest you wear more to warm up." Reid's warm breath stirs the baby hairs behind my ear, his smile hungry after a glance towards the just-low-enough neckline of my tank. *Thank you, Emily.*

My turn. "Never have I ever sung on stage." I know I'll be in the minority in this room full of film and theatre types.

"Diabolical," Reid says, his voice a low hum, admiration in the smirk he gives me before he joins everyone else in another shot. The beginnings of a buzz make my head swim, and I fight not to sway towards him like a magnet towards a steel bar.

Reid turns to the room, aware that it's his turn even if I'm aware of little beyond him. "Never have I ever... kissed a guy." All four girls roll our eyes and down our half-shots, and I realize I'm on my way to a colossal hangover. Good thing there's no filming tomorrow.

"Way to out me right away, dude." Tadd throws back his shot, smiling wickedly. "And let me know if you want me to fix that for you."

Graham downs his shot as well. "Damned independent films," he growls good-naturedly as Quinton hoots with laughter.

"Never have I ever eaten lobster." Quinton says, and everyone in the room grabs their shot glasses.

Tadd makes a "T" with his hands. "Time out, time out, that *can't* be true, I call bullshit."

"Wrong game, baby. Chill." MiShaun tousles his pale, poker-straight hair.

Brooke waits until Tadd curses once and drinks. "Never have I ever been in love," she says, staring at Reid. He stares back, neither moving. Graham takes a drink, watching me. I'm not sure what being in love feels like, but I sense that what I felt for Justin from Newark, or certainly anyone else since him, wasn't it. I don't drink.

"Never have I ever been to Hawaii," Graham says. I'm

the only person who doesn't drink, and he smiles at me from the opposite side of the circle. Hawaii is where my father and Chloe honeymooned.

"Never have I ever—" MiShaun pauses for effect, "played this stupid game before." She clinks glasses with Jenna while everyone else takes a drink.

Tadd admits that never has he ever learned to ride a bicycle, and everyone else groans and downs a shot before Jenna admits that she's never learned to swim.

"What?" Brooke downs her half-shot. "We need to get you out to the pool. What if you land a part in a film where you have to dive into a lake, and come up wet and sexy?"

"That's a good point." Jenna chews her lip.

"Wet and sexy? Really?" Quinton fans himself with the discarded *Cosmo*. "Does everybody need to be able to pop outta the water looking like your *Life's a Beach* poster?"

"Yes, and I'm well-qualified to teach that sk-skill." Brooke's poster was issued the month she turned eighteen. She stands in calf-deep surf, holding a surf board and clad in a wetsuit, unzipped to mid-chest, with her finger through the zipper pull as though she's still unzipping. Emily's brother has it prominently displayed in his bedroom.

"I'd be willing to assist with that worthy cause," Quinton says, lying back on the carpet. "Be sure to let me know when lessons commence."

"We'll send you a memo," Brooke says.

By the time we get back around to Tadd, we're stumbling over each other's names and any words containing more than one syllable, the slip-ups seeming beyond hilarious. Graham is more subdued than the other guys, his smile easy and genuine at the silliness around him. I catch his dark eyes on me a couple of times, but he watches Brooke, too.

"Let's make this more interesting," Tadd says, leaning back on his elbows. He waits until everyone is quiet. "Never have I ever… hooked up with a costar."

"Hold up. Are we talking hooked up or hooked *up*,"

Quinton asks. "'Cause I do not believe for a second that your horn dog self hasn't found a twin on a set."

"Either. Let's say the make-out hook-up."

"*What*? You are ly-*ing*," Quinton says.

"Nope." Tadd crosses his heart. "I'm pure as the driven whatever, on location. But don't worry—one of the extras is on my list of things to *do*."

MiShaun swats Tadd's head too gently to be much of a reprimand. When everyone drinks, including Jenna, there's a shocked silence before the room is filled with laughter and Quinton leans across to high-five her as she blushes red. Tadd eyes her blearily. "You are an enigma," he means to say, though what comes out sounds more like *you are an enema*. We laugh until our sides hurt; Quinton laughs so hard he's crying.

Next to me, Reid's gaze sweeps slowly from my face to my breasts, over the ribbon tie at my waist, to my pink toenails and back up. I want to know how he feels about me—not just my body (when he's drunk and paying attention), but *me*. After our scenes this week, I was reduced to mush, and he ignored me at the club. I *should* be pissed. Which proves to be impossible when my head is spinning and he is sitting right next to me, looking so crazy gorgeous.

Balls. The tequila caught up with me quickly.

"What should I do with you, Emma Pierce?" He's inches away, his mouth turned up on one side, his eyes slate blue in the dim light of the room.

"What do you wanna do?" I flirt back.

"Hmm." His eyes are locked on mine, and I feel the vibrations to my toes. "You don't know?"

I shake my head, immediately wishing I hadn't. The effects of the tequila are building, even though I started cheating half an hour ago, feigning shots. My thoughts spin along with my vision. I close my eyes for a moment, and hear Reid's soft laugh.

Oh, man. I can't let everything move this fast with Reid;

I'm not sure yet what he wants. Correction. I'm pretty sure what he wants, but I don't know what it means. The hot/cold game is confusing. Is he trying to slow it down? Does he regularly hook up during films? Is a hookup what I want, if it's all I can get with him? I'm far too buzzed to think clearly.

"Let's play spin-the-bottle," Quinton suggests. "Or seven minutes in heaven. We can use the balcony."

MiShaun stands. "This is where I call old lady privilege, children." She zigzags across the floor to the door, waving off protests. "I've *done* junior high."

"MiShaun, I think you're just afraid to kiss me," Tadd says.

She turns, one hand on the curve of her hip. "And you may be right."

As she leaves the room, Tadd quips, "I believe I've just been insulted."

Graham's eyes meet mine, but I'm sure there's no way he remembers what he promised me several hours ago until he stands, stretching. "I'm beat. And just so you know, Tadd, I'm *not* afraid to kiss you." He picks up his guitar. Like a postscript, he turns and adds, "Emma, you said something about running in the morning?" reaching a hand down to me. I link my hand with his and he pulls me up. The room tilts back and forth, but he holds my wrist firmly. Half a minute later, we're in the hallway walking towards our rooms, one of us less steadily than the other.

"Maybe I'm weird, but those kissing games feel so awkward." My words slur together—*kissygamesh feelsawkward*—which makes me giggle.

He passes his door, his warm hand at my waist, keeping me from bumping into walls or falling down. "I agree. I'd rather control who I kiss than leave it to fate and an empty bottle," he says softly, taking my key, unlocking my door and pushing it open.

"I wasn't ready to go out onto the balcony with… well. I mean, we're all kinda smashed. Balconies aren't safe.

Somebody could fall over the edge. Or something." I lean against the open door, a blush creeping up my neck.

"You know, it might have been me you ended up with out there, not him," I look up at him then—his brown eyes so dark they're nearly black as he teases me about seven minutes we might have shared on Brooke's balcony, doing… who knows what.

"Huh."

He hands the key card back to me and smiles. "Goodnight, Emma."

He turns back to his room, and I watch until he unlocks his door and pushes it open. "Emma?" he calls softly as I stumble into my room.

I catch my door before it closes, my heartbeat drumming in my ears, and answer without looking around the corner. "Yeah?"

"That's definitely four." He's chuckling as his door closes with a click.

Chapter 13

REID

Emma and Graham are gone before I can react, thanks to the number of shots I've had. With exception of that one look between them, he seemed focused on Brooke all night, so the idea that he'd leap up and take Emma with him at some point was out of nowhere.

Tadd gets to his feet unsteadily after a quick glance between Brooke and me. "Quinton, help me get this baby into her room." He gestures to Jenna, who's curled up asleep on the floor. We've successfully set a fifteen-year-old on the road to corruption, as others did for each of us. Tadd nudges her semi-awake and he and Quinton each take one of her arms. "Thank God she weighs as much as a postage stamp," Tadd says, propping her up.

Quinton closes his eyes, steadying himself with one arm around Jenna. "I'm going to hate myself in the morning."

"I hate you *now*, man. I still don't believe you've never had lobster."

They both laugh, weaving towards the door, Jenna barely conscious between them.

"G'night. You two behave," Tadd leers at Brooke and me, eyebrows raised, as the three of them stumble into the hallway.

The door closes behind them and we sit, staring at each other across the expanse of carpet. Neither of us says anything for a couple of minutes.

Finally, I incline my head towards her bed. "Once, for old times' sake?"

Incredulous, she blinks, measuring how serious I am. Given that Emma just left the room with Graham, Brooke is drunk and looking hot and doable, and we're in her room alone, I'm game if she is. For a few seconds—one, two, three—I think she might be. And then she shuts it down. "Not on your life."

"So serious and bitter." My mouth twists in amusement. "It wasn't so bad."

She gasps lightly, her mouth a small "O" as she blinks, and again, before she shutters it, there's more naked emotion in her face than I thought she possessed. She gains control of it quickly, her eyes locked to mine. And then she crawls across the ten feet of space between us, onto my lap, straddling me, her knees at my hips. Kissing me, at first softly and then hard, like punishment, she wraps her arms around my neck, her nails piercing the skin through my t-shirt as her fingers rake across my shoulders and she grinds her pelvis against mine. Despite the alcohol in my blood, my body responds, though perhaps *because* of the alcohol in my blood, I don't realize what she's doing.

Without warning she recoils and slides off my lap, forcing my hands away from where they grip her waist. "It wasn't so *good*, either." Her tone is disinterested and her smile, glacial. She pushes herself upright and walks an erratic path to her bathroom, dismissing me. "You can go now, Reid. I want nothing from you."

I stand and laugh, watch how her shoulders tighten at the sound. "Right. I forgot for a moment what a cold bitch you are, Brooke. I remember now. Don't worry, you're not nearly as difficult to leave as you assume."

"Fuck you, Reid," she says as I pull the door open. I chuckle as it shuts behind me, seemingly unaffected.

When I get to my room it takes every effort of restraint not to put a hole through the goddamned wall. Brooke was my first, and I was hers. We were young and stupid and for a brief space in time, I thought I loved her. I hadn't, of course, any more than she loved me. As much as I wish I was unaffected by her, that's impossible. No reason I can't conceal it, though.

Emma

While the room spins, I lie across the bed, calculating how many shots I had tonight. Definitely more than I've done before in one sitting. Running in the morning is out of the question; so much for new good habits. I remember to text Emily just before my battery dies, though the message is probably an incomprehensible jumble of letters, since the buttons on my phone keep shuffling.

I wake to a tapping noise and at first I'm convinced it's coming from inside my head. I crack an eye open. My mouth feels like someone has wallpapered it with felt. *Tap-tap-tap*. Nope, definitely the door. The clock on the nightstand says it's not quite ten a.m.

On my toes, I peer out the peephole. I unlock the door, open it a sliver and squint in the bright hallway lighting. "Graham?"

He holds up a lidded cup with a Starbucks label and smiles. "Go brush your teeth and splash some water on your face."

"Graham, I look, and feel, like crap."

He slips into my room. "Go on, it'll help. How do you

take your coffee?" He walks to the desk with the coffees, pulling packets of sugar and cream out of his pockets.

I sigh, unable to argue with a head full of cotton. "Gimme the works." Obediently, I go into the bathroom and close the door behind me. I wash my face, brush my teeth, and pull my hair into a ponytail, avoiding the mirror as much as possible while doing so, which isn't too difficult since my eyes refuse to open fully.

When I come out, he hands me the cup.

"How are you *up*, and feeling this—" I snap my fingers "—this… what's the word…" I gesture towards him, then rub my eyes and sit on the bed.

"Unhungover?"

"That's the word."

"Well, I outweigh you by at least seventy pounds. That's pretty much the secret." He moves a pair of shoes from the desk chair to the floor and sits down.

"So you never get hungover?"

"I wouldn't say that. But I took it easy last night while everyone else got plastered with the help of high school party games."

"Didn't have any fun, huh?" I say, taking a sip and closing my eyes.

"Last night was fun in its own way."

"Meaning?"

He watches me, sipping his coffee and sitting back with one foot resting on top of the opposite knee. "Mmm. I'd like to know what you thought."

"I'm just glad we didn't play spin-the-bottle or… well, I'm not a fan of the whole, uh, kissing game concept…"

He sips his coffee, considering. "Yeah, me neither."

"I thought guys liked those kinds of games."

His lashes sweep down, hiding his eyes. "I'm not really a games sorta guy." I think about that while he sips his coffee, and then, in what I'm starting to realize is a typical maneuver for him, he changes the subject completely. "Think you might be up for brunch and some shopping?"

A guy who wants to shop? "You aren't going to lure me into a sporting goods place or a comic book store, are you?"

"I was thinking bookstore. But if you're into comics…"

"No, please. Bookstore yes; comics no." I briefly dated a guy last year who was into comics. He never stopped talking about them, even when I threatened to start talking about *Gilmore Girls* reruns. I know more about comic books than any girl ever wants to know.

"Finish your coffee, get ready, and I'll be back in, say, forty-five minutes?" He stands and moves towards the door.

As I shower, I realize that Graham completely sidestepped my question about his comment that last night was "fun in its own way." I'm definitely not running on all cylinders, as my father would say.

My phone is recharged and flashing when I get out. There's a text from Emily answering what I sent her last night:

Me: er oksyrf * becer smf o ;rgy brfpre dpom tnr vorrle
Em: I assume, from your text, that drinking was involved. Hello? Something I can READ???

I text her back and she answers immediately.

Me: Sorry, tequila attack. The keypad kept moving around.
Em: You promised to tell all. Start telling!
Me: What i meant last night was we played i never, and i left before spin the bottle
Em: WHAT??? HOLY SHIT!!! Calling you.

"You guys seriously didn't play *I never* and *spin-the-bottle* did you?"

"Yes and almost."

"Somehow I've always pictured celebrity parties as more… sophisticated?"

I laugh. "Yeah, me too. I left when Quinton suggested spin-the-bottle or seven minutes in heaven."

"Are you *insane*? There was a possibility of seven minutes in heaven with Quinton Beauvier, and you left *early*?"

"Em, you know how I feel about those games…"

"Yeah, I know. I just don't see why I can't body-double for you during times like this! It would be a grueling task, but I'd make the sacrifice for you."

I recognize Graham's one-knuckle *thunk-thunk* at the door.

"Um, I'm about to go to brunch, so I'll call you later?"

"Sure. Don't worry about me. All by myself in boring Sacramento. Alone. No life."

"Emily, you know you're always with me in spirit."

"Bite me," she says. "I wanna be with you in *person* playing spin-the-bottle with Reid and Quinton."

"Now who's whining?" I tease.

"Fine. But one of these days, I expect to reap the benefits of having a big star for a best friend."

"Absolutely. You'll be first in line."

Chapter 14

REID

I wake up just before noon and call room service for coffee, then my voicemail to retrieve a message received early this morning from Dad. Like he didn't know I'd still be asleep when he called.

I got charged with pot possession earlier this summer, and he's avoided communicating with me directly since then. I was at a party, passing a couple of joints around with some people when John texted me this:

John: pass the joint to the girl next to you and walk to the back door NOW

While John may lack anything resembling judgment, he *always* knows what's going down. So I obeyed. He pulled me into the alley where his girl du jour was waiting with her car, just as the police came in the front door. There were photos of me smoking, but it was dark, and they were too indistinct to be incontestably me, or weed, for that matter. With no physical evidence to prove that I was present or in possession, Dad's firm claimed hearsay and the case was thrown out… which didn't preclude Dad from going ballistic.

We pitched a fortune at my PR firm to ward off the tarnish to my image. The money came straight from *my* account, but for some reason, who paid for what wasn't a viable argument. My straight-laced father has never stepped out of line in his life, and as he's expressed stridently on multiple occasions, he can't comprehend why I live my life the way I do.

I assumed his message would involve some account information I needed, or a contract I forgot to sign that he's overnighting. So I don't expect this: "Reid," he sighs heavily, "I'm calling to let you know that your mother has decided to check into a rehab program." He doesn't say *again* but it hangs there, unsaid, nevertheless. "Exclusive facility, by the ocean, not too far from home. She'll get good care. Ninety day program. She hopes to be back home for the holidays, possibly before you're done filming."

He goes silent for several seconds, and I'm not sure if that's the end. Then he adds, "She'll be able to take phone calls in a couple of weeks. I'll let you know the number, in case you… have time to call her. Just don't… say anything upsetting." He has a lot of nerve saying that. I'm usually not the one who upsets her. "If you have any questions, call me. Otherwise… well. Call if you need anything."

Awesome.

I should have seen her rock-bottom coming. Even though I was seldom around, she had a drink in her hand every time I was. With the exception of when I was really young, and for short, varying periods of time after any rehab experience, this is how I picture her: Mom, drink in hand. It's her prop, part of her costume. Sometimes I wonder if her despondency stems from trying to be something she isn't—someone constantly sober, without the ability to dull the knife-thrusts of reality. Maybe Mom-with-a-drink-in-her-hand is who she really is, and thinking that it's immoral or makes her a bad person is what causes the crisis.

Or maybe I'm a classic enabler, as one of her therapists yelled in a fit of untherapist-like vocal exasperation.

Or maybe I look in the mirror every day and am scared as shit that I'll see either of my parents looking back at me.

Emma

"Thanks again for the coffee." Graham and I are walking along 6th street. He's shortened his stride to match mine, like he does when we run. "That was nice. Otherwise, I'd still be hiding under my pillows, feeling like I just ate a dirty t-shirt."

He smiles. "A dirty t-shirt? That's... disgustingly descriptive."

"Disgustingly fitting, unfortunately."

He's walking with his hands in his pockets, and he bumps my arm lightly with his elbow. "So you think I'm nice, huh? Maybe I'm actually a complete jerk with ulterior motives."

I tap my lip with a finger, peering at him. "You'd have to be a nefarious individual with seriously evil intentions, to bring me coffee and be a jerk at heart."

He looks down at me, eyebrows raised. Out here in the sunlight his eyes, while still dark, seem more deep caramel, less onyx. His hair has a reddish tint in the sunlight, too, something completely invisible inside. It's like being outdoors turns his color dial a notch or two lighter.

"Good deducing. And use of the word nefarious," he says. "Especially with the hangover and all."

The day is warm already. I assumed as much, and dressed in shorts and the pink t-shirt I'd left on the bed last night in favor of the black tank. I grabbed my red canvas Chucks instead of flip-flops, since I had no idea just how much walking Graham had in mind. Good thing, too, because we've walked about a hundred blocks by now.

"How much farther?" The good news is I may actually

feel like having brunch at some point in the near future. The bad news is I don't know if we're planning on walking to the next county first.

"I take it you're a suburbs sort of girl. I grew up in New York City—lots of walking. This feels like nothing." This guy is a freaking *master* at dodging questions.

"Yes, I'm a lazy suburban girl… who, lest we forget, is suffering from a killer hangover because I don't weigh a hundred pounds more."

"Seventy. And I hate to tell you, but—" He takes my shoulders and turns me, guiding me up a pathway to the front door of the restaurant, located in a renovated old house. "We're here."

I give him a haughty look. "In that case, I'm glad I don't have to kick your ass, since I'm too pooped from walking a thousand miles for that type of exertion." He smiles and shakes his head, pulling the door open for me.

Twenty minutes later, I'm eating the fluffiest blueberry muffin ever made and mumbling an apology. "Sorry about the cranky."

He forks a bite of omelet, dabs it into the pool of salsa he poured on one side of his plate, and sticks it in his mouth. Chewing, he appears puzzled. "What cranky?" He lines up another bite. "Oh, you mean when you looked like you were about to stage a mutiny for having to walk a couple of blocks?"

"A couple? It was at least fifteen!"

"Actually, ten."

"Nuh-uh." I was certain it was closer to twenty.

"Yep. Ten exactly."

God, I'm in worse shape than I thought. "Huh."

"That's five," he says, before I even have time to hear myself and cringe.

"Know-it-all."

He laughs. "Would you rather be in your room, buried under your pillows?"

"No." I sound like a sullen toddler. Sipping my chicory-flavored coffee, I relax, and the house seems to sigh with me, the refinished wood floors creaking as a waiter walks by with a full tray over his head. "This place is great."

"Told ya."

After brunch we backtrack and spend a couple of hours at the bookstore. There's a puppet show going on in the kids' area, and he insists we sit on the floor and watch. This is when I learn that Graham and his older sisters used to make sock puppets and put on shows for their parents. This whole idea is so foreign to me that I'm sure he's making it up. On the walk back to the hotel, I ask him what kinds of shows.

"We'd make puppets of ourselves, or our favorite book characters, like *Where the Wild Things Are*, gluing on wiggly eyeballs and yarn." I try to imagine a sock puppet Graham. "One time we made penguins, coloring popsicle sticks like lightsabers and hot gluing those to the flippers, and then we did a *Star Wars* reenactment for my Dad's birthday. He loves penguins, and anything *Star Wars*."

Penguin puppets with lightsabers? There's no way he could make this up.

"So according to one of the shots you tossed back last night, you're an only child," he says. "What was that like—being the center of attention all the time?"

My first thought is that after my mother died, I felt more like the invisible kid than the center of attention. And then I begin stressing about how I'm going to talk about my mother being dead. The subject of family always, sooner or later, brings the story of my mom forward. There's no simple way to say it, no way to fully express everything those two words mean to me: she died. The feelings are muted most of the time, something only accomplished by the passing of time, but they'll never go away. I know that now. There are moments I wish the pain would disappear, but mostly, it's a comforting ache. I lost her, and I feel it—sometimes like a bruise that doesn't hurt until it's pressed, sometimes like a knife.

"I bet you were spoiled rotten," Graham says, slowing at the window of a narrow storefront of skateboards and boarding gear.

"I seem like a brat?" I pout, ruining any defense against it.

"I didn't say *that.* But I can picture you as a little girl: adorable, no one else around to steal the spotlight. That's all it would take to wrap your parents around your little finger. I mean at that point it's self-preservation, right? Darwin's lesser-known theory: survival of the cutest."

I smile, willing myself not to blush. "I guess I don't really know if I was spoiled or not."

"Fair enough. I was the youngest, and a little monster. Or so I hear from my sisters."

He has no idea how relieved I am that we've strayed from talking about my family. "But aren't they disqualified from judging, as your competition for attention?"

"You'd think… but my mother agrees with them."

Examining hand-made jewelry through a store window, I'm caught off guard and can't stifle a laugh. "That's terrible!"

He shrugs as though resigned. "There are allegations of extreme tattling, tantrums and cookie hoarding. But don't ask for details. I plead the fifth." His phone beeps and he pulls it from his pocket, reading the text and typing a quick response.

"I have a career-related question," I say, after we walk for a minute in silence. "What made you want to play Bill Collins? Have you read *Pride and Prejudice*?"

"I read it after I was up for the audition. I *could* say Collins is a complex character and playing him will widen my range, but honestly, I'm supporting myself as an actor. If my agent recommends a role and I get it, I do it. Being too picky would be economic suicide."

"Huh." I stick my tongue out at him when he smiles and holds up six fingers, which makes him laugh.

"What about you? Why Lizbeth Bennet?" His phone rings and he glances at the display. "Oh—I've gotta take this. Can we—?" I nod and he steps out of the path of foot traffic. "Hello?" I gesture to let him know I'm walking on to the hotel, half a block away. He nods before turning, his voice warm, happy. "Yeah, I'm here, what's up?"

When I reach the hotel entrance, I look back. He's moved to the edge of the sidewalk and is slipping his lighter back in his pocket, laughing, a cigarette dangling from his fingers.

Chapter 15

REID

After ordering a room service breakfast at noon, I text Tadd and Quinton to see what's on tap for tonight, knowing I might not hear from either of them for hours. I have the barest excuse of a hangover this morning; it should be worse. I think my adrenaline during and after the exchange with Brooke burned off most of my buzz. The last thing I need tonight is more of her. A guys night out is in order.

The more I think about Emma and Graham's exit last night, the more premeditated it seems, at least on his side. I haven't figured him out yet. He's unanticipated competition for Emma, considering how he's hanging around Brooke, too. Frankly, I'm not used to having to compete for a chick at all. I should probably find it refreshing. I don't.

Tadd calls half an hour later. "First, god*damn* it don't let me drink that much again, and second, I'm up for guys night out. But I warn you, if I get lucky, it may turn into guys night in."

"Yeah, yeah. I'll text Quinton… I don't have Graham's number, but I assume we're inviting him." No way I want him left here with Emma down the hall.

"He's next door to me; I'll pop over and ask."

Perfect. I get the feeling Graham would suspect an invitation coming from me; I can't imagine that Brooke has kept her opinions of me to herself. I knew we hadn't left things on congenial terms, but I had no idea she'd be that hostile. "Cool. Eight? Nine?"

Tadd does a hangover groan. "Nine. We've got tomorrow off."

"I'll call Bob and let him know we'll need a bodyguard and a car, possibly separate cars on the way back." I'm bringing somebody back with me, that's for damned sure. Emma is proving more elusive than I expected her to be, and I need someone to take the edge off.

When we meet downstairs at nine, Bob and Jeff are waiting to usher us to a car. Tadd comes down last. Alone.

"Is Graham meeting us later?"

"He said he's staying in tonight."

I pull to a stop in the middle of the lobby. "What?"

"He said he's still recovering from last night and he's going to stay in." *Liar*. He was the least drunk person in the room last night. Tadd bumps me and keeps walking. "Come on, dude. What's the big deal? Let's go."

I have no choice but to follow. The paparazzi are handled deftly by Bob and Jeff and two minutes later we're in the car heading to a martini bar Tadd heard about.

"What are the girls doing?" That didn't come out as offhand as I'd intended, but luckily Tadd doesn't care.

"I ran into Brooke and Meredith earlier—they were planning a girls-only night. Brooke looked as relieved to have a night off from you as you look about a night off from her." He has the nerve to smirk that I'm relieved to know where Emma's going to be tonight. Wow. This is already *way* more high-maintenance than I'm used to.

Quinton leans up. "What's going on between you two

anyway?"

"Nothing, man." I share a quick look with Tadd and shrug. "We had a thing, like years ago, and she's apparently not over it."

Quinton bumps my fist with his, grinning. "Here's to always leaving them wanting more."

I don't tell him that *wanting more* is not exactly what's between Brooke and me.

Emma

My hangover is gone, but I need a quiet evening. I *was* planning on a long talk with Emily, but she has a date with a guy who works at Abercrombie, a few doors down from Hot Topic, where she works. (I pointed out that this scenario contains serious odd-couple potential, which she didn't appreciate as much as I did.) She's been through a long dry spell, and the possibility of starting her senior year with no boyfriend and no prospects is "intolerable."

There's more to my recuperation plan than ditching the lingering headache. My father and Chloe are arriving tomorrow and will be in Austin for five days. I'll need my strength to deal with both the grueling filming schedule and the stress of having her that close at the same time. It's too much to hope that she'll recede to the background. Chloe doesn't do background.

I've excused myself from tonight's Austin nightlife tour—guys in one group, girls in the other. Room service delivers a spinach salad and the television plays music videos, volume low. Feeling restless, I wander onto the tiny balcony that overlooks the street and lean on the stone railing, staring at the big black sky, where I can only make out a few of the brightest stars. Downtown is too illuminated for star-gazing. People mill around below, and even this far up, I catch jumbled bits of conversation and laughter. And a trace of tobacco?

"Emma, hey." Graham is two balconies over, straightening from the railing, smoking. His eyes, meeting mine, are black with the darkness and distance. He takes a drag, the tip of the cigarette glowing red near his silhouette in the dim light from the streetlamps and headlights below.

"Hey, yourself. I assumed you'd gone out with the guys."

A momentary breeze kicks up, and he shakes the hair out of his eyes, exhales a trail of smoke that dissipates in all directions. "I decided to opt out tonight."

I nod. "Me, too."

He takes another drag and resumes his posture of leaning on the railing, staring down at the swirls of color and noise at street level. He doesn't speak again, and though I'm curious about the call that interrupted our earlier conversation, I can't think of a casual way to ask about it. I walk back into my room without interrupting his thoughts. I consider hauling one of the cushy chairs out onto the balcony to read, but if Graham is still outside, it might be awkward.

After perusing the dessert menu and convincing myself not to order a slice of double chocolate cake, I grab the novel I bought this morning and settle on the bed. My stomach growls in protest, unshushed when I mumble, "Shut *up*." Opening the book, I feel the familiar brush of pleasure—the crackle of the pages and the binding, the inky smell. And then I nearly jump out of my skin when the phone on the nightstand rings at full volume.

"Hello?" I answer, heart pounding, looking for the sound control switch.

"Emma? It's Graham. I, uh, don't have your cell number…"

"Oh."

"So… I ordered this chocolate cake from room service, and it's even more monstrous than it looked in the menu… and I was thinking we could share it. If you want. I understand if you'd rather be alone, though."

I smile, having planned for an evening of precisely that, just as I'd originally planned to run alone every morning. "I *just* convinced myself that I didn't need that cake... But I guess if I share yours, it won't really count."

"Exactly. I'll be down in a minute."

"I could order up coffee?" Because that's what I need at nearly 10 p.m. when I had intentions of going to bed early—*coffee*.

"Sounds good."

I call room service and then run to the bathroom and brush my teeth. I have just enough time to sweep on lip balm before Graham taps lightly on the door. When I unbolt and open it, he's holding two forks and the most massive slice of cake I've ever seen. "Wow. That thing is enormous."

"Yeah. It's basically an entire cake." He runs a hand through his hair and a couple of strands towards the middle stick straight up. He's barefoot, wearing jeans and a worn t-shirt inscribed with the name of an indie band I vaguely recognize. Emily would know it.

We drag the chairs and one nightstand out onto the balcony, where we sip coffee and eat from opposite sides of the cake without dividing it. The muffled din of Saturday night floats up from the street below. After a few minutes of clinking forks and sighs of contentment, Graham asks what made me want to play Lizbeth Bennet, returning to this afternoon's conversation as though the interruption occurred moments ago, rather than hours.

"What girl wouldn't want to do an adaptation of *Pride and Prejudice*?" I hedge.

"She said mysteriously," he returns, one eyebrow raised. He takes another sip of coffee, waiting, slouching into the chair, turning more fully towards me, his long legs extended.

I pull my knees up into my chair, angling to face him. "Well, like most girls in the English-speaking world, I adore Elizabeth Bennet. She's the ultimate heroine, strong-willed and independent, intelligent, loyal, but at the same time, she's not flawless, she's not above mistakes, or falling in love."

He nods. "So as soon as you knew about the film, you wanted to do it?"

Wow, he's good.

"Not exactly. I mean, it isn't Elizabeth Bennet, after all. It's *Lizbeth*, this Americanized version. And some of the screenplay lines… I guess I'm a purist about some things, and Jane Austen is one of those things."

"Fair enough. So when did you first read *Pride and Prejudice*?"

Here we go. "I don't know. It was my mother's favorite book. I remember her reading it aloud to me when I was very young." My stomach pitches and I blame the sugary cake and caffeine-laden coffee, when the origin of this uneasiness is all too familiar. I evade this discussion whenever possible. I could do that now, with Graham, but I'm not going to. I want to tell him.

"So what does she think? Did she want you to do the film, or is she a Jane Austen purist, too?"

Here we go, here we go, here we go. I pick at a fingernail, staring at my hands. "She died when I was six." The words spill out quickly, but softly, and I want to tell him everything, all of it, though I can't say any more because I can't quite face the bits and pieces I always fold away and shove under the surface. My father and the way we haven't connected since we lost her. My inability to have a normal childhood because I've been in front of a camera, pretending to be someone else, since before she was gone. Chloe and the way she always expects to be the center of every universe near her. And I'm okay, I really am, most of the time. But sometimes, I'm just not.

Graham doesn't speak until I look at him. His eyes hold mine, and they don't slide away, uncomfortable with the fact that mine are brimming with tears. "I'm sorry, Emma," he says.

I nod, take a breath, and pull a napkin from under the nearly-empty plate, pressing it under my eyes. "Thanks."

We sit outside for a while longer, eventually talking about other work we've done. I tell him about the Nazi director of the grape juice commercial, and he tells me about the attractive forty-something star of an art house film he did at a few years ago who showed up at his trailer door wearing a robe and nothing else.

"Do I want to know how you found out about the 'nothing else'?"

He grimaces. "The exact way you're thinking."

"Eww… so did you—?"

"Um, *no*. I told her I had to get up early, and she said, 'you don't have to be scared, Graham,' and I just blustered through it, of course, something like, 'oh, no it's not that, I'm just really tired.' And then I didn't answer my door after that. She got the idea eventually."

"Wow."

"Yeah," he says, laughing. "I may still need therapy over that night."

We end up sitting on my bed, six or so inches of space between us, watching a movie on pay-per-view. I fall asleep about halfway through it. When I wake up just after 4 a.m., he's gone. The chairs are back inside, the balcony door closed and locked. The comforter is folded over me like a cocoon, and there's a note on the nightstand.

Thanks for helping with the mountain of cake.
I'll be downstairs at 6 if you want to run -
Graham

I set the alarm on my phone for 5:40.

Chapter 16

REID

I should be asleep until noon. Instead, I'm wide awake and staring at the ceiling by nine a.m., deciding how pissed I should be.

Between the late dinner and the martini bar last night, we drove past Brooke, Meredith, MiShaun and Jenna going into a club. Tadd pointed them out. "There go the girls—small world, huh?"

"I didn't see Emma," I commented.

Quinton yawned, glancing back at them through the rear window. "Yeah, I talked to Meredith earlier, on the way to the elevator. She said Emma was wavering over whether to go or not tonight. Apparently she had a monster hangover this morning."

Meaning Graham and Emma both ditched.

"Son of a *bitch*," I swore.

"What?" Quinton asked as Tadd grinned at me and shook his head. He's always been a big fan of any girl who gets under my skin.

We were three-for-three last night, soothing the

annoyance somewhat—at least until this morning. There was a bachelorette party at the bar—nine girls and three guys, and *all* of them looked hot. Quinton was ready to lead the offensive, but Tadd cautioned that when encountering a group like that, you have to watch out for the Cheerleader Effect: the inexplicable consequence of a few extreme hotties in a group bringing less attractive friends up to par. Possible hazardous situation. As a man of action, Quinton was skeptical.

Tadd glanced at the group surreptitiously. "Okay, look. At first glance, all three of those guys are candidates. But in reality, only one of them is one-nighter material."

Quinton and I checked them out. "I don't see it," Quinton said.

"Easy—it's the blond guy," I said.

Tadd sighed. "Reid, you obviously have a blonde predilection—"

My palms turned up, shoulders shrugging. "Blondes are my gold standard."

"Don't get distracted by hair color." He shook his head, hair falling perfectly around his face, and leaned closer. "Dudes. It's *obviously* the Hispanic guy. Look again."

Quinton stared, frowning. "I still don't see it."

Tadd rolled his eyes. "That's because *you* are disproportionately straight."

"Excuse me! Unless disproportionately means *all*—then guilty as charged. And BTW, Reid, dibs on the sister who looks like Halle Berry's reincarnation."

Tadd pursed his lips. "Dude, Halle Berry isn't dead, thus she can't be reincarnated."

Quinton emptied his drink and got to his feet. "Whatever, man, I'm going in."

Tadd and I each grabbed an arm and sat him back down. "Hold up, noob," Tadd said. "Let's get Halle and Mr. Tall Dark and Gay to bring their most attractive girlfriend and trot over *here*."

Quinton sat, still unconvinced. “We can do that?”

“Watch and learn.” Tadd turned to me. “Reid, you’ve just said something incredibly amusing.” And then he laughed his patented Tadd-Wyler-Sexy-Laugh while I smiled and chuckled along.

A dozen pairs of eyes shifted to us. Tadd made eye contact with his target while Quinton—who’s a remarkably fast learner—did the same with his. I appeared oblivious, staring into my martini, pulling the olive from the tiny plastic sword with my teeth. Tadd broke eye contact, only to glance back a few seconds later. Quinton smirked, straightening and stretching his arms behind his neck in a blatant display of biceps. And then we sat back and waited for recognition to flicker.

A few hours, several dirty martinis and two cigars later, Bob was escorting the bride-to-be from my hotel room to a waiting Town Car. Personal policy—I don’t wake up with them still in my bed. And don’t worry—there was no way she was going to pull off wearing white, long before I came along.

Emma

My father and Chloe have landed—she texted me to gripe about some lady in a wheelchair at the front of the plane who was “holding everyone up.” They have to collect Chloe’s bags after deplaning (she can’t travel without at least two colossal suitcases and several smaller ones), so I have about an hour before they arrive, which I spend wishing we were filming today, chewing on a hangnail, checking my clothes, changing my clothes, and straightening my hotel room in a state of total anxiety.

She texts me again from the shuttle, annoyed that there wasn’t a limo to pick them up. They booked a room in the same hotel, and she wants me to come down to the lobby to meet them when they arrive. When I exit the elevator, I catch her irate voice at the front desk one second too late to scramble back in. She's pissed that their room isn't on the same floor as the cast and crew. The producers left strict instructions for hotel management with a list of approved guests for rooms on our floor. There are no exceptions, for privacy and security reasons. Unfortunately, "no exceptions" isn't something Chloe accepts.

I do the only thing that makes sense in that moment. I make a beeline across the marble elevator bank and hide behind a column.

"But our *minor* daughter is on the fourth floor!" Her voice pitches higher, and I picture every head in the room swiveling towards her, just as she likes it. The concierge begins to speak in soothing tones, assuring her that there's a lovely room reserved for them one floor down from me. He adds that he'll be sending up a complimentary bottle of champagne shortly, in hopes of making their stay more enjoyable.

As I scoot around the pillar to avoid being spotted, Chloe harrumphs her halfhearted consent and they board the elevator with their overloaded luggage cart. The doors close and the dial shows their assent to the third floor, and I'm stuck inadvertently eavesdropping on the concierge chastising the desk clerk.

"In the future, simply say, 'I'm sorry, ma'am, that floor is fully occupied.'"

I inch around the column. The desk clerk is young, dark-haired and slender, with classically pretty features. Chloe would hate her on sight. Red-faced, she stares at the marble countertop.

"Relatives of celebrities can be unreasonable, and if the relative becomes offended, we risk losing the celebrity's patronage."

"Yes, sir," the clerk mumbles. Thanks to Chloe's furor,

the "celebrity" being discussed is *me*. Awesome.

"Um, Emma?"

I jump, caught skulking between the column and a massive potted plant. "MiShaun," I gasp. "God."

"Who are we hiding from?" She peers around the immediate area.

"My stepmother. She and my father just got here, they haven't even seen me yet, and she's already bitched out the desk clerk and the concierge. They'll be here *all week*. They're going to be interacting with everyone." I close my eyes. "Oh. My. God."

MiShaun takes my arm and leads me to the elevator. "Emma, let me share a liberating truth concerning our relationships with our parents, especially as we become adults." She pushes the fourth floor button and the doors shut us in. "The people who know and love us will not hold our parents, or their crazy-ass behavior, against us."

"But what about everyone else, all the people who don't know and love me?"

"Screw everyone else."

Chloe and my father have been invited to dinner by Adam Richter. This event would be doomed enough in itself, but a few of the cast members are going as well. I'm considering excuses (sore throat, seizure, untimely death?) when the concierge calls to say the taxi is here; an impending sense of disaster follows me down to their room. Chloe answers the door wearing a black dress and black patent stilettos; the dress is shorter and tighter than ideal, but for my stepmother, it's practically demure. Just as I release the pent-up breath I've been holding since I got off of the elevator, her eyes sweep over me. "Emma, when are you going to start wearing adult clothing? Stylish jewelry might be an improvement, too."

My outfit: aqua tank and gauzy skirt with a fluid watercolor pattern in various shades of aqua. I'm wearing small silver hoops in my ears and my mother's ring on my right hand—a single princess-cut diamond, channel set into a solid platinum band.

Chloe sighs, refreshing her dark lipstick in the mirror. "And another thing." She blots her lips with a tissue. "Some makeup wouldn't hurt, either."

My father exits the bathroom, knotting a tie. "I think I look beautiful just as I am," he says, hugging one arm around my shoulders, oblivious to her attack on me, as usual.

"Oh, *Connor*." She pushes him playfully in the chest.

Screw everyone else, screw everyone else, screw everyone else.

Chapter 17

REID

I arrive at the restaurant with Richter and one of the production assistants. “Reservation for Richter, party of eight,” she tells the maître d, whose eyes widen when he sees me. Waiters scramble to get our table ready as Graham and Brooke come in, followed by Emma and her parents. Her mom is hot.

At a circular table, Emma takes the seat between her dad and Laura, the PA, and I sit next to Brooke. Graham is on her other side, of course, and she leans pointedly away from me and towards him.

“Hi, I’m Chloe, Emma’s stepmother.” She drops into the seat next to me.

“And I’m Reid, her costar. Nice to meet you.” I extend a hand and she giggles. I shake her dad’s hand as well, smile at Emma.

“Emma,” the PA says. “Ready for tomorrow?”

“Yep, all set.” Her smile is nervous, and I wonder why until half an hour later when Chloe is on her third glass of wine, talking to me. My mother would say Chloe is not familiar with using her inside voice. Or any discretion whatsoever.

She rests her chin in her hand, elbow propped on the table, and leans close. "So what's the *wildest* thing a woman has ever asked you to autograph?" With her free hand, she's playing with her distractively flashy earring, after which she rests her hand on my forearm a beat or so too long—classic flirt mode. She couldn't be more Emma-opposite.

I lean closer. "Well, I once had a beautiful woman ask me to sign her panties."

"You're *kidding* me!" Chloe's laugh is loud and a little high-pitched, and when I glance at Emma, she looks ready to bolt. Her pulse quickens at her throat and her wide eyes flick to Richter, Laura, Brooke.

And then Graham. I register the fact of eye contact between them, though I can't see his face from this angle. She inhales slowly. Her expression becomes more composed.

Hmm.

Richter asks her a question about her last movie, some holiday made-for-television crap about a deaf woman whose hearing daughter teaches her to play the violin. Chloe's conversation with me, meanwhile, gets raunchier by the minute ("Was she *wearing* them at the time?"), and Emma's doing everything she can to ignore it. If it was anyone else, I'd be amused at the way she's letting this get to her. As it is, I find myself wanting to shield her, but I have no idea what to do. The concept of using a personal filter in public escapes this woman.

Brooke eyes Chloe briefly, then leans to Graham and whispers something. Straightening, she laughs. "Don't you think so?"

Without replying, Graham refills her wine glass and then Emma's, whose hand is clenching a fork as though she's considering its effectiveness as a weapon. Or a suicidal device. Her eyes connect with Graham's for a split second and she calms visibly, again.

I don't like this at all.

Emma

This evening is a nightmare. When I look at my father, he seems tolerant of his wife's behavior rather than mortified. I've never understood their relationship, and I guess I never will. Towards the end of the meal, Chloe bats her lashes at Reid, loud and effusive over something he's just said. His expression is veiled, but not enough for me to miss the fact that he's regarding Chloe the way a scientist would examine a strange new species. Oh God.

What does a panic attack feel like? I can't breathe, and my heart rate is erratic, it's all over the place, I wish I was dead. My *director* is sitting here, and my costars. Everyone is staring at her, staring at me. I look at Graham, and he's watching me, again, his eyes sympathetic and calming. I take a deep breath. Tell myself that this night has to end eventually.

Then Reid announces that he's meeting Quinton and the others for a night of club hopping along 6th Street. "Emma, you're coming, right?"

Before I can reply, Chloe says, "Of course she's going! Oh, Connor, can we go, too?" She does her wind-up monkey clap as my father shrugs and agrees. I want to strangle him.

I pull my phone out in the taxi while Chloe blathers to my father about how cute and sweet Reid is.

Me: FML. Chloe is coming clubbing with us. Where is my invisibility cloak?!?
Em: OMG. When do they come home?
Me: Thursday. The buildings here are not tall enough to leap from!
Em: DO NOT SAY THAT. I'll cross my fingers that she breaks an ankle. Or her pelvis.

Emily's text gives me an idea, and I when we arrive, I manage to convince everyone that I sprained my ankle running this morning and can't dance. Biding my time, I perch on a barstool and tip the bartender ten bucks to give me water refills. The first chance I get, I am so gone. My chance comes when Chloe and Reid move to the dance floor, right after my father slips away without me—one more strike against him, as far as I'm concerned.

The hotel is only two or three well-lit blocks away. Despite the semi-buzzed crowd and a few typical hey-baby comments, I feel fairly safe. But when a hand grips my upper arm lightly from behind, I spin around, ready to shove the heel of my palm into some guy's nose.

"Whoa, hold up." Graham releases my arm, hands up in surrender.

"Ohmigod, Graham." I wait for my heart to slow as the crowd parts around us.

"I thought your ankle was critically injured." He smiles down at me as we begin walking towards the hotel, side by side. I didn't see him at the club, though I spotted Brooke and Quinton dancing.

"Well."

"Ah, creative subterfuge," he says, removing a cigarette and lighter from his pocket.

"Did you leave just to get a smoke?"

He cups his hand over the cigarette and flicks the lighter. "I probably left for the same reason you did."

"I *seriously* doubt that."

"Oh?"

Please, do not make me say it. I look at Graham, willing these words into his brain. He nods, holding the cigarette to the tiny flame and taking a drag, turning towards the street to exhale. The smoke trails behind him.

"Graham... I assume you wouldn't like to be thought of as hypocritical?"

He gives me a puzzled look. "Correct..."

"So if you're going to call me on my compulsion of constantly saying 'huh,' then I think it's only fair that I call you on a little addiction called *nicotine*."

"Uh-oh." He takes another drag, stubbing it out before we enter the hotel. "Yeah, I know you're right."

Wow. That was easy. "So what are you going to do about it?"

"I don't know. I've tried quitting a couple of times. Didn't go so well." He runs a hand through his hair as we wait for the elevator. "A miserable failure, in fact."

"Well, you're helping me quit saying 'huh' every five seconds, so maybe I can help you. How did you try to quit before?"

"Cold turkey." The elevator opens, and we get on. He jabs the 4 button.

"I've heard cold turkey doesn't work so well."

"Oh?"

"Yeah. I, um, Googled quitting smoking." We walk down the hallway, reaching his room first.

"Really," he says, smiling. "So, what *does* work? According to your research."

"Well, the patches and gum increase your chances of success, also quitting with someone, or having a support group. And anti-depressants help; but you'd need a prescription for those."

"You looked this stuff up for me? To help me quit?" There's a small crease between his brows, and I wonder if this is over-the-top interference.

"Yeah…"

He peers at me, his mouth pulling up on one side. "Thanks."

"You're welcome."

He pulls out his wallet, removes his key card. "Do you want to come in, watch a movie or… induce another cake coma?"

"God, no, I couldn't eat anything more today."

"Oh. Okay, well, I'll see you in the morning, maybe?"

"Yeah, sure." I realize then that I'd only meant to turn down more food, not his company. I turn to walk to my room, opening my door when he says, "Emma?" His gaze wanders over me. "I like your outfit. Kinda gypsy. Suits you."

Maybe this night wasn't a total waste.

Chapter 18

REID

Emma disappeared last night. *Again.* I half expected to find a glass slipper this time on the way out. Not that I don't get Emma's reaction where her stepmother is concerned. When she vanished, I was sympathetic.

Then at some point, I noticed that Graham was gone too. What the *hell*? My brain tells me to just back off, there are millions of chicks to be had. I could walk outside and come back in with several right now. And most of them would be ecstatic to do whatever I want, however I want it. So why am I responding like this to Emma? The challenge? That's how I felt about Brooke, once upon a time—and look where that got me.

Today, we're filming one of the earliest scenes: a party at the home of Charlotte Lucas, best friend of Lizbeth. When I arrive on location, I feel like I've been trapped in a Pottery Barn catalog. I watch MiShaun and Emma do their opening scene, and I don't care if it makes sense. I want her. No marginal, semi-talented, indie-film asswipe like Graham is going to keep her from me. Besides, what the hell *is* he doing with Brooke?

Laura tells me Tadd and I are up next, so I turn away and do my breathing exercises. Time enough to think about this shit later.

INT. LUCAS HOUSE - NIGHT

WILL and CHARLIE look over fellow partygoers as LIZBETH hides just around the corner and listens to their conversation:

CHARLIE

(speaking over music)

Isn't this awesome? The girls here are gorgeous.

WILL

(condescendingly)

Charlie, there aren't any hot girls at this party, except the one you've been chatting up. I'll give you that one, but that's it.

CHARLIE

Jane Bennet is the hottest girl here. But her sister Lizbeth is cute - I talked to her for a few minutes. She seems nice, and intelligent. Just your type. You should talk to her.

WILL

She was okay, I guess, but not worth the effort.

CHARLIE
God, Will, you're freaking impossible. Does anyone ever measure up enough for you?

WILL
I wouldn't hold my breath here.

LIZBETH, indignant, straightens away from her hiding place and marches past them, crossing the room to Charlotte, who's picking up discarded soda cans and napkins.

"Cut!" Richter says.

Emma

"Emma, good scene." Reid holds a venti doubleshot caramel macchiato, his caffeinated beverage of choice. He drinks at least one a day, sometimes two or three, at which point Richter forbids him more caffeine, because he starts talking so fast he runs words together—like a younger, better-looking version of my agent, Dan. Scary. "When you stormed past me and Tadd, it was like a tornado moved past. I definitely wouldn't want to get you mad."

"You know, they call it 'acting' for a reason," I retort, trying not to smile.

"You're very convincing as a woman scorned, that's all I'm saying." He attempts to look stern, his eyes teasing.

"Are you suggesting that I have experience in being scorned?" I'm aiming for playfully sarcastic, hoping it's not resembling resentfully bitchy.

He looks down at me, eyebrows raised. "I'm suggesting

no such thing. I just can't see any guy being as stupid as Will, if Lizbeth was as hot as you." I can't stop the blush that creeps across my face. "What happened to you last night?" He's so good-looking up close that it takes my breath away. I feel like I'm standing next to a work of art. "I looked up and you were gone."

"Yeah, I've been craving more sleep lately." I turn to grab a bottle of water from the cooler, breaking the mesmeric connection.

I almost tell him I've been getting up early and running every morning, but I don't. Graham and I are the only ones from our cast up and on the street that early, though we've crossed tracks with a couple of the production people. Not that Reid would bother getting up early to run with me. I tell myself I don't want the complication.

The assistant director calls for attention. "Okay folks, let's get some general party shots, dancing, some semi-inappropriate touching, etcetera, and we'll be finished for the day." This announcement earns an exhausted cheer from everyone. "Places!"

This morning, Graham was waiting in the lobby when I got downstairs. As we headed for the trail, deciding to reverse our usual direction to mix it up, he examined the sky. "It's overcast this morning." The clouds were dark and heavy, the air laden with a metallic pre-storm smell. "We may get rained on."

The sky remained merely ominous until we were at our halfway point, when it opened up a couple of seconds after a single deafening crack of thunder shook the ground and forced an embarrassing yelp from me. As it started pouring, we looked at each other and burst out laughing. We were drenched in five minutes. When a covered picnic area appeared just off the path, he sprinted towards it, and I followed. We sat on the table with our feet on the bench, staring out at the wet landscape.

I combed my fingers through my hair, squeezing the water out of it. "So what did you decide about the smoking?"

"I want to do it. Quit, I mean." He ran both hands through his dripping hair, pushing it back and off of his face. "It won't be easy, though." He bumped my knee with his. "So, are you prepared to be my support group?"

I smiled. "I guess I sorta have to, since I'm the one who goaded you into doing it."

He stared at me like he was trying to read my thoughts, and I was abruptly conscious of his proximity, his dark eyes examining my face. "Maybe I don't deserve your help after teasing you so mercilessly about your cute little 'huh' habit."

Raising a hand to my face, he gently swept a strand of wet hair off of my forehead, tucking it behind my ear. (Cute. Little. Huh. Habit?) I swallowed, my pulse thrumming so loudly in my ears that it drowned out the deluge pounding all around us. Our eyes held as his hand lowered, grazing past my ear, my shoulder, and down my arm, raising a wake of goosebumps in a trail behind his fingertips to my hand where it rested on my thigh.

Taking a deep breath, he hopped down from the table, tugging at my hand. He looked out at the rain, my hand still loosely caught in his. "I don't think it's going to let up soon enough. We're going to have to brave it. Just think *coffee*." He looked back at me and smiled. "And I'll try *not* to think *cigarette*. Though no promises until I get those damned patches."

"Okay." My voice was weightless, too insubstantial to be heard.

"You ready?"

I nodded. He squeezed my hand once, and then let go and jogged out into the rain. I followed him, a million more questions in my head than were there ten minutes before.

Chapter 19

REID

Walt Riggs, an LA friend and front man of a band, is in Austin for a gig tomorrow night. I'm exhausted as hell after filming a twelve-hour day, but I don't have any scenes tomorrow, so I told Walt we could hang out tonight. I pick him up from the airport in the limo, and Bob insists on going along. The man takes his bodyguarding duties seriously.

While we're waiting outside the arrival gate, Bob and I are playing Call of Duty. I've gotten used to playing Tadd and Quinton, so I think nothing of shooting Bob's guy in the head after a campaign. We do it all the time. Bob, however, is unfamiliar. His mouth drops open and he just looks at me. "What the hell, man?"

"Er, sorry, Bob. Didn't know you'd have an issue."

"We're *partners*. We just kicked ass together, Semper Fi and shit, and you *shot* me. That's just wrong, man. That's just so wrong." He shakes his head, crestfallen. Jesus. Note to self: don't play Call of Duty with Bob.

Walt comes out then, his jagged punk emo hair hanging in his eyes, leather bands wrapping both wrists, fitted t-shirt, jeans tight to his ankles. He's always dressed like this, caught constant crap about it from his jock older brothers and dad until recently, when all of a sudden he's a rock star. His bag is slung over one shoulder, along with his guitar case. I hit the button to lower the opaque window, calling his name as he's glancing around. He sees me and smiles, sauntering over as the driver exits to take his stuff. People crane their necks to look at him as he hands it over.

He's unlikely to be recognized by many people at this stage, but he will be, and soon. *Rolling Stone* sent someone to do an interview and photo spread with his band a week or so ago. In addition to his half Irish, half Korean looks—pale skin, coal black hair and piercing green eyes—the boy has serious vocal talent.

"Hey, man. Nice." He appraises the limo as I push the door open and he gets in, shoving the hair out of his eyes.

"Better get used to it."

"Yeah, we'll see." He glances at Bob, immediately thrusting a hand out. "Hey, I'm Walt."

Bob gives him the bone-crushing shake I know from experience and barks, "Bob." Walt doesn't even flinch.

"Groovy." He looks at me. "So what are we doing, man? I'm totally wired, but I need a shower. That flight was a bitch—the air wasn't working right or something. It was like hell in the sky." He stops, pulls out his boarding pass and scribbles something on the back of it—my best guess is lyrics.

I check the time on my phone. It's a little after eight. "We can drop you at your hotel, come back at like ten?"

"Brilliant."

When Bob and I get back to my hotel, Bob says the car will be ready at 9:40. He lumbers off the elevator, less effusive than usual, and turns left towards his room. I probably should've apologized again for killing his Call of Duty guy. I shake my head, turning right to go down the hall to my room, and look up just in time to see Graham going into Brooke's room. They are *so* hooking up.

Emma's room is a few down from Brooke's, and since I know where Graham is—and therefore where he *isn't*—I think about inviting her to go out with Walt and me. But she had a more demanding day than I did—more scenes, which equaled more retakes due to flukes like the A/C not keeping up with the temperature in that house and everyone looking shiny. Plus she has to film tomorrow and would need to be back in early.

I'm a patient guy. Okay, that's bullshit… but I can be patient with good reason. The concert tomorrow night will be perfect for testing Emma's and my off-screen chemistry. I'd already planned to invite the whole group. Brooke is a total music beast, especially little-known but growing hotter breakout bands like Walt's. She'll *definitely* be there, and will no doubt keep Graham's attention, leaving Emma to me. I pass Emma's room, having a couple of vodka shots in my room to loosen up instead.

Emma

After the day's filming, I was too tired to think clearly, let alone do any more than change into boxers and a t-shirt, order a bowl of fruit from room service, take a few bites, and collapse. Thank God my parents decided to entertain themselves tonight.

I could have sworn Graham was going to kiss me this morning, and I *wanted* him to, but instead, he turned away. Or ran away, more like. Because of Brooke? And then I went on set and Reid was attentive and flirting with me all day, but I'm not sure he wants more than a fling. I don't think that's what I want.

I fell asleep way too early, thoughts of Reid and Graham swirling through my head, and wake at 10 p.m. to the thrashing images of a Nirvana video on the TV—*Come as You are*. I've been sleeping for two hours, and I can tell I'm not going to be able to get back to sleep for another couple of hours, at least. I putter around the room, restless, eat some peanuts from the mini-bar, brush my teeth, watch a few videos, do some sit-ups.

Finally I grab my room key, open my door and peek into the hallway. No one's out. I pad down to Graham's door and knock softly, wait twenty or thirty seconds and knock again, a little harder. Nothing. As I turn to go back to my room, I hear a door open farther down the hall. I glance back and see Graham, leaving Brooke's room. *Craaaap.* Practically running to my room, I jam the card into the lock and for once it immediately blinks green and I'm in, shutting the door behind me. *Dammit. Dammit. Dammit.*

A minute later Graham knocks at my door; I know it's him without looking. I chew my thumbnail, deliberating. He maybe almost kissed me this morning, and he just came out of Brooke's room. But we're friends, and nothing actually happened this morning, and it's silly to refuse to talk to him because he was in her room.

I take a deep breath and open the door, employing every acting skill I possess to fix a pleasant expression on my face. His arms are propped on either side of the doorframe, his lanky, muscular body filling up the space. I'm aware of nothing but how casually sexy he is: barefoot, in jeans and a white t-shirt.

"Hey." His dark eyes search my face. "Did you need something? I just… thought maybe you were knocking on my door just now…"

"Oh, no. I mean, *no*, I don't really need anything, and yeah, I knocked on your door, but it's cool. I'm just bored. I fell asleep for a while, and now I'm awake and kinda wired…" *Shut up, Emma.* "and… uh… that's all."

"Bored, huh? What did you have in mind?"

I try to push away the answers that crowd in, most

notably *come in and finish what you started this morning.*

"I don't know. I was just thinking maybe you were still up, or something…"

"Well, you were right." He smiles, stretching against the door frame, hands gripping the top, his shirt teasing up and displaying a sliver of taut abdomen. "So. Can I come in?"

"Oh," I back into the room, "Sure. I'm sorry. Jeez. I guess I'm still a little fuzzy from the late nap."

He walks past me and drops into one of the chairs and I sit on the bed, folding my legs under me. "Do you wanna watch something?" he asks, tilting his head towards the television. "Or… I could interrogate you, find out all your secrets."

My bed is unmade, covers and pillows askew, the only light in the room coming from one small lamp and flashing MTV images. From a lifetime of reading scene settings, I know this setting is the definition of intimate. "You already know more than a lot of people know about me," I say. "I'm relatively boring."

"Mmm, I don't think that's true. And I don't even know the basic stuff. Like, how old are you?" He leans forward in the chair, elbows on knees.

"Well, *that's* certainly a stimulating topic. I'm seventeen, for another two months and…" I count in my head "…three weeks."

"So, eighteen in less than three months."

"Yeah… is that surprising?"

"Well, you look as though you could be younger than that, but you seem older, more mature. It isn't surprising; I just wasn't sure."

"So how old are you? Twenty?"

"Yep, since June. How'd you know?"

I am *not* telling him that I Internet stalked him. "Well, you *seem* younger than that, very immature, in fact, but you *look* older…" I laugh at the shocked look on his face, and then he growls and starts out of the chair. Backing farther onto the bed, I shake my head, still laughing. "Noooo…"

"So I look like an immature old guy, is that what you're saying?" One corner of his mouth turns up as he puts a knee on the bed, following me.

"Positively decrepit." I hold my hands out in what's clearly simulated protection as he advances. I'm almost to the other side of the bed when he grabs both of my hands in one of his, sweeping his opposite arm around my waist and pulling me towards him. In two seconds, I'm flat on my back and he's on his knees next to me.

He releases one wrist long enough to catch it with his other hand, and he flattens my hands to the bed on either side of my head. His eyes are black in the low light of the room. "Do you surrender?"

My heart is pounding, and I'm tingling from head to toe. "Surrender to what?" I whisper, my chest rising and falling, my eyes locked on his.

His gaze doesn't waver. "A kiss."

Images flash through my mind: the sincerity of his concern when I told him about losing my mother. The feel of him sitting next to me this morning, soaked through and touching my face. The jolt of seeing him exiting Brooke's room a few minutes ago. None of this adds up, or makes sense, and I want to care about that, but I can't find the will to resist—not just him, but my own desire, or curiosity, or something. I don't care what. I want that kiss.

He loosens his hold, starts to draw back because I haven't answered.

"Yes," I breathe, and he freezes.

"Yes?"

"Yes."

He trails his fingers over the side of my face, temple to neck, tracing a path, neck to waist. His right hand moves palm to palm with my left, intertwines our fingers as he lowers his head, and then his mouth is moving over mine, softly, carefully. I squeeze the hand holding mine and shift closer to him, clutching his shirt in my free hand, and he deepens the kiss, stretching out next to me, one knee hooked over my thigh. The hand at my waist progresses down over my hip, moving over my bare leg to the sensitive spot behind my knee. His hand is warm on my skin, drawing my leg over his until we're tangled together in the middle of the bed, his opposite shoulder under my head, his arm encircling me. His tongue traces my lips softly, parting them, thrusting inside. I moan, opening my mouth and pressing as close to him as I can get.

Too soon, he pulls away, both of us panting, sucking air as though we've been underwater. Teasing his fingers through my hair, he pushes a strand behind my ear, and I close my eyes as he cradles my head in his hand, the pad of his thumb stroking my cheek and jaw. Our heartbeats slow as we lie there, hardly moving, for several minutes.

"I'd better go." His voice is low and rough, full of what he doesn't say.

I open my eyes to stare into his, wanting to protest, but no coherent words come. His eyes are so dark there is no color to them at all, just guarded depths, full of thoughts and motivations I can't decipher.

"I'll see you tomorrow," he says, extracting himself slowly from my legs and hands. He leans over me, kissing my forehead, turning and padding from the room without a backward glance. I lie motionless except for the in and out of my breath, the beat of my heart, the pulse through my veins. Almost convinced I've dreamed the entire interlude, I fall asleep, and do dream it. Over and over.

Chapter 20

REID

Walt is into a my-body's-a-temple phase. I don't judge—I mean maybe he hit a wall. He was going pretty hardcore for a while, getting into shit I won't even touch. And I've touched a lot. We're at the bar they'll be playing tomorrow, and while I'm on my second beer, Walt has charmed the chick bartender into heating water for a cup of *tea* (he brought his own Tazo).

Yeah, the half-Asian guy is having tea *in the bar*. And I'll be goddamned if it couldn't get him play from some of the girls nearby.

Bob, obviously still offended that I shot his avatar, sent Jeff with us tonight. Jeff is plenty imposing. He's as much of a land mass as Bob, covered in tattoos, and has a single, thin scar running through one eyebrow, touching the cheek below and continuing off the jaw. At some point I'm going to be drunk enough to ask him how he got it. I just hope I remember his answer, if he gives it. Must be some story.

The band is good. Not as good as Walt's, but decent. The floor space below the little rise on which the band performs is full of people dancing—mostly girls. As the evening wears on, they begin to notice Walt and me… and Jeff. That's the thing about bodyguards. The main purpose of them is intimidation, with protection a close second. Enough intimidation and the protection element is never called into play. This is all great when there's a threat, which is not the case at the moment. I'm about to tell Jeff to get invisible when a couple of girls break off from the herd and come over.

"Excuse me," one says. "We were thinkin' you guys look lonely." None too original. But they're both drop-dead hot, so who cares.

Apparently, Walt cares. "Nah. I'm enjoying the music and just watching you girls dance. Reid?"

The girl's face goes through the emotions of having been rejected and complimented, and then her eyes widen and she looks at me, blinking. "Are you *for real* Reid Alexander? I mean we thought you looked like him but you're really him? You're not shittin' me?"

Jeff sits up straighter, crosses his arms over his chest. The posture doesn't go unnoticed, but it doesn't dissuade them, either. "Seriously?" the second girl says. "Ohmigod." She looks back at Walt.

"I'm nobody," he says, and sips his tea, observing her through a black fringe of bangs.

She looks as though she doesn't believe him. "Then it'll be okay with him—" she gestures to Jeff "—if I take *you* with me?"

Walt laughs. "I suppose so, in theory. But I'm not interested in going anywhere. You're welcome to have a seat, though?"

She looks at his lap as he hooks an empty chair at a nearby table with his foot and pulls it over. As she's considering, some recorded pop song comes on because the band is taking a break. The girls both squeal and ask us to dance. Something about Walt's expression says *holy mother of God, no*, but he sort of smiles. "No, thanks."

Right then the guitarist for the band, a curvy chick with purple hair, multiple piercings and huge blue eyes, glides between the two girls and sits in the chair, ignoring the girls and me completely and leaning towards Walt. His foot is still hooked around the leg of the chair. "You're Walt Riggs." She sticks her hand out. "I'm Carrie." Walt takes it, turns her hand over to read the tattoo on the inside of her wrist, which looks like Latin. "It basically says 'been there, done that,'" she says.

"Cool… You sure you've been there enough, done that enough, to have it permanently inscribed?"

She shrugs. "Maybe not. But I'm getting closer, and I've already got the ink saying so when I get there."

He gives her a genuine smile, and she laughs, throaty and full. I have to hand it to him, she's hands down the most intriguing chick in here.

"BRB," I say, taking both of the other girls, neither of whom Walt is paying any attention to, onto the dance floor.

Jeff and I drop him off at his hotel a couple of hours later. I thought he might take Carrie back to his hotel room, because they talked whenever she wasn't playing, but he said, "No, man, that's a professional relationship, you know? Ever heard the rule 'don't shit where you eat'?"

"But you just met her tonight, so how professional could that relationship be?"

He chews the inside of his cheek, thinking. "That's the thing. How professional could it ever be, if we just use each other for sex now?"

Huh. "If you were playing her, I guess that reasoning makes sense. But if it was mutual?"

He smiles, shakes his head. "It's never mutual. Somebody always wants more. People's psyches are complex, man."

I consider that for about five seconds. "Okay, so text me tomorrow with what time you want us at the back entrance.

There'll be between five to ten of us."

"Awesome. See you tomorrow."

Emma

The last thing I expected, after a kiss like that, was to run the trails alone this morning.

The lobby was deserted but for the desk clerk and me. Nothing unusual for the early hour, and I've beaten Graham downstairs before. Grabbing a section of the newspaper off of a table in the lobby area, I stood while reading it, sure he'd be down any minute. I was nervous, hands cold and stomach shaky, but I was sure that once we started running, once we started talking, those sensations would subside.

"Ms. Pierce?" I turned to find the desk clerk standing four feet away. "I have a message for you." She passed a folded sheet of paper to me, *Emma Pierce* scrawled on the outside. I recognized Graham's handwriting from the note he left on my nightstand a few nights ago.

> *Emma –*
>
> *Something came up and I had to go home. I'm sorry I won't be able to make our usual run in the morning. I may be gone a few days. I'm not sure. Just didn't want you waiting around for me - Graham*

For a few minutes, I wondered if there was a hidden message in the last sentence. And then I ran alone, glad for my renewed morning habit, which gave me something nothing else could: the ability to concentrate on little more than putting one foot in front of the other, marking time by counting each stride, until finally I was back in my room, standing under a hot shower.

"Earth to Emma." MiShaun breaks through my inattention. While the film crew is working on backdrop shots in the front of the Bennet house, I've been sitting at the kitchen table, staring out the back window, reconsidering Graham's kiss in light of his abrupt absence and possibly cryptic message.

"Sorry, MiShaun." I make no attempt to come up with an excuse, having overplayed the lack-of-caffeine defense, when the actual reason has nothing to do with drinkable stimulants. I can't get that kiss out of my head. Plus, before we kissed, he'd just come from Brooke's room. I have no idea what he was doing with her, even if I did shove that thought out of my head before we kissed.

"I was going to see if you wanted to go over lines, but if you need to zone out, far be it from me to intrude..." She looks curious. I must be more distracted than I thought.

"No, I'm fine, just... a lot to think about lately, with my parents still here." The truth is, I've all but forgotten they're here. "I guess we aren't doing the mall scenes this week?"

"I heard they're holding off until next week to do mall scenes, since Graham's in them."

"Oh, yeah, Graham..." I say this as though I haven't been thinking of him all day. My finger traces circles on the table. "Why did he leave Austin? Did anyone say?"

"I heard family thing in New York."

I feel instantly guilty. "What kind of family thing?"

MiShaun shrugs, shuffling through sides. "I'm sure we'll get the story when he gets back."

I have all the emotional weight of a ping pong ball, flying back and forth between my own feelings for Reid and Graham, nevermind what either of them feels. On the surface, Reid is paying attention to no one but me, while Graham is often occupied with Brooke. Reid is a known player and Graham—who knows what he's doing? Last night, he went from Brooke's room straight to mine, and like an idiot I let him kiss me. This should be clear-cut… but the kiss last night felt so right.

And then Graham disappeared this morning and everything is more confused than ever.

"MiShaun? You're pretty good at giving advice…"

"You need more? Shoot, baby."

I swallow. "Okay. So… how do you know whether to follow logic or intuition? I mean, when something *looks* like one thing, but *feels* like another—how do you know which is the truth?"

She puts the pages down and levels a look at me. "Is this about Reid?"

"What? No, just a general question, not relating to anyone in particular." Just *two* anyones. I should be crossing my fingers under the table.

She presses her lips together, a crease forming on her forehead. Finally, she sighs. "Sometimes, you just can't tell. But I'll say this, if what looks like the facts of the matter are conflicting with your feelings, then you need more information before deciding."

"Even if your feelings seem *really* sure of themselves?" I ask, knowing the answer.

"*Especially* then." She narrows her eyes at me, one eyebrow raised. "You sure this isn't about Reid? Because this seems like the sort of questions a girl would start asking herself after being kissed senseless by him."

"We haven't—I didn't—"

"Mmm-hmm."

"So I noticed you being dropped off at the hotel Monday night," I blurt out. "And the driver looked sorta familiar…" Emily calls this redirecting the subject. She's a big fan of this tactic when losing an argument with her mom. "MiShaun, are you *blushing*?"

"Don't be ridiculous. My people do not blush." She puts

on her prim and proper face and I smirk at her, because she's *wrong* about that. "Well. I'm obviously not as sneaky as I think."

"So what's he's like? What does he do?"

"He's a computer guy. I don't know the details and I already told him not to bother trying to tell me, because I get disoriented if I have to do any more to my laptop than turn it on."

"Computer guy, huh?" I wonder vaguely if this 'huh' counts towards Graham's tally. *He isn't here to rule on it, so I rule no.*

"Among other things." A wistful smile crosses her face.

"Such as?"

"Now, Emma. You know I don't kiss and tell."

"Right," I say. "But you can ask me about kissing Reid Alexander."

As if on cue, Reid walks around the corner, stops and puts his hands on the back of the chair next to me. "What was that?" He smiles, and I know he overheard me.

"Um, we're just, uh…"

"Going over lines," MiShaun says, straightening the sheets and placing them between us. "What are you doing here, Mr. Alexander? This afternoon is a Lizbeth/Charlotte scene. And as much as the producers would like your pretty face in every shot they can squeeze you into, you are not in it."

"I had to discuss something with Richter. Also, there's a concert tonight. It's an LA band; I know the lead singer. He says we can come in the back way, separate from the crowd, and have our own cordoned-off area so the bodyguards can do their thing. You guys up for it?"

I nod at MiShaun, and she says, "Sure, we're in."

"Cool. We're meeting in the lobby at eight to go get food, and the band goes on around ten." He drums the top of the chair, blue eyes twinkling. "I'll let you get back to… whatever you were discussing."

Chapter 21

REID

"Party of seven for Alexander." The hostess glances up, her expression morphing into the wide-eyed look I'm used to outside of LA or NYC. You'd think celebrities are imaginary beings, the way people react when they see us in public. Like aliens have landed, or Jesus has risen. My presence alone would have been enough for her, but the addition of whoever else she recognizes in the group renders her incapable of unstuttered speech. Brooke, MiShaun, Quinton, Tadd, Jenna and Emma are along for the ride. Graham, apparently, went home to New York last night, and I'm just *so* bummed about that. Not.

I'm careful that there's no overt touching between Emma and me, just grazes here and there—my hand at the small of her back from the car to the door of the restaurant, and again walking to the table. My arm across the back of her chair. Our shoulders and thighs pressing against each other intermittently while we're all talking and interacting during dinner. If things go as planned, she won't have to wait for the movie release to be famous, because everyone wants to know who I'm hooking up with. Paparazzi. Gossip rags and Internet sites. She's going to have to get used to this—the way that people know who I am, and because of that, they think they know me. Fame is people screaming your name, loving you, hating you, all on a whim.

When we arrive at the club, we use the band entrance Walt offered, rather than walk through the crowd. The hallways in the back are a cramped, dim maze, and I take Emma's hand as we're led through by the manager. We follow him to a restricted area, just off-stage, where we can sit and watch without being recognized or pestered. Bob and Jeff hover nearby.

I love my fans, but I wish they'd fade off occasionally and let me live my life. I escort Emma to the front spot near the wall. The way the chairs are arranged, there's no one behind us and no one in front of us—it's as private as possible. Quinton is next to me, and Brooke, of course, is as far from me as she can get. My arm is propped across the back of Emma's chair as the warm-up band winds up their last set.

The music is deafening, so there's not a lot of talking. In between sets, Emma asks if I know any of the other band members. "I met the guitarist when I was hanging out with Walt in LA. The other guys, no."

"Cool," she says.

The music is *good*, and Walt is damned incredible. Girls gathered in front of the stage jostle for position in front of him, but he's not staying in one place. He plays the whole audience, and everyone's into it. The floor pulses with bass notes, sending waves of vibration up through my legs. I glance at Emma and she smiles, leans closer and says, "He's amazing."

"I know, right?" My hand moves to her shoulder, kneading the muscles absently. She relaxes under my touch as my fingers slide through her hair at the base of her neck and the moment says *now, now, now*. When I lean in, twisting the brim of my Lakers cap to the back, she doesn't pull away. Cradling her head against my shoulder, with the beat pounding through us and the weird sense of privacy provided by the smoky darkness and a few hundred people all focused elsewhere, I kiss her. There's no script, no film crew, and this is unlike anything we've done on camera, where I have to do the leading man thing, choreographed for shadows and camera angles and a hundred other aspects of filming a scene. I slide my tongue across hers and deepen the kiss until I can taste her hesitation melting. When I pull away, her eyes open slowly, staring into mine.

When we get back to the hotel, I deliver her to her room, kissing her once more, short and sweet—nothing like the kiss during the show—despite the pleasantly evil ideas of everything I'd like to do to her pounding through my head.

My friend John will be in town tomorrow—he says he's always wanted to visit Texas and he's bored as hell in LA. That's John. Too much money, too much time, no celebrity on his own. I think going out with me is like a drug for him—it's like he's famous, too, and he loves it. Guess he needs another hit.

Tadd and I talked earlier today about going south for a couple of days to go tubing on the Guadalupe river. Disappearing for a couple of days would be a good idea, because this is how girls like Emma operate: they need just enough attention to let them know they're on your mind. A text or two per day, just on edge of naughty, and she'll be ready to go by Saturday.

I think I might like this going slower thing.

Emma

All morning, I keep blushing for no apparent reason—every time I think of the fact that I've kissed two insanely hot guys in the last two *days*. I still haven't heard from Graham. Reid sent me a text this morning wishing me good luck with filming today.

His fans know where we're filming, and they showed up early to stand just outside the barricades surrounding the house. But *he* isn't filming today, so all but the most tenacious of them eventually trickled away. Chloe and my father are visiting the set this afternoon, and when their taxi arrives, there's renewed excitement among the dozen or so fans until they exit. Chloe's outfit today consists of skintight lowrise jeans, wedge heels, and a low-hanging peasant blouse that would look more appropriate on someone in high school. And I don't mean someone who *teaches* high school.

When I go outside to authorize them through set security, a couple of the fans holler, "Emma!" I turn and wave, surprised they know who I am.

The afternoon's schedule consists mainly of a scene including Tim Warner and Leslie Neale as Lizbeth's parents, a fact that sends Chloe into insufferable enthusiasm overdrive. As Tim and Leslie are discussing the interaction they'll be filming first, Chloe interrupts to tell them how she's been a huge fan since she was a little girl. Tim stops talking, flabbergasted, and Leslie stares at Chloe for a moment before saying, "Thank you dear, and who are you?"

"Oh! I'm Emma's mother!" I cringe at both this semi-fabrication and the appalling fact that she's legitimately connected to me at all.

As I dream of trap doors and the benefits of quicksand, Leslie and Tim turn towards me, and I try to make myself think *screw everyone else* even though the last thing I want is for these two distinguished actors to have a poor opinion of me, even if MiShaun is right and it isn't fair for them to judge me based on Chloe.

Leslie recovers first. "Well, I'm sure you're proud of her. She's so talented. At the moment, though, we've got to get this scene set up. If you'd just make yourself comfortable and enjoy watching Emma work…" She leads Chloe to a chair off-set and motions to an assistant to the PA, asking her to get Mrs. Pierce something to drink. As she turns from a stunned and silent Chloe, Leslie winks at me.

I think I love her.

At the end of the day, I'm exhausted and running on five or six non-consecutive hours of sleep, but Chloe insists on going out to dinner since they're leaving early in the morning. I want nothing more than room service, a conversation with Emily about all the kissing going on, and some sleep.

"We'll make it an early night," my father says. "I haven't gotten the chance to tell you how great you were today." Unable to help myself, I warm under his words, leaning my head on his shoulder as he pats my knee.

Over dinner at a local barbeque place, Chloe talks about how awesome Leslie was for an hour and a half straight while my father squeezes in a sentence or two praising *my* performance. In the taxi, I dig my phone from my bag to text Emily. There are two missed calls and two texts from her; the restaurant was so loud that I didn't hear the phone alerts. The first text says: CALL ME. That's scary, considering the all caps, but the second, sent half an hour ago, is way more frightening: GOOGLE YOURSELF AND THEN CALL ME.

Once in my room, I boot up my laptop and type my name into the search box. And there, spread across the Internet, in multiple locations including every Reid Alexander fanpage, are indistinct photos and rampant speculation about Reid Alexander and his current costar, Emma Pierce, who were kissing, offscreen, at a club in Austin.

Oh. God.

I'd texted with Emily about the kiss the previous night, but there's a vast difference in getting the unadorned facts via text, and seeing it in grainy color on a 17-inch monitor, accompanied by assorted enhanced close-ups of the action.

"I had no idea anyone could even see us. Oh, God."

"No reason to panic. Let's be logical. Okay, *Reid Alexander kissed you*, for real, not lights-camera-action. And like what practically ninety-nine percent of girls would do if faced with Reid Alexander's lips, you went for it."

"Yeah."

"So what's the problem, exactly, besides the whole thing getting outed to the world? You said he was an amazing kisser."

"He is… but… there's this, uh, complication I was going to talk to you about tonight, before I knew all of this. Remember the guy I've been running with?"

"Graham, right?"

"Yeah. Well, he kissed me. Monday night."

"Okay, back up. *What?*" I visualize her waving her hands around. Emily can be on the phone and *driving*, and she'll wave both hands around. She says it helps her think. "Is this the same Graham you said was 'just a friend' or some *other* Graham?"

"Oh, God."

"Sorry, Em. You know sarcasm is my coping mechanism. Go on. Spill it."

I curl on my side in the middle of my bed, exactly where Graham and I were. "I've felt this… building attraction to him, and we spent all Saturday evening talking, and then we were watching a movie, and I fell asleep and when I woke up he was gone."

"So. Talking *in bed* on Saturday. Interesting. And then Monday, what?"

"I couldn't sleep, and I knocked on his door, thinking we could talk, or something…"

"*Emma…*" Emily says.

"Okay, well, he didn't answer..." I gulp, anticipating how she'll react to the next part. "So I was walking back to my room… and he came out of Brooke's room."

"Hold on. Brooke *Cameron*, aka Kristen Wells—evil

incarnate?"

"Emily, you know she's not as horrible in real life as her character on *Life's a Beach*."

"Yet she's got this Graham guy in her room. Why?"

"I don't know. I didn't ask." Wow, that sounds even worse out loud than it did in my head.

"Emma, *what*?" She sighs, and I know she'd shake me if she wasn't several hundred miles away. "This kiss took place after he emerged *sans explanation* from Brooke Cameron's *hotel room*?"

I take a deep breath and leave out the humiliation of him seeing me run back to my room like a frightened rabbit scurrying for a hole in the fence. "He came to my room, and we were talking, and then playing around, and somehow we ended up kissing."

"Somehow you ended up kissing." I see her dubious expression in my mind's eye—mouth in a grim line, one eyebrow raised just so.

"I know. It sounds ridiculous..."

Emily is quiet, except for the sound of her tapping a pencil against her front teeth, which drives her mom insane. "Well, which of these two guys are you interested in?"

I think about Graham pushing a strand of hair behind my ear when we'd ducked out of the rainstorm, the feel of his fingers sliding over my skin, how he listened when I talked about losing Mom. I think about the hunger in Reid's beautiful eyes, the heated difference in his off-screen kiss, and the way he teases me. "I like them both. They're just… different."

"Well that complicates matters. What happens after this film? Do you see either of them being in your life after it's over? Do you want that?"

"*Oh my God.* I kissed two guys within 24 hours of each other—one in my hotel room and one out in public and now it's all over the Internet. What am I gonna *do*?" I don't really expect an answer. I'm thinking about running away to join the Peace Corps, which seems more appealing every minute.

"Emma. Besides looking a wee bit slutty, and let's face it, most of Hollywood is a little slutty, what are you *really* worried about?"

My answer surprises me. "I guess I'm worried that Reid will think we're a thing… and I'm worried that Graham will think that, too."

"So you don't want Graham to think you and Reid are hooking up..."

"I think I'd feel the same if it was the other way around," I say, while my brain goes *you sure about that?* and I think *YES* a little too forcefully and Emily would say *methinks thou doth protest too much* to if she heard me having this conversation with myself.

"Even though Graham and Brooke might be hooking up? Hmm."

"Uh, one more thing. Graham left Austin sometime during the night after that kiss, and I haven't seen him or heard from him since then. Some family emergency, I think. But he hasn't called or texted or anything."

"Weird," Emily says, pencil going *tic tic tic*. "What else do you know about him?"

"He's older."

"How much older?" I hear a prepared-to-be-horrified note in her voice.

"Two and a half years."

"Thank God, I thought you were gonna say he was like thirty or something. Look, I think the reason you're in this predicament now is you're letting *them* determine everything. Maybe you should decide what *you* want, Em."

"Right now I want to come home and hide in your closet."

She laughs because that's exactly what I used to do when Chloe came to pick me up and I didn't want to go home. "Look, you don't need either of them. Don't do anything else until you figure out what you want. Or *who* you want."

I'm suddenly extremely homesick for my best friend, my usual routine, and my uncomplicated life—which didn't include photos of me, locking lips with a bona fide teen idol, splashed across the Internet.

Chapter 22

REID

John arrived last night. Picking people up at the airport is starting to feel like a second job. Quinton tagged along and we all went out for a late dinner, then back to my room to plot the trip down the Guadalupe, which Bob is none too happy about. He came by the room to tell me he's sending Jeff and another security guy with us. "If anybody drowns, it had better be *that* guy," he said, pointing at John.

"What the hell, man?" John blinked. Bob growled at him as he left the room.

At this point, we'd already put down a load of whiskey sours, so this exchange was hysterical as far as Quinton and I saw it. Tadd joined us around midnight after some don't-ask-don't-tell activity, which he usually tells anyway. Especially if we ask.

I'd intended to be awake early enough to see Emma before we left, but given the level of inebriation that occurred and the fact that it was three a.m. by the time everyone left my room, that didn't happen. I texted her once we were underway, and she answered when she was on lunch break.

I'm less worried about competing with Graham than I was before I kissed her. Never hurts to draw an obvious contrast to potential rivals, though. Especially if it seems to be unintentional:

Me: Going tubing for a couple of days with quinton, tadd, and a friend from home. Thought I would tell you and not just disappear. :)

Emma: What's tubing?

Me: Basically you get in a huge inner tube and float down the river. I will def bring you along next time.

Emma: Sounds dangerous...

Me: Nope, lol. Just fun.

Emma: K. Have fun. :)

We rent three cottages and six tubes, and buy as much beer as the coolers can carry. If we're doing this, we're doing it all the way. Our assigned bodyguards, Jeff and Ricky, are less unhappy than Bob was about our impromptu excursion. Even though they technically aren't allowed to drink on the job, we assured them we didn't consider beer consumption *drinking*, per se. Plus they're both legal and can buy the beer.

"How do you even know about all this?" Tadd asks, while we meander through a convenience store, all wearing hats and sunglasses, grabbing water shoes, sunblock and mesh nets to hold the empty cans.

"I used to know somebody who lived in Austin. The locals do this for fun during the summer—I figured we might as well try it while we're here, right?"

Brooke is the somebody. Once upon a time, she told me stories about her older sisters, who planned tubing trips with their friends every summer. "They drink beer all day and float down the river, flirting with boys, and then everyone meets up at a bonfire, where my sisters trade in their Baptist roots to become river whores and hook up with every cute guy they bump into."

"Sounds fun," I'd said, and she punched me in the arm.

"Ow!" We were watching a movie in my trailer, something so boring we'd long since lost interest in favor of making out. At fourteen and fifteen, nobody knew who we were yet, but we wanted the fame, we craved the industry recognition, and we were both willing to work our asses off to get there. The movie we were filming together then was ultimately a flop, but we weren't the stars so it didn't reflect on us.

She leaned over and kissed the spot she'd punched. "I don't want you hooking up with a bunch of girls." Leaning back, she regarded me with a slight pout, an expression that had, at the time, melted me every time she did it.

"I don't want any other girls," I said.

"I don't want any other guys," she answered, leaning closer.

"Good." I kissed her, pulling her onto my lap, my hands wandering under her shirt as hers wandered under mine. Maybe that was the first time we went a step further than making out.

That conversation went like this: "Do you think—?"

She looked at me a long moment before nodding. "Okay."

Emma

We're filming at the Bennet house again. Graham and I have the first scene. I don't know when he returned to Austin, only that I haven't heard from him in the two and a half days since he kissed me. Meanwhile, the photos of Reid and me at the concert have pretty much gone viral, and considering Graham's silence, it seems clear enough how he feels about that.

The kitchen is packed, between craft services people setting up breakfast and snacks, crew members standing around eating, discussing camera angles and scene layouts, and the cast taking bites between bits of line rehearsals. More than once I start to leave the kitchen and go to the living area, where it's less crowded and noisy, but something keeps me hiding in the throng of people, and I know exactly what that something is.

Waiting to see Graham yanks my emotions back and forth, as though I'm either facing a starting gate or a firing squad. I'm as jittery and nauseated as I would be after four cups of coffee. I can't quite get a grip, giving me five seconds, from the moment I finally hear his voice in the other room, to pull it together.

Epic. Fail.

He comes around the corner, sides in hand, talking with Richter, wearing jeans and a rumpled button-down shirt, sleeves rolled and pushed above his elbows. Running a hand through his hair, he glances around the room, his eyes not stopping on anything or anyone until he reaches me. Expression unreadable, he nods once in my direction and turns back to Richter.

"Let's get you into makeup," Richter tells him. "Fifteen minutes?"

"Sure." I don't see him again until right before we're on camera.

I don't recognize Graham when he comes back. My concern that they wouldn't be able to make him look goofy enough for Bill Collins was dead wrong. His hair is slicked back with gel and he's wearing pleated khaki pants, a coral golf shirt—tucked in—and a pair of gold-framed glasses with spherical lenses. His walk and his mannerisms are timid, yet self-important. He's perfect.

We're filming the absurd proposal scene between Bill and Lizbeth. The assistant director lays out the scene and we listen without looking at each other. Graham hasn't looked at me after that first glance, though he'll be contractually obligated to in a few minutes. I would have felt so comfortable doing this scene a week ago, before he kissed me, before he disappeared and returned not speaking to me.

"Action," Richter says.

INT. Bennet Kitchen - Day
LIZBETH is loading dishes into the dishwasher as BILL walks in from the dining room with a stack of plates.

BILL
Lizbeth, I have something to ask you.

LIZBETH
(taking dishes from him, rinsing them in the sink)
Yes?

BILL
As you know, I am an integral part of the Rosings firm, with a lucrative career in front of me.

LIZBETH
(rolling eyes to the side)
Yes, so you've said.

BILL
My boss, Ms. DeBourgh, believes that a man in my position is best suited to an advantageous career if he is settled down, domestically speaking.

LIZBETH frowns.

BILL

So, I'm asking you, Lizbeth Bennet, to marry me.

LIZBETH swivels to face him, dropping a plate into the sink where it clatters and breaks.

(The expression on Graham's face is so guarded that I have a difficult time staying in character—Bill Collins is supposed to be comic relief. Graham seems… angry.)

LIZBETH

(incredulous)

But. But. I'm in high school.

(I'm determined to fix that parenthetical incredulous expression on my face. I try to focus on his ridiculous glasses, the stupid slicked-back hair, *anything*. Nothing works.)

BILL

The engagement won't be official until you're eighteen, but that needn't stop us from planning.

(He sounds much too persuasive to be the idiotic Bill Collins; even his nasally whine is absent. Richter is going to notice; *everyone* is going to notice. Suddenly I'm *livid*.)

LIZBETH

(stunned)

Are you insane?

BILL
(laughing carelessly)
Girls are all such teases. It's nearly impossible for a guy to know where he stands!

(And I'm blushing again…)

LIZBETH
(horrified)
I am not being a tease. If I've done something to make you think I'm interested, well, I'm sorry. My answer is still no.

BILL
You don't need to worry about the choice of ring, by the way. I didn't purchase one yet because I wanted to make sure you had your choice.

LIZBETH
You didn't even know me a month ago. You couldn't possibly have come here intending to just fall in love with someone you don't even know?

(My voice cracks and I can't keep my lip from quivering. *Dammit.*)

BILL
It's true, I didn't know you, but I had every intention of making

up for my dad's mismanagement of Bennet Inc. by hooking up, legitimately of course, with you. I knew you were beautiful. I was sure I would feel a connection. And I did.

(Graham is staring into my eyes, and I have trouble remembering my lines.)

LIZBETH

(slinging soapy water into the sink)

This is crazy. I'm not getting married to anyone, certainly not to you.

"Cut," Richter says, and I can tell he's less than happy. He eyes Graham and me, his hand over his mouth, as though he wants to make sure not to say anything until he knows exactly what he means to say. "Everyone but Emma and Graham take five." *Crap*. "On second thought, make it ten." *Oh, crap*.

Our accomplished director leans a hip on the table and crosses his arms over his chest, regarding the two of us. I imagine this is what it feels like to be called to the principal's office for fighting or talking in class. Graham and I both look anywhere but at Richter or each other.

"So. Graham," Richter begins. "You realize your guy is a silly, shallow character?"

Graham nods, crossing his arms over his chest, too. Defensive response, as any actor knows.

"So what's with the brooding stares? You've been spot on playing this guy as clueless and superficial. And now, he's staring at Lizbeth as though he's deciding whether to kick a chair across the room or throw her over his shoulder and retreat to his cave."

I'm blushing again—*throw her over his shoulder*—and

Graham is silent for a full minute. "I know. I'm sorry," he answers, arms loosening, one hand gripping the countertop while he almost runs the other through his hair, stopping when he realizes it's gelled back. "If I could have a few minutes, I'll get into character. I'm a little off today."

"All right. Take ten minutes. Be ready to reshoot, but let me know if you need longer."

Graham nods and leaves the room without looking at me.

"Everything okay between you two?" Richter asks when Graham is gone.

"Yeah." What else can I say?

"Well. I think you were responding to Graham's lead in that last take. Remember that Lizbeth isn't angry. She's shocked and incredulous."

"I know. I'll get it right next take. I'm sorry."

"Take a few minutes and we'll hit take two."

We film the scene again, and Graham has pulled himself completely into character. We do several partial scenes and a few minor retakes. Richter wasn't far off, though I should have been professional enough to stay in character, and I can't blame Graham completely. "Perfect," Richter says. "Let's take a break, and we'll come back and do the next bit with the Bennet family." Graham walks out the front door dialing his cell.

The last scene before lunch, which doesn't include Graham, goes well. When we're done, I turn and he's leaning against a door jamb, watching me. We lock eyes briefly before the PA claims his attention. I don't know if that kiss meant anything to him, or if it was a regretted impulse. I don't know if I'm interrupting something between Graham and Brooke that has nothing to do with me. He's seen the photos of Reid and me, or at least knows about them, and I hate that he's angry, or hurt, or disgusted. I hate that we aren't talking.

Taking a turkey sandwich, a Diet Coke, and this afternoon's sides, I go out back to the covered patio. The weather is hot, but in the shade it's passably warm. When the door opens behind me, I hope it isn't someone from makeup, since they'll have to touch up anything that gets shiny, which is inevitable now that I'm hiding out in the heat.

"Hey, Emma," Graham says, walking around the cushioned bench where I sit and taking the seat opposite me. He sets a bottle of water on the low table and reaches into his pocket for his pack and lighter.

"Hi."

"I'm starting the patches tomorrow, as soon as we're done filming," he says, tapping a cigarette out of the nearly empty package, lighting the end. Taking a drag, he stores the pack and lighter away, leans back, exhales above our heads. "That way I start when I'm not filming."

"You bought the patches, then?" Hearing his voice makes me happy. Just knowing he doesn't hate me is a relief.

"Yeah. When I was in New York." He doesn't elaborate, taking another drag on the cigarette and looking out over the parched yard.

"Is everything okay… with your trip to New York? Someone said you had a family emergency."

"Oh. Yeah, everything's fine," he says, falling silent again.

"Okay. Well. Good." I look back down at the sheet in my hand, not sure what to say now that he's here. I've forgotten how Graham is with silences, though. He's comfortable in them, never determined to fill them unless he has something to say.

He finishes his cigarette and starts another before he speaks. "Sorry for earlier, getting you bitched out with me. I was just really off today, for some reason." His eyes are sincere, the earlier judgment in them dissolved, gone.

"It's okay. I was off, too."

"Well. I wanted to apologize. Actors tend to play off of each other in a scene, and I really screwed up the first time around." He starts to run a hand through his hair again and stops abruptly, yanking his hand down and taking a last long drag, like his nicotine cravings know that he and cigarettes are about to go their separate ways, and they want to stock up.

I can't help smiling at him. "That stuff in your hair is driving you crazy, isn't it."

He grins back at me. "Man, you don't even know. I had no idea how often I touched my hair until all of a sudden I *can't*. This stuff feels like glue."

I eat the last bite of my sandwich and finish the Diet Coke while he smokes. I fiddle with the wrapper, wad it up and balance it on top of the empty can.

"Have you been running, while I was gone?"

I look up at him. "I skipped one day, but I ran today."

"Going tomorrow?"

"I was planning to."

"Mind if I join you? I haven't done so much as a pushup since we ran last."

"Sure."

The PA pokes his head out the door. "Five minutes, Emma."

At the end of filming, Graham leaves the set without speaking to anyone but Richter. I want to talk to him again, but I feel so guilty over kissing Reid that I lose my nerve any time I consider initiating a conversation. And then I think of Brooke, and I'm not sure if I have anything to feel guilty *for*.

Reid: Hey, just thinking about you and wanted to say hi
Me: Hi back. Having fun? Using sunscreen?
Reid: Yes... and yes... but after that many hours in the sun, I may come back saturday a little pinker anyway.
Me: Lol. See you then.
Reid: Hope so ;)

Chapter 23

REID

Brooke got one thing right: river whores.

I'm talking about the guys and me, of course. The past two days have consisted of watching for hours as groups of girls float nearby with their tubes hooked together, clad in bikinis and frayed denim shorts with straw cowboy hats or baseball caps shielding their faces. Last night was after-hours partying and inviting a few girls (and a couple of guys—Tadd's no more angelic than the rest of us) back to the cottages. Being on this river the past couple of days, I remember what made Brooke so fascinating.

I grew up in LA, and thanks to a multitude of factors including Dad's career trajectory, Mom's ancestry, and their collective net worth, I've run in exclusive circles my whole life. The majority of women in those circles of southern California, and their daughters, have a look. An untouchable beauty, a not-quite-real quality, everything pampered and flawless. My mother has this look, as do her friends. The socialites, the actresses, the wannabes, they all have it.

When I met Brooke, she was fifteen and new to

California. She'd been discovered in Texas—in Austin, in fact, and she was so raw and fresh and *different*, she took my breath away. She was beautiful, but natural. Her hair wasn't highlighted, and she wore no makeup off set. She had tan lines from laying out at the community pool and muscles from playing soccer since she was five. Since she'd grown up in a relatively large city, her accent was mild, but definitely there.

She'd confessed that her manager was sending her to speech classes to lose her "horrible drawl." I remember telling her that was the most idiotic thing I'd ever heard, but when I begged her not to go, she'd laughed and said, "You don't want me to sound like some brainless hick, do you?" That was just the first thing LA changed about her. Now she's as perfect and soulless as the others there. Not that I can talk.

The girls here all have her former accent, in various concentrations. In some, every other word is *y'all*. Others just soften syllables and liaise words. All of them tend to drop any *g* at the end of any word.

A few of them figured out who we are. Not difficult when we're all together like this, which is what had Bob freaked out. When I'm outside LA by myself or with John, I sometimes get away with saying, "Yeah, I get that all the time," if someone discovers who I am. With Quinton and Tadd along, it's nearly impossible. Hats and sunglasses help, but a few people know our identities despite the camouflage.

The last thing I need in my campaign to win Emma over all the way is photos of me with other girls popping up tomorrow on the Internet. Wherever there are cameras, or wherever cameras might be, I'm doing no more than hanging out with the guys, maybe a little drinking, a little dancing. Anyone following me into the cottage is subject to leaving all personal items with Jeff and Ricky. One girl objected, which was no big deal—Ricky just escorted her back to her friends' campsite. Her friend, on the other hand, surrendered her bag and phone to Jeff and asked if she needed to give him her clothes, too. I told her no, she and I would take care of that ourselves.

Emma

"So what, exactly, are the boys doing?" MiShaun asks over dinner Friday night.

"They went tubing." Brooke answers.

"Pardon me?" MiShaun says, one eyebrow raised.

"A shallow, slow-moving river, inner tubes—like from tires—and a day of doing nothing but floating downstream. Add beer and girls in bikinis and it's a guy's wet dream. Ha, ha."

"Sounds like a guaranteed sunburn to me," Jenna says.

MiShaun agrees. "Richter will have their hides if they come back looking like well-done lobsters."

"Excuse me, are you Brooke Cameron? From *Life's a Beach*?" Two girls stand hesitantly by our table, apprehensive but determined.

Brooke turns, a wide smile replacing her blasé expression. "Yes, I am."

"Oh, we *love* you!" the second girl says while the first nods. "You're so bitchy and awesome!" Both girls blanch. "I mean, I know Kirsten is just your character, that you aren't really, uh—."

"Don't worry—I *strive* for bitchy and awesome." She laughs and they relax. "Would you like to take a picture or something?" A whirlwind of activity occurs as the two fans dig their phones out of their bags.

The rest of us slide looks towards each other that say *Who is this person?*

While Jenna takes a photo of Brooke with one of her fans, the other girl glances around the table. "Ohmigod,

MiShaun Grant! Wow, you guys are *friends*? That's so cool!"

"We're in Austin filming a movie," Brooke says, motioning for the second girl to get into the photo Jenna is about to take.

"You *are*?" That's when they recognize *me*. I don't know if they think they're being subtle, or if they don't care. They stare and whisper behind their hands. "Wait. Hold on. Are you talking about the movie with *Reid Alexander*?" Both girls scan the restaurant.

"Yes," Brooke says, a new edge to her voice. "And he's not *here*." Meredith and I exchange another look.

Their disappointment is palpable. "Can we at least get a photo with you, too?" one of them asks MiShaun, who flashes Meredith and me a smirk.

"Sure thing. Always happy to do impromptu photo ops with my *adoring* fans." Her sarcastic tone is gently veiled by the words. Meredith bites the inside of her cheek and examines her silverware as I cough-laugh into my napkin. MiShaun leans towards the fans, smiling, while Jenna snaps the photos. The photo requests are repeated with me, and suddenly I can hardly wait to get back to the hotel.

"You girls have a nice evening," Brooke dismisses the two girls and turns back to Jenna as though they'd been interrupted in the middle of a scintillating conversation.

"God," Brooke says as they walk away, "Reid's a pain in the ass even when he isn't around."

Chapter 24

REID

John's CEO father called last night and ordered him home. Apparently he has orientation for college starting Monday morning, and he's supposed to check in tomorrow. Oops.

No matter how loud and intimidating my dad is, he doesn't compare to John's dad, a CEO who handles everyone he encounters, no matter who they are, as though they work for him. That includes John, who nicknamed him the Dark Lord when we were sixteen. John doesn't work and is completely financially dependent, so when the Dark Lord says jump, he jumps.

John and I are sharing one of the cottages, and he knocked on my bedroom door at, shall we say, an inopportune moment last night. The girl—let's call her Macy because I like that name and I can't recall her real name—shot up like she'd been hit with a jumper cable.

"*What*?" I called, annoyed.

"Hey man, a minute," John said on the other side of the door.

I glanced at Macy, who was mostly undressed but looked

like she might bolt. "Don't move." I put one finger on her sternum and pushed her slowly back down, smiling. "It's just my dumbass friend. I'll be right back."

I padded across the small room, shirtless, jeans unzipped, and cracked open the door. "What the hell do you *want*, man? I know you had more condoms that you could use in a week."

"My dad just called. I, uh, have to be home tomorrow."

"And?"

"On a ten a.m. flight."

"What? *Why*?" I shook my head. "Nevermind. I'll text Jeff—God knows I'm not disturbing *him* right now. He'd kick your ass, only because he's not allowed to kick *mine*."

"Yeah, that's kinda why I didn't knock on his door…"

"I'll handle it. Now leave me the hell alone the rest of the night. Seriously."

He smiled. "Don't worry, man. Thanks."

"Whatever." I shut the door with a snap, locked it and turned, grabbing my phone from the rickety dresser and tapping a message to Jeff, Tadd and Quinton as I walked towards the bed, staring at Macy. "Where were we?"

There's a flurry of activity this morning to get out of here before eight. Macy's just been coaxed into one of three taxis, looking severely hungover and pouting that I'm leaving. There's no reason to tell her that my leaving has nothing to do with putting her in a taxi this morning. No offense to hot girls everywhere—but newsflash—there are hot girls everywhere. I don't do seconds.

I'm not including Emma with that—she's not a one-nighter. I assume she'll keep me happily occupied for the duration of filming. Maybe longer, who knows. If you mess around with costars, there's generally an assumption of being a couple, at least temporarily. I don't believe in love, and even though my parents have been married forever, I don't believe in marriage either. They just exist and rotate around each other's lives. There's no emotional relationship there. It's a social, fiscal relationship. That's not for me and never will be.

I don't lie to girls like Macy (whose name is Tracy, by the way—I was close). If she goes into something like last night assuming a relationship might come out the other end—and I don't care if we're talking about me or John or *any guy*—she's fooling herself. It has nothing to do with a lack of respect or any of that shit they try to scare girls with. It's way more simple than that.

If I met you last night, and brought you back to my place, or followed you to yours, and we had sex, that's what we asked for from each other. It's what I got, and what you got. I don't know you. You don't know me. Thanks for playing, and we're done. If by some fluke anything was said at some point during this entire exchange that made me curious enough to see you again, I would.

Has that happened before? A couple of times. Did it last? Clearly, no.

Emma

Graham and I barely spoke yesterday morning while we ran, and at lunch he was running lines with MiShaun while I worked with Tim and Leslie. I don't know what he did last night while the girls went out.

This morning, he hasn't spoken since murmuring, "Good morning," in the lobby, and we're almost halfway through our regular trail. In contrast to our comfortable silences, this quiet is awkward, as though there are words in our mouths, trapped. There's no sound beyond our separate strides synchronizing to a singular, rhythmic footfall, the reverberations from the engine of a small plane circling above—a car dealership ad promising *NO DOWN*

PAYMENT! undulating behind, and the drone of cars on a nearby street.

After another five minutes, I can't take the disconnection any longer. Any conversation, no matter how dull, would be better than this uncomfortable void. "Any nicotine cravings yet?"

I read relief in his glance, in the way his shoulders relax, like he was waiting for me to speak while I was waiting for him. "I'm actually still buzzing from the patch."

"Where'd you put it?"

He pulls back the sleeve of his t-shirt to reveal the patch, stuck to his more-muscular-than-I'd-realized-before bicep. "I'm supposed to put it in a new spot every time, I guess to give the skin a rest."

"Huh," I say, hearing myself the second it leaves my mouth. A moment passes, and I wonder if he'll say anything.

"You've grown careless in my absence. What are we up to now? Forty or so?"

I shove him, inexplicably pleased that he hasn't given up teasing me, and he laughs, swerving off the path for no more than two steps. "Peace, girl, chill! You're still under ten. But we're on the honor system here, so you'll have to let me know if you start racking up penalties when I'm not around."

I pretend to scowl.

"Hey, you know I'm just messing with you, right? I really don't care if you use 'huh' in every third sentence."

"I don't know," I pout. "Seems like it really bugs you."

He smiles. "Nah. It would take a lot more than that for you to get on my nerves."

We exit the elevator on the fourth floor to the energetic banter of our costars, who've returned from the tubing trip. Quinton is kneeling on the floor, digging through his bag, clothes strewn all around it, while Reid and Tadd stand nearby, watching him. "I *know* that damned card is here somewhere."

"I'll call down to the front desk; they'll send someone up with a new one," Tadd offers.

"Dude it was *just here*, I saw it this morning as I was packing…"

When Graham and I come into sight, Reid's more tanned (somewhat pink) face lights up. "Emma!" he says, as though we haven't seen each other for weeks.

He walks straight over and puts his arms around me, twirling me around once, leaving one arm around my waist as he says, "Hey, Graham," and sticks out his hand. Graham shakes it without comment. "Too bad you couldn't make it, man, it was *awesome*. Nothing to do all day but drink and float."

He looks down at me. "Aren't you the cutest thing in this little tank and shorts combo. Out exercising early, eh?" Before I can form an answer, he leans in and kisses me.

The kiss isn't more than a peck, not more than a split-second meeting of our lips, and is nothing like the passionate kiss three nights ago, but the action holds unmistakable familiarity. Graham's face is void of expression as he turns towards his door. When I'm free from Reid's embrace, I walk across the hall and push my key card into my door, annoyed at Reid for claiming me with that kiss, annoyed at Graham for surrendering so easily.

"Ah-ha!" Quinton locates his key card at the very bottom of his bag.

"Hey, let's all go out tonight," Reid suggests.

"I need a nap first," Tadd says, yawning. "A *long* freaking nap."

"It's only like 10 a.m." Reid punches his arm and dodges away. "You can get a full eight hours of beauty rest and still have plenty of time to put on your makeup."

Tadd lunges forward and trips over a mound of clothing, and Quinton recoils, saying, "Man, I am in *serious* need of some adult company," as they crash to the ground, rolling and laughing like five-year-olds.

"What?" Tadd rolls off of Reid, his innocent expression contradicted by the leg he immediately sticks out to trip Reid as he rises.

My door unlocks and I push it open as Reid says, "See you tonight, Emma?"

He has no idea what he just did. "Sure."

"Cool. I'll text everyone; we can all meet up and go together."

Graham is already in his room, his door shutting with a soft click.

I spend the afternoon in my room, finishing a novel that leaves me full-on depressed. The main character is giving a party, and the entire story is the day leading up to the party. But all during that day, as she's getting everything prepared for this party, she's recalling her past, and the people who'll be attending: one guy in particular, someone who was in love with her years and years before, someone she didn't choose. And it's not like she's miserable; it's worse, like she sometimes feels dead inside. At least that's what I got from it.

Reading a story like that makes you either want to go out and party or stay in to contemplate slitting your wrists.

I'm still deciding.

Me: Everyone going out tonight, prepare for compromising internet photos tomorrow. Still confused. Call when you get a break?

Em: Trying to feel sorry for you... 2 hot guys, 1 you...

"Hey, I'm on dinner break. Jasper gave me a whole twenty minutes," Emily says when I answer. "God, today's been a nightmare. Some of Derek's anti-Goth friends strolled through the store to check me out, and I didn't disappoint. You *know* how I dress when I'm working."

"Yeah."

"Hold on a sec." I hear her ordering a slice of pizza and a

lemonade, the buzz of hundreds of conversations and the squeals of children in the background. I can almost smell the oregano and tomato sauce of the food court pizza place, mixing with the aroma of constantly frying baskets of French fries at the Hot-Dog-on-a-Stick next door. It feels like months since Emily and I were there together, contemplating my looming celebrity.

"Okay, I'm back. So. What are you more hesitant about, how you feel about Reid, or how he feels about you?"

"Not really how he feels, but what it means, you know?"

"Like the 'What are your intensions, Mr. Alexander?' kind of what it 'means'?"

"Too nineteenth century?"

"Kinda. Plus this isn't some tool who works at the Gap, this is *Reid Alexander*."

"I know. And I'm 17, not 35. It's not like I need promises of forever."

"Just because you don't want somebody to pull the rug out from under you doesn't mean you're asking for forever. You've had enough grief, Em. I've always wondered how *I* turned out to be the one who pens binders of melancholic poetry, for chrissake."

My father and I never talk about how my mother died.

It was cancer, and it was quick. What I've deduced in the past eleven years: she was too young to have known to start looking; there was no family history, no pressing need to be diligent about checkups. The malignant cells were masters at camouflage, with so few telltale signs that photos of her, taken mere months before she died, didn't contain a single warning. I know. I looked. She appeared healthy and beautiful, but appearances lie.

The discovery was accidental. Her dentist, troubled about the amount of blood loss she sustained from a simple dental procedure, badgered her to go see her doctor. She gave in to shut him up, and I picture her getting the phone call two or three days later, sitting down hard at the kitchen table, speechless.

I was a child, so the truth was kept from me until there was no avoiding it. I don't know how long I had with her, from the knowledge that I was losing her to the moment she was gone. I have a few strong memories from that time. In the hospital, the tubes and needles that seemed to anchor her to the bed scared the living daylights out of me. Once home, she lay propped in the center of her bed with so many pillows that she seemed to be floating on a cloud of them. Six-year-old reasoning told me that being home meant she was getting better. Bits and pieces of the funeral are vivid. I cried because my father did, because my grandmother did, because everyone did, even the priest, and because my mother wasn't there to console me, and I didn't completely understand why.

My grandmother moved in for a week or two, but she finally had to go back to work. She lived nearby, and she became the one I turned to most often when I missed my mother, the one who felt it like I did. Like a giant hole had opened in the middle of my chest, and nothing would ever fill it.

My father was so completely withdrawn and silent after Mom was gone that I began to forget that he was ever easygoing and cheerful. I forgot the way we had chased each other around the house, our food fights, and how he'd get me to help him wash his car and I'd splash him with a bucketful of soapy water. He'd spray me with the hose, and Mom would put her hands on her hips and say, "Connor, I swear to God, I am a single mother of two." Mouth turned down, eyes big and blinking, he would do what she called his puppy dog look, holding my hand while I mimicked his expression, and she'd throw her hands up in surrender, walking away, hiding her smile. He'd stage-whisper, "She's no match for our green-eyed charm."

For a brief time, when he began seeing Chloe, he was like that again—happy. He looked at me instead of through me.

And then at some point he belonged to her, and even if he was still there in my life, it was like we'd come apart. I was outside of his embrace again, fighting in vain for a way back in that I never found.

They married thirteen months after my mother died.

I know my father loves me, in his own way. That's how they say it: *He loves you in his own way*. Well, what about my way? What if I need for him to love me in *my* way?

Chapter 25

REID

Everyone meets in the lobby for tonight's outing, including Brooke and Graham, who stand inches apart, speaking quietly. I take Emma's hand and lead her to the first taxi, Bob following us, everyone else taking the two remaining cars. Not many photographers out tonight—they probably didn't know I'd come back from New Braunfels since we got in so early and I didn't leave the hotel today.

Emma's wearing a little black dress, straps criss-crossing over her shoulders and meeting the dress halfway down her back. Her shoes look like funky heeled Mary Janes, very schoolgirl, totally hot. Continuing that theme, her hair is swept into a high ponytail. I have a weakness for ponytails—something about the bareness of the nape, the innocent feminine look of it. "You look adorable tonight," I tell her, and she smiles into her lap before glancing up at me. When I hold my hand out, palm up, she takes it. Her hand is small, delicate, absolutely feminine, and this awareness makes me want her even more. "Cool ring. Princess cut diamond—I like it."

"Me, too." Her finger brushes over it. I get the feeling there's a story behind that ring, but for whatever reason, she's not ready to share it.

The club has a VIP area in a loft overlooking the dance floor. We commandeer the space, pushing the low tables together in the center with four sofas surrounding them. Brooke plops next to Graham, across from Emma and me, leaning into him to whisper something. I keep a peripheral eye on Emma to see if she's watching them. She was definitely tense this morning after I kissed her in the hallway in front of him. Did it feel like I was marking my territory? Unfortunately, yes. Did it feel necessary at the time? Also yes.

My arm rests behind her now, and we're sitting close enough that our thighs brush with the slightest pressure. Everyone orders drinks while Tadd, Quinton and I talk about the parts of our trip we can discuss in mixed company.

"Look at this." Tadd pulls up the leg of his jeans to show a huge purpling bruise on his shin. "Stupid invisible underwater branch."

"Dude, I thought the Guadalupe had an alligator," Quinton says. "You screamed like a little girl until you saw it was just a stick and started cursing like a strung-out ho."

Tadd smoothes the fabric over his leg carefully and points at Quinton. "Like you didn't launch yourself outta that tube like a rocket when that fish bit your ass."

My hand moves to Emma's bare neck, massaging lightly as she laughs with everyone else.

"No one warned me there were carnivorous fish in that damned river!" Quinton says.

"Reid and I didn't get so much as nibbled. It was all Quinton," Tadd says.

"You're just jealous that none of them wanted a piece of you."

"Yeah, *that's* the reason."

A new song comes on and I stand up, taking Emma's

hand. "Let's dance." She allows herself to be pulled up, and Meredith and Tadd decide to follow us.

"You sure you can hit the floor after that life-threatening injury?" Quinton quips.

Tadd flips him off and keeps walking.

Emma

I don't look at Graham as Reid and I move to the stairs and start down. Even with the dim lighting, descending the staircase is like entering a debutante's ball. Practically everyone downstairs looks up to see who's coming down. At least half of them seem to recognize Reid. One bodyguard shadows us, and another waits just off the dance floor.

Reid is either oblivious or faking oblivion; more likely the latter. Clad in a blue t-shirt that exactly matches his eyes, a pair of jeans that fit him like they're custom made, and worn-in cowboy boots, he's a living breathing incarnation of male beauty. He's every bit the guy in an Armani suit on the cover of *GQ*, with a spread inside in which he sports a tight black tank, doing pull-ups on a tree branch, showing off his enviable biceps and shoulders.

He pulls me into his arms on the floor, ignoring the fast tempo of the song and swaying slowly, dragging my arms up and around his neck. Bending to my ear, he says, "Don't be scared, I've got you."

"Do I look afraid?"

"Mm-hmm." He smiles down at me, resting his forehead on mine, his hands on my lower back, pressing me closer. "Positively terrified."

"I'm more brave than I look."

"That's good to know." He pulls me deeper into the crowd, which parts for us. The bodyguards look nervous, but Reid acts as though we're the only people on the floor, and everyone else allows it. This boy could charm just about anything out of anyone, and he's quite conscious of that fact. Just another reason for my apprehension.

I try not to think of Graham upstairs. I'm convinced he left my room the other night because of Brooke. They're probably already involved, possibly they have been for a while. Maybe they argued, maybe he just slipped—our kiss was a mistake and nothing more. He's become a good friend. I like talking to him and running with him, the way he teases me, the way he seems to look out for me. Trying to turn it into anything further will ruin it.

That's what I tell myself, locked in Reid's arms, dancing within a crowd of people as though no one else exists. But Reid and I will never be invisible, as much as we might pretend it, and I never feel like everyone else disappears. I feel them staring, the whole time we're on the floor, like they can see right through me.

"Let's go to the café, get some coffee. I'm not ready to go up yet," Reid says quietly to me as we enter the hotel hours later in groups of two and three. We're last in.

"Do you want to ask anyone else—?"

"I've had enough of everyone else for one night." Holding one finger to his lips, he pulls me towards the café, out of sight of the elevator.

He asks for a booth by the window and slides in beside me instead of across. We order coffee and share a slice of cheesecake, most of which he eats. I'm still trying to work off that cake I shared with Graham.

Don't think of Graham.

There are still people in the street, and we watch them parade by. "I like watching people making idiots of themselves, like that guy." He points to someone performing a drunken dance for a few friends who are attempting, unsuccessfully, to stop him. "Or fall in love, like those two." A couple standing under a streetlamp are kissing passionately enough to make me blush.

"Me too. I like getting to be the audience."

"So," he says then, his fingers on my chin, turning my face. He kisses me lightly, at first. And then his arms slip around me, one hand moving from my lower back to my hip to my thigh, his mouth more urgent. Finally he leans his forehead against mine like he did at the club, his eyes closed as our breathing slows.

"Come to my room with me?" He asks so softly that I'm almost unsure he said it. His meaning is clear. Crystal.

"I… I don't know, Reid…" My mind is casting about for some response, not wanting to push him away, but not ready for what he's asking.

"I just want to kiss you, nothing more." He laughs softly. "Okay, that's entirely untrue. What I mean is, there will *be* nothing more, if it's too soon for you. Just please, let me kiss you in a room where there isn't a waiter hovering or a camera rolling or a million people watching."

I nod, and he slaps a fifty on the table for what is probably a twelve dollar ticket, takes my hand and tucks it under his arm as we walk across to the café exit and to the elevators.

When the doors open, he sticks his head out first, glancing one way and then the other, as though we're spies. Or fugitives. The hallway is deserted. We dash to his room, giggling. His room key is in his hand and in a matter of seconds we're in, and he's letting the door swing shut behind us and locking it. I'm not giggling anymore, and neither is he.

"Do you want something to drink?"

I feel dry-mouthed and nervous. "Water?" For a moment I feel silly; it isn't like I've never made out with anyone before. And then I remember that I'm alone in a hotel room with Reid Alexander.

"Coming right up. Make yourself at home." His room is a suite with a king-sized bed dominating one wall, a sitting area with a sofa and two chairs, a bar, and French doors at the south-facing balcony. There are fresh cut flowers in the middle of the dresser, and dry-cleaning bags hanging on the closet door. I perch in the middle of the sofa.

He brings two bottled waters from the bar fridge, hands me one as he sits next to me, leaning into the corner of the sofa, leaving several inches of space between us. My anxiety is building rather than decreasing, but I'm not sure how to calm myself.

For no good reason I recall how comfortable I felt with Graham in my room.

Don't think about Graham.

"Emma." Reid leans up to place his bottle on the coffee table, and fixes me with the smoldering stare I recognize from every magazine spread he's done in the last two years. The difference is this look is real, in person, and directed at me. "Come here."

I place my bottle next to his and move closer, until our knees are touching. He kisses me softly, one hand on my waist, the heel of his hand pressed to my ribcage. Some minutes later, he stands, pulls me up by both hands and puts my arms around his neck as he had on the dance floor. Kissing me again, he lifts me by the hips, settles my legs around his torso and sits back down, never breaking the contact of his mouth on mine. We kiss for five minutes, ten, fifteen, I have no idea. When I finally break away, as breathless as if I'd run a mile, his mouth moves to my neck, kissing an erratic pathway to my ear.

Kneading my lower back with one hand while the other cups the base of my skull, he runs his fingertips from my shoulders to my hands, back and forth, finally circling my wrists with his hands, pulling my hands to lay on his chest. I feel his heartbeat under my palm, and his hands move to my thighs.

"Are you very sure," his lips blaze a path from my chin to the base of my throat and my hands grip his biceps as though

I'm suspended over a sheer drop, "that you don't want to stay?"

I have to get out of here before I surrender to something I'm not ready for. I can't think straight, and with what he's doing, stopping him, let alone myself, isn't going to get any easier.

"I can't, Reid." My God, I couldn't sound less convincing.

"Mmm, I think you can," he says, his hands moving over the bare skin of my shoulders, pushing the straps aside. As he presses me gently back on the sofa, looking down at me with a subtle, perceptive smile, I know he can read my longing to give in. And then he's kissing me again and it's a full five minutes before we come up for air.

"Reid, please. Not… yet."

"I understand," he says, taking a deep breath, eyes closed. He opens them and smiles wryly. "Can't blame a guy for trying." He kisses me one more time, quick and sweet, hands surrounding my face. "You know where I am if you change your mind, Emma."

I leave his room, my legs shaking as though I've been at sea for a month, and I feel a weird mixture of regret and relief. It takes me four tries to get the key card to unlock my door.

I lie back on my bed and push my mental replay button… until my phone beeps, startling me. It's Meredith, probably wondering what happened when Reid and I disappeared.

Meredith: You okay? Not that I'm checking up on you or anything. ;)
Me: Yep. Reid and I decided to stop by the cafe downstairs for a few minutes.
Meredith: Wanna get lunch and go shopping tomorrow?
Me: Sounds good. Noon?
Meredith: Sure. I'll come to your room. cya then

Chapter 26

REID

Time for a re-eval.

First up, I'm certain Emma's a virgin. The way she's holding back isn't just wariness of me—though that's part and parcel. She's new to the whole rodeo. Though there's nothing about her that says *I'm saving myself for marriage* or any such crap, most girls want to save themselves for something—usually love, in which, as I've already established, I don't believe.

Given the above, her kissing skill is incredible. I know it's subjective, and not everyone likes the same things, the same way. Honestly, if I'm going to get laid, I tolerate just about anything. But Emma requires no toleration, and with a *lot* of past history to use for comparison, I know better than to take that for granted. She's responsive, following every move I make like she did on the dance floor, tentative and sweet while managing to drive me crazy with wanting her, no matter how much control I seem to have over myself and the situation in the beginning.

It's been a while since I've been this infatuated with

someone. Jesus, what a rush. I can't screw this up, and the best way to insure success in that is to cut off any other action for the duration. After the hour or so the two of us spent in my room last night, I've lost all interest in everyone else anyway. I want her. Period.

So then, Graham Douglas.

I don't know him. He's a puzzle. He's done nothing but indie films, with some student films mixed in. No acting jobs before he was seventeen, and it looks like he started college before that. No idea if he continued or gave it up or what. He's two years older than me, a year older than Brooke. I assume the two of them met on some previous project. They seem too chummy to have just met.

I can't find that he crossed paths with Emma before *School Pride*, but anything is possible. Maybe they hooked up at some point, but not all the way. All the same, he doesn't seem like the sort to dispute boundaries—if he thinks she's mine, I think he'll retreat. After I kissed Emma in front of him yesterday, he backed off without a word. Caveman tactics aren't in my repertoire, generally, but neither is losing a girl I want this badly.

Emma

Over lunch, Meredith grills me. "Emma, *what* is going on between you and Reid?"

I shrug one shoulder. "Honestly, I'm not sure."

"Hmm. I thought I might not to get an answer to my text until this morning...."

"Well, I answered last night—from my room." She arches a brow. "Where I was *alone*."

"Okay, enough interrogation, I get it." She takes a sip of her iced tea. "I'm still depressed over breaking up with Robby, even if it was for the best."

"What happened?"

Her mouth twists. "When we're together, everything is fine. When I'm away on location or whatever, it goes to hell. He loses all trust in me. If he can't get me on my cell, he leaves angry messages. He accuses me of doing things I'd never do. Then he says he loves me and he's just scared. The night we broke up, I told him I can't be with him if he can't trust me. And he said, 'Then I guess you can't be with me,' and that was that."

"Wow. That sucks."

"Seriously."

My phone beeps and I dig it out of my bag.

Reid: Dinner tonight? Alone? Be at your room at 7?
Me: Sure

"Reid?" Meredith asks.

"He wants us to go to dinner alone."

"Yet you're 'not sure' what's going on." She smirks. "Look, he obviously likes you, you like him… unless there's someone else?"

I think of Graham, and my teeth clench. *Why* can't I stop thinking of him that way? Because of *one* kiss that he obviously thinks was a mistake? I stack my fork and knife on the plate, not looking at her. "No. I just need to get over it."

"I hear that. Robby and I have broken up three times in the last two years, and I *really* just need to get over it." Her eyes well up with tears. I wish I could find this Robby guy and dead-leg him, like I'd done to a kid who broke Emily's heart in second grade, when retribution was easy.

"So. What are we wearing tonight? Casual hot, or dressy hot?" Meredith asks, smiling, blinking her tears away. "We're about to shop this town's rocks off. We need to know what we're hunting for."

Me: Casual or dressy?

Reid: Preference?
Me: No?
Reid: K, lol. Casual it is. See you at 7.

While I'm dressing for my date with Reid (dark jeans, purple silk tank), I think about my run with Graham this morning. He didn't ask what happened to me last night, thank God. He asked about my upcoming classes. Those of us who haven't graduated and are under eighteen are required by law to attend class on set during the school year. Next week, Jenna, Meredith and I begin timed blocks of instruction with tutors. I'll have enough credits to graduate by November.

"So then what?" We single-filed around a slower couple, for the third time in ten minutes. "College?" The paths are busy on Sunday mornings, which makes carrying on a conversation a disconnected and sporadic event.

"I've never planned to go."

He smiled down at a toddler in a stroller as we passed, and she smiled back. "Why not?"

I shrugged. "I've never considered it a requirement. Or an option." I felt myself getting defensive. "I'm not that bright. I do okay in my coursework, but nothing spectacular."

"You're underestimating yourself, Emma. And most people in college are *not* geniuses."

"So you've taken some sort of poll? Or perhaps did some research?"

He laughed, falling in behind me as we passed a group jogging the opposite direction. "If research can be defined as being aware that you could run brainy little circles around most of the people I've gone to class with," he said, "then yes."

The warm sensation that flowed through me was both similar to yet nothing like some guy telling me I'm hot. Some guy like Reid, for instance.

"MiShaun says you completed a degree in New York?"

"Not quite. My final semester is this spring, after *School*

Pride wraps."

"How'd you get so far ahead?"

He bit his lip. "With academic parents and older sisters, I was precocious. I skipped kindergarten, moved from second grade to third mid-year. I liked being younger than anyone else in class, even though I got beat up occasionally for being pretentious."

"*Were* you pretentious?"

"Yeah." He laughed. "I was completely full of myself, pretty much all the time."

"So you finished high school when?"

"Sixteen." He smirked at me. "Clever diversion, getting me to talk about myself so I'll quit asking you about your future plans, which you haven't made."

"I wasn't trying to divert. I was curious."

"Uh-huh." I guessed he was wearing the same expression that got him creamed on the playground.

"Besides, if you're trying to convince me that people who go to college aren't brilliant, you totally suck at the persuasive part of your argument."

He sighed. "I'm *not* brilliant. I've just always been a bit more… driven… than my peers. Another thing—certain classes and instructors make you think and generate approaches to issues you didn't know existed. As an actor, it gives you more depth to pull from."

Almost exactly what Jenna said on the plane.

"Hu—" I caught myself and clamped my lips shut.

"Nice catch," he said before taking the lead so we could pass another slowpoke walker.

I'm ready to go at 6:45. By 7:00, I've retouched my hair four times, checked my teeth twice, sat down on the bed and stood up again countless times. At the knock, my stomach drops. Without checking the peephole, I pull the door open, and there stands Brooke, dressed to go out, but her hair is straight on one side, wavy on the other.

"Brooke? Hi?"

She walks into my room. "Hey, cute tank. *Please* tell me you have a Chi flatiron. Mine shorted out or something. Goddamned thing made a *zzzzt* noise when I was halfway done, as you can undoubtedly see with your own eyes, and now I have a date in like twenty minutes with the super *hot* manager of that band we saw the other night? And my hair looks like complete crap."

Band manager? She has a date with a band manager? "Uh, sure. I'll get it."

"Oh, thank God. I seriously wanted to kill someone but couldn't think who'd be culpable except for whoever put that thing together, and they're probably making three cents an hour and working out of a windowless factory in southeast Asia."

As we exit the bathroom, a confident knock sounds at the door. Brooke's eyes slide to me. "Date tonight, Emma? Who is it? Reid?" She peers through the peephole. "Yep, there he stands, Mr. Everything." I'm wondering what she means by *that* as she pulls the door open and stands in the doorway. "Hey there."

He's wearing jeans and a white jersey Lacoste shirt, and he looks like he got up from a nap, ran a hand through his hair and pronounced it fine. And that's the thing—it *is* fine. This is the most unfair and strangely subtle characteristic that he possesses: the more blasé he is about his appearance, the more beautiful he gets.

Over Brooke's shoulder, I watch a number of emotions flicker over Reid's face. Glancing at the number on the door and back to her, he blinks, his head tilting sideways just slightly. His eyes narrow, spotting me behind her. "Brooke. Nice hair."

"Well. I'm off to repair my split personality. You children have fun." She turns to me. "Thanks for the Chi. I owe you big time." She and Reid are like five-year-olds in a stare-off as she walks around him, until she breaks it off and walks towards her room, humming.

“Odd girl,” he says, turning back to me. His gaze appreciative, he looks me up and down. Taking my hand, he twirls me around slowly. “You look *so* hot. Are you ready to go?”

“Yep. I’ll get my bag.” I take a calming breath as I cross the room, trying to remind myself that he’s just a guy. On this date, *he’s just a guy*.

Right.

Chapter 27

REID

Bob and Jeff are standing at the hotel exit, which tells me everything is about to get a lot more interesting. When we step outside and the flashes start, Emma's hand tightens in mine. With our bodyguards running defense, I slide an arm around Emma and lead her to the waiting car. She's clearly a little freaked out and unused to this level of media attention.

One of the many alarming and unexpected things no one tells you is how *close* the people with cameras come. Don't they have professional zoom lenses? Do they really need to duck under Bob's meaty arm to snap a flash right in our faces? The photographers call my name, trying to get me to glance up so they can get the money shot. When that doesn't work, they try Emma. She follows my lead and ignores them. Smart girl.

Some of the paparazzi follow us to the restaurant, which is at least half an hour away, and the flashes start up again before we even get out of the car. Bob and Jeff, as usual, are worth every penny production is paying them, supplying a wall of muscle on either side of us as we dash inside.

We're greeted by a deferential maître d, dim lighting, thick carpeting, limestone walls and wood beams. The wait staff is dressed in formal black and white, tables boast crisp white cloths and frosted candlelight, and tiny white lights wrap around columns and dip overhead like stars. I give my name and we're ushered to a table near the window in the back, as I requested, with a view of the lake. There's outdoor seating and a dock, which is trimmed with more firefly-sized lights.

I watch her face as she takes it all in. "Like it?"

Her wide grey-green eyes drift over everything, returning to mine. "Yeah. It's beautiful."

"True." I'm staring at her. Haven't stopped since we sat down. She smiles shyly into her lap. The table is small, and I lean forward and take her hand, the ghost of a smile playing across my mouth, and bring it to my lips, kissing the knuckles one at a time. Corny, I know. Just the sort of thing guys are usually too dense to actually do. Her cheeks glow a little pink.

"So Emma. Are you ready to be famous?" I release her hand, leaning back as the waiter arrives with a bottle of wine. "Because this film is going to do it for both of us."

She smirks at me while the wine is tasted and approved, doesn't speak until the waiter disappears. "You're already famous."

I frown, lips pursed. "I am? What makes you say that?"

She laughs. "Oh, I don't know… the photographers who follow you around, maybe? The girls?"

"What girls? I haven't noticed any girls," I say, and she laughs again. "Well, I've noticed *one* girl. And I haven't been able to see or care about any of the others lately. They might as well be invisible."

Peering at me, head angled, she says, "Hmm."

I don't want to say too much too soon. She seems oddly perceptive where bullshit is concerned. "You didn't answer. Are you ready for it yourself?"

She shrugs. "I don't know. It's still a little surreal. I want to be successful, of course. But part of me just wants to be a normal girl."

That's a new one. Who wants to be normal? "Normal how?"

The self-consciousness is back. She bites her lip, fingers tracing the base of her wine glass as she debates what to reveal. "Like… high school. Theatre class. Homecoming football games. College plans. Prom."

"Prom, eh?" I laugh softly and she smiles. "How long have you been tutored?"

"Since sixth grade."

"I started then, too."

She leans up. "It never bothered you—the friends you left behind? The athletic teams you never played on, the class president spot you'd have easily won?"

No one's ever asked me about this before. I never gave much thought to what I may have left behind or given up. I finished my degree credits a year ago, and was more than happy to be done with classes, assignments and tutors. "I never did public school, so my situation was never all that normal to begin with." I lean closer, too, elbows on the table. "You realize, don't you, that there are millions of kids our age who'd desert all of that stuff in a heartbeat to have what we have, to be who we are?"

"So I hear." She colors slightly and I smile.

"What?" I ask, and she blushes harder, smiling into her lap again.

"Nothing. Just some stuff my best friend said to me recently. About doing this movie." I tilt my head, an acknowledgement that there's more she isn't saying. She rolls her eyes. "With you."

I can't help but chuckle. "So I have a loyal fan in—where do you live?"

"Sacramento."

"Sacramento. Not too far from LA." I know what I'm

implying the moment this is out of my mouth.

She does, too, and she's studying my face. "It's like 400 miles. Not exactly next door."

I shrug. "No. But not as far as say, Texas, or New York." I know what I'm implying with this, too, but I've got the innocent look down. Growing up with my dad taught me to either lie like a pro or not bother.

In a feat of perfect timing that will earn him a thirty percent tip, the waiter arrives with our meals.

Emma

Strangely, I haven't given much thought to where Graham lives, in relation to me. But New York is on the other side of the country from Sacramento. In comparison, Los Angeles seems right down the street. I should pinch myself right now for thinking about Graham at all. I'm on a date with Reid. And I'm enjoying it.

The meal is amazing, the waiter attentive but not intrusive. We talk about jobs we've done, people we've worked with or want to work with, and he's funny, especially when discussing Hollywood gossip, and how petty and catty people can be. How fake. Which makes me think of Brooke.

"So how do you know Brooke?" I ask, not thinking this question will get the reaction it does. I just recalled the animosity that seems to be between them and wondered at the reason. He reins in his response quickly, but not before I see what flies across his face. Even still, I'm not sure how to interpret it. "I'm sorry—I'm not trying to pry… I just… noticed you guys seem… uh…" Oh my God, I've talked myself into a corner.

"Noticed that, did you?" His voice is careful, calm. He doesn't seem angry.

"I'm so sorry—it's none of my business."

"It's okay. I've never really… discussed what happened with anyone." He shifts in his chair, waits while the waiter takes his plate. "We were involved. A long time ago." His blue eyes sweep up and he sighs. "To say it didn't end well would be an understatement."

"Wow. I'm really… sorry." I'm dying to know what happened, but there's no *way* I'm asking that of him.

"Seriously, it was a *long* time ago. I'm way over it, believe me. I know she is, too. This is just the first time we've worked together since then." He smiles pensively, then twitches his hair back and seems to shake off any negative leftovers. "There's no reason for either of us to be bitter at this point. She seems happy enough with Graham."

Boom. Just like that.

"Are they—? I mean, tonight she said…" Oops, this is probably going against the girl code. Even if Brooke and I aren't exactly best friends.

He arches a brow. "What?"

Ugh! What if he tells Graham? Should *I* tell Graham?

"Well, um, she said something about a date tonight…"

"With someone other than Graham, is that what you mean?"

"Yeah." I feel uncomfortable having divulged this, until Reid answers.

"Emma… you're not used to Hollywood people. You're still inexperienced—not that you should be anything else." He snaps a credit card on top of the bill and sends the waiter away. "I'm almost positive Brooke and Graham, living as far apart as they do, have an understanding."

"You mean… to go out with other people?"

"Either that, or they're just fooling around while we're on location here." I guess the look on my face takes me directly from inexperienced to downright naïve, because he says, "Oh great. I've shocked you. Look, I'm *sure* whatever they're doing, they've agreed on between them. The best thing to do in this business is adopt a live-and-let-live attitude."

He signs the receipt, an illegible scrawl, and stands, taking my hand. "Come on, let's get out of here."

When we reach the hotel, he shields me on the way in as he did hours ago, on the way out. Once we're inside, he takes my hand as we cross the lobby. I feel more comfortable with him than I ever thought it possible to be, but my pulse is hammering by the time we get into the elevator. When the doors shut, he leans against the side wall and pulls me forward, his feet spread just far enough apart for me to stand in between them. "I'm going to kiss you now," he says, his hands pressing my low back. And then he does.

We stop at my door, and he says nothing about us continuing to his room. "I know you have filming at an offensive hour tomorrow, so if you'll let me have one more kiss just inside your door, I'll go to my room, where I'll sit and smile for a bit before falling asleep."

"No killing zombies tonight?"

He laughs. "Ah, who was it—Tadd, or Quinton? That addiction is supposed to be our secret. It's like Fight Club for guys with faces that have to stay pretty."

I laugh, unlocking my door. We step inside my room, where I've left a single lamp on and curtains open, because it was light outside when we left. Reid lets the door shut and immediately presses me to it, his hands on my shoulders. Inverting his hands, his fingernails lightly skim down my bare arms. When he gets to my hands, he takes them in his, dips his head and kisses me.

"I have to go now or I'm not going at all," he says, minutes later. I can't do any more than nod. He kisses me again, pulling away and murmuring, "*Damn*," before opening the door and slipping into the hallway.

Production interrupted the Bennet house filming schedule in favor of completing some scenes at the mall. We have to be on location and ready to go by 5 a.m. so we can wrap filming before the mall opens. No one can blame us for whining about morning coming too soon when we're dragging ourselves out of bed at 4 a.m.—which I'm sorry is *not* technically morning. Graham and I decided yesterday, when we got news of the change, to sacrifice our morning runs for the week.

Five of us stumble into the limo and collapse on the seats, clutching Starbucks cups and battered sides, going over lines. Reid, Tadd and Brooke don't film until the afternoon, so at the moment, everyone hates them. Quinton sprawls next to me, eyes shut and Ray-Bans in place, despite the darkness outside and the tinted windows, as if the mini-lights throughout the interior of the limo are an outrage. "Why am I awake? Sun's not even up yet," he complains.

Next to me, Graham's mouth turns up on one side and he bumps my foot with his. We're used to being up before the sun, familiar with the gradual warmth on our backs as it rises, the erratic, elongated shadows it creates ahead of us as we jog west along the river paths, its rays on our faces as we circle around to head back to the hotel. "I miss running already," he says.

"I hear mall walking is popular with the older folks," I say. "You could stick around after we're done filming, get a few laps in…"

He shakes his head, fighting to repress a grin. "Funny girl." His gaze moves to the window across from us, and we both watch the cityscape passing by for several moments. "What if the *running* isn't the only part of it I miss?"

I glance at him, but his gaze doesn't shift from the window. *God.*

Em: Details from last night?? I saw photos online, but it isn't the same as the straight dirt.

Me: It was nice. We talked a lot. The paparazzi stuff is all a little scary.

Em: You're going out with a guy who has his own posters, i mean holy shit.

Me: I knnnnoooooowww. It didn't feel like that last night though…

Em: Are you guys official? Fan pages say your people and his people are not commenting.
Me: I have people??
Em: Apparently
Me: Ugh. Gotta go film. I'm supposed to start classes this afternoon. Zzzzzz

Chapter 28

REID

For the past three days, any time I can get away with it, I'm monopolizing Emma's time. Her afternoon classes are an annoying interruption, plus now she has assignments to do during the free time that I'd rather she spend with me. We have next Monday off, due in part to it being Labor Day and in part to Adam Richter's wife having a scheduled C-section that day.

For me, a long weekend means two things. First, Emma's going home to Sacramento on Saturday, so I already won't see her for three days. And second, my mom's first two weeks in rehab, which I've consciously refused to think about, are almost up. Dad's just informed me that I'm leaving for LA Friday night—meaning tomorrow.

"We're expected to be at a family session with her Saturday morning," he says.

I feel myself responding emotionally to his dictatorial bearing before I even process the words. And then I process the words. Family. Session. The *last* thing I want is to talk to another useless therapist. "What," I say, my voice devoid of inflection.

"Look, I'm sorry if this interrupts your routine partying, but this is your *mother*, and she should be important enough to give up *an hour* or so of your customary time-squandering activities. George has you set up for Austin to LA Friday night, and I'm driving us out to Malibu Saturday morning."

Okay so first, he thinks he's going to lecture *me* on making Mom a priority? What about all the dinners he misses? The charity shit she does that he pays no goddamned attention to? He spends evenings and weekends in do-not-disturb-I'm-important-and-working mode, even when he's home. Now, because she's in rehab again, he's going to play the concern card? Really?

I run a hand through my hair, grabbing and pulling it while my jaw clenches. He pushes every goddamned button I have. "Fine. Friday night. Tell George to have a car waiting at LAX."

"It's already set up—you know George."

"Fine," I say again. I'm done talking to him but for some inane reason can't seem to just hang *up*.

"You'll be in a little late for dinner—" he begins.

"No thanks anyway, Dad. This week is killing me. Just have Immaculada leave me something I can heat up when I get there."

"All right. I'll see you tomorrow—"

"Right. tomorrow." I push end, hurl my phone at the bed. It bounces once and off, hitting the thick carpeting. "*Goddammit*."

Emma is in tutoring for another few minutes. She's coming to my room when she's done. The past few days, we've been dancing around the subject of sex. Any time I take a step up and she responds by stepping back, so do I. But I *really* don't want to go home without this in the bag. If home and Dad and family sessions weren't looming, I could keep hold of my patience better. If I hadn't decided to terminate local hookups, I could just grab Quinton or Tadd and go out, find someone... if, if, if. *Gah.* I keep telling myself that she'll be worth the wait. If the chemistry we have so far is any indication, she'll be more than worth it.

Most of us were in the Gap this morning, where she and I did scenes in which our characters were involved in a heated exchange. I swear we were both so into it we were half pissed, half turned on by the time Richter called *cut*. While waiting for production to get the lighting repositioned, I angled my head away from the crush of people all standing around. "Come 'ere."

She followed me, puzzled, as I walked to the opposite side of a ten-foot high partition hung with board shorts on one side and sundresses on the other. "Reid? What—?"

I didn't let her finish, drawing her into the rainbow of sundresses and kissing her, pushing her up against the makeshift wall, the gauzy cotton at her back like a cushion. When I lifted my head, she blinked, her hands braced on my chest, not exactly pulling me forward, not exactly pushing me away, either. "What was that for?" She was a little breathless.

"That was 'Have dinner with me tonight.'" I started to lean in again and she put a hand over my mouth, laughing quietly and glancing over my shoulder to make sure no one had discovered us. I guess someone had to care about that, because I sure as shit didn't.

"We have to be here early again tomorrow. We won't really have time to go out—"

"Dinner in, then." Her hand muffled my words, and the careful one-day scruff of beard I have to keep for filming tickled her palm.

"Are you going to behave?" She began to slide her hand away, carefully, like she didn't trust me. I tried not to smile and failed. When she arched a brow at me with a look of authority, I imagined her with a ruler in one hand and a piece of chalk in the other, wearing glasses, a tight little skirt, high heeled pumps… definitely not helping.

I nodded, holding up two fingers. "Scout's honor."

She narrowed her eyes. "Somehow I can't imagine you as a Boy Scout."

I blinked innocently. "Oh—that's a Boy Scout thing?"

She rolled her eyes and I leaned in and kissed her. "*Reid.*"

"Emma… my room or yours? Your choice." I grazed her temple with my lips and lowered my voice to a whisper. "Lots of this." I kissed her again. "And all clothes stay on."

She peered at me, lips pursed, and I held up two fingers again, which made her laugh and shove my shoulder. "Okay. Yours."

Just then we heard the PA, Laura, coming around the corner saying, "They couldn't have gone far…" I stepped two feet back, yanking my sides from the back pocket of my jeans while pulling Emma from the vertical mattress I'd pressed her into.

When Laura appeared, I was pointing to the middle of the sheet and Emma was looking on. "And that's your cue to give me the evil eye."

"Oh! I see," Emma said, as though we were discussing the script while standing amongst a buttload of sundresses. Out of sight from everyone else. Good thing we're actors.

Laura spotted us. "*There* you are. What are you two doing over here? Nobody knew where you went! They're ready for you." Emma gave me another little shove when Laura looked away. I mouthed *what?* with the most angelic expression I could muster.

Mall filming should wrap early tomorrow. A couple of retakes, a few distance and tracking shots, and we're out. Even still, I've got to pack and get to LAX to check in by five. So it's tonight, or we're talking next week. Damn.

Emma

The big screen television is still on, but we're not exactly paying attention to it.

When I got to his room, he pulled me inside and locked every bolt on the door. "Um…" I said, and he told me he didn't want housecleaning coming in, but he thought I probably wouldn't want him to hang the *do not disturb* tag on the door. Definitely not.

Now, we're sitting on the floor, our backs to the foot of the bed, and he's just told me that if the zombie apocalypse ever happens, I'm going to be in deep shit. I pretend to be insulted. "I'm not convinced that my inability to avoid getting my brains eaten on a video game directly correlates to certain death in an actual zombie attack."

Smiling, he tosses the controllers next to the television and pulls me up from the floor. "Maybe not. But you have to admit, it doesn't bode well." We pick our way through the dinner dishes littering the blanket he'd spread on the floor when room service arrived. Very little remains of his butter poached jumbo shrimp or my artichoke cream cheese crepes; nothing remains of the chardonnay. I feel just full enough and pleasantly fuzzy, but not drunk. As we sit on the sofa, though, I'm so aware of him, of every detail, that I'm buzzing hard.

"So. Where were we earlier today, while we were hiding from the film crew…"

His hands run over me, so focused and expert that the existence of clothing makes little difference. We make out on his sofa, kissing and touching until I'm lying flat, melting into the cushions as he stares down, his eyes navy blue in the dim light, his tousled hair hanging over his forehead. "You're incredible," he says, his voice soft, face propped on one hand while the other carefully teases from the hollow in my throat, over a breast, triggering a gasp when his fingers graze the nipple, down over my stomach, dipping into my shorts.

He makes no move to unfasten them, but I know what he's thinking. He knows that I do. He's a hypnotist, and he doesn't intend to snap his fingers and count to three, removing me from this trance. "I know what I promised. Clothing on. But you promised nothing, and if you want to, I'd be happy to let you make me a liar."

The difference between us? He knows exactly what he wants.

"Reid. It's only been a week." Five days, actually. Five days of kissing and making out, half our encounters ending in some sort of skirmish of yes and no.

"That long?" I roll my eyes and he laughs. "I'm sorry, Emma. I know I'm being pushy. You're so adorably irresistible, and I'm just a guy, you know?"

He's overly fond of that excuse. As though I wouldn't pull him into his bed right now, if not for that nagging feeling that I need a few more days. If he's this persistent with every girl he runs across, the majority would have been in his bed five days ago if they were in my position. And that's what's bothering me. How many have there been, and how many are waiting in the wings? I need some time alone, to think. And I need Emily.

Reid Alexander wants to sleep with me. And I keep telling him no.

I must be insane.

No one checked out of the hotel in Austin, preferring to keep our temporary quarters intact, so I've only brought one bag with me on this trip to the home that's never felt like home.

When my father married Chloe, she moved into our house. Within months, she began pleading for a new place. "We need a home of our own," she pouted, her arms around his neck as I eavesdropped from the laundry nook off of the hallway to their bedroom. "Let's move to Los Angeles or San Francisco. Somewhere not so horrible and suburban." I held my breath. Leaving Sacramento would mean leaving Emily and Grandma.

"Chloe, my *job* is here," he answered.

The compromise was a big new house, where the furniture was child-unfriendly and my bedroom was decorated in something Chloe called shabby chic, the walls a mustard-gone-bad color that I hadn't known existed. I spent weekends with my grandmother as often as possible, where it was acceptable to talk about Mom, and I was permitted to put my feet on the sofa and keep a kitten I named Hector.

One weekend, after Chloe had taken it upon herself to sit me down and deliver the Sex Talk, I stammered through asking Grandma some follow-up questions. I wasn't sure if she'd know the answers, but I figured she'd had my mom, so she must have had sex at least *once* in her life. When I repeated some of Chloe's basic explanations, my grandmother's usually-composed face turned a mottled purple, and I was afraid I'd just given her a heart attack. But she just took a deep breath and said, "This discussion calls for some cocoa, with plenty of tiny marshmallows."

When I was fourteen, Grandma died of a brain aneurysm. She'd been diligent about good diet and exercise, cancer checks and heart disease prevention. I researched and found out that they're virtually undetectable, especially if there are no symptoms like headaches or double vision. And even if they'd found it earlier, they might not have been able to do anything about it, nestled in her brain. She would have hated knowing there was a ticking time bomb in her head.

I begged my father and Chloe to allow Hector to come live with us. I swore to vacuum and use pet rollers every single day, promised to feed, water and scoop litter. All Chloe said was, "I'm *allergic*, Connor!" I'm convinced that the only thing about Hector that Chloe was allergic to was the thought of his fur attaching itself to her garish clothes and furniture.

"I'm sorry, Emma," my father said as I stomped to my room. "We'll find him a new home." He sounded remorseful, but unwavering. In a conflict, Chloe's desires always overrode mine.

Emily, livid in my defense, pleaded with her mother to take in my orphaned cat. Mrs. Watson wasn't thrilled about Hector's beautiful long white hair, but to our shock, she consented. Hector, no dummy, transferred his feline displays of adoration—infrequent lap sitting and frequent tail hugs—to Emily's mom. My cat is ten now, a senior citizen in feline years.

"Only one bag?" My father eyes my duffel dubiously when I exit the airport. He's used to Chloe, with whom there's no such thing as skipping the baggage carousel.

"I'm only here for a couple days." I toss it into the backseat and climb into his SUV.

"How's the filming going?" he asks, pulling into traffic as I take a deep breath.

"Fine." I'm trying to focus on seeing Emily, and her mother, and Hector. If they hadn't been waiting for me in Sacramento, I'd have rather stayed in Austin for the weekend, even if I was completely alone there. I wouldn't have come home to see Chloe, not in a million years. I wouldn't have come home to see my father.

Opposing viewpoints war inside my mind. On one hand, I want to ask his advice about Reid and Graham, and college, and the fact that I'm going to be a legal adult soon. I want him to know that it scares the hell out of me because I have no plans for my life besides continuing what I've always done.

On the other hand, I don't want to speak to him at all.

Every developmental psychology website I've searched says that the desire to separate is natural in adolescents. But what I'm feeling can't be natural, and the freedom I have wasn't gained normally. I grew up with no religious commandments, not much of a curfew, and no pressure to succeed academically. Grandma and Mrs. Watson loved me, but they couldn't parent me. That authority was always with my father, and all he's ever exerted it to do is urge me to become a star. I'm a seventeen-year-old who's raised her*self* for a solid freaking decade. I've done a pretty good job of it, but that fact is so incredibly sad that it's infuriating. Sitting here in the front seat of my father's car, I realize that I *am* furious.

In an effort to fill the silence, he begins to talk about work, and the kitchen redesign Chloe initiated, and a problem with the sprinkler system that required the entire yard to be dug up and a new system to be installed.

I don't respond.

And he doesn't notice that I don't.

Chapter 29

REID

We're halfway to the rehab facility, and neither of us has said a word. Once we leave LA proper, the haze that domes the city almost 365 days a year abates. A bright blue sky seems painted above the landscape; the only clouds are wisps of smoke in the distance.

I have no idea what to expect from the therapy session, or from Mom. I have no faith in the process. Why should I? The process has failed her multiple times. She struggles to stay sober while I struggle to avoid it.

That's not exactly true. While it's true that I push my boundaries as often as possible, I have it under control when it needs to be. I like getting hammered sometimes, sure. I'm young. It's fun. Why not? I'm not using alcohol to "numb the pain" or any stupid shit like that. I'm not using it when I'm working. Any number of Mom's therapists would say I'm in denial, that I'm making excuses. I'd say I'm explaining. They'd say there's a difference between explanations and excuses, and I'm doing one and calling it the other. Then I'd say I don't give a flying goddamn which it is. And that would be the end of that.

John's texting me—says there's a party tonight we've got to make it to. He wants to know if I want to stay over at his apartment near campus. He starts classes Tuesday, not that he's stressed about it. I doubt he's even got an idea what his schedule is—his father required him to apply as a finance major. I can't imagine how that's going to end, but it'll be explosive. John is riding the ragged edge of pretending to follow in his dad's footsteps. I'm glad that at least I don't have to do that. I've got my own path, and while Dad may not get it, he seems to support it. At the very least, he's never tried to mold me into a younger version of himself: Mark Alexander, brilliant, respectable attorney at law.

I doubt he thinks I'd even be capable of turning out like him, not that I can argue the point, and not that I ever *wanted* to be.

When we arrive, Dad charges straight across the lobby to the reception desk and I trail him, not taking my sunglasses off until I get past the reception area and anyone hanging out there. The woman behind the desk recognizes him and immediately looks at me, blinking rapidly even though her expression remains neutral, confirming that she knows who I am by association. I wonder if my fame makes being here more difficult for Mom, where everyone knows, or will know—that she's the mother of Reid Alexander. She can't be anonymous, any more than I can. But at least my notoriety was/is my choice.

The place is posh, no surprise, and Mom seems as fragile as always, also no surprise. We are only allowed to meet with her in the counselor's office for this visit, and frankly I'm hoping this time will be the only one required of me.

There are two sofas—one of them is more like a loveseat—and two chairs, surrounding a low table. The therapist, Dr. Weems, takes one of the chairs, crossing her legs and opening the file on her lap, giving us no direction on where to sit. I sense a test, but I'm not sure what arrangement she'd accept as positive, or if she perceives that I know she's analyzing each of us and how we relate to each other based on our choice. By the time these thoughts make their way through my brain, Dad is sitting in the middle of the long sofa, mom next to him in the corner. I plop down in the middle of the loveseat because that choice doesn't require anything but sitting straight down. Dr. Weems is scribbling, already finding my faults, or maybe she's doodling a cartoon of funny cats while waiting for us to stop playing musical sofas.

"Mark, Reid, I'm Dr. Weems—please call me Marcie. It's good to meet both of you." She smiles that calculating therapist smile, the one that doesn't quite reach the eyes, as Dad greets her politely and leans up to shake her hand. When she turns to look at me, I'm leaning forward, elbows on knees, ready to bolt out of here at the first opportunity. I raise my chin once, acknowledging her. That's the best I'll do, and my peripheral awareness of Dad's glower won't change it.

She's undaunted. I doubt asshole adolescent males are new to her. "We've made some really solid progress in the last two weeks." The heel of Marcie's pump is hanging slightly from her foot, as though she's actually playing dress up and wearing her mother's shoes. "I'm pleased that the two of you could join us so you could see for yourselves that your loved one is doing well, and so we can do a little work as a family unit."

Our "loved one" is sitting right there, being spoken about in the third person with an epithetical term rather than her name. I'll admit I have issues with therapists in general. I think they're a pretentious group of people who believe they know your innermost secrets from body language and what they trick you into saying. Marcie is all that plus attributes from your least favorite, most biased teacher ever.

I watch Mom, the way her fingers shake with the slightest tremor, barely perceptible, whenever she has to speak. When she looks up, I try to catch her eyes—dark blue, identical to mine—wondering if she wants someone to just grab her hand and get the hell out of here. But no, she's determined to tackle the demons. She clenches her jaw, frowns at the flower arrangement in the center of the table or the stack of magazines on either side. And then she pushes her small voice forward, and answers Marcie's probing questions and Dad's careful inquiries.

Marcie squints at me a few times during the hour. I'm not saying anything unless asked directly, and even then, I'm the opposite of forthcoming. What I don't say: I don't want to be here, I don't want to contribute, and I don't see why I have to when it isn't *me* in rehab. When the hour is up, I feel like I was just released from prison.

When Mom hugs me goodbye, my arms slide around her and I realize she's even smaller than usual. "Thank you for coming," she says into my shoulder. "I'm sorry. I love you."

I close my eyes. *Say it, say it, say it*. "You too." Both not good enough and better than nothing. She gives me another squeeze before letting go. She walks into my dad's arms and I turn towards the window. He's the worst kind of hypocrite—pretending this level of give-a-shit *now* when she's spent years flying along behind him like a kite, just trying to stay airborne.

Emma

"Where are Reid's posters?" I'm reclining on Emily's bed, Hector draped over my abdomen, purring an atypical welcome. I stroke his silky back and scratch behind his ears.

Emily closes her bedroom door, where two sexy-beautiful close-up posters of Reid are attached with double-stick tape. (Emily's mom has two rules for posters: double-stick tape, not thumbtacks, and on the doors, never the walls.) "You downgraded him to the back of the door?" Emily's system: the favored boys go on the closet door, visible all the time; the lesser ones go to the back of her bedroom door. Quinton's is still on the closet door, and has in fact moved to the number one spot: face level above the door knob.

"It didn't seem right to have Reid in a prominent spot when you two are practically a couple. I can't cheat with my best friend's guy. Even theoretically."

"So he's like a brother to you now."

"Don't be crazy," she answers. "*Look* at him."

"I do look at him. Practically every day."

She mock-glares at me and I laugh.

"I found a few pics of Graham, by the way." She plops onto the bed next to me, grabbing a pillow and propping her head at the foot of the bed so we can see each other over the lump of Hector fur. "He's hot, though more in that intense, introspective sorta way, rather than Reid's all-American look. My coworkers would be all over him."

I breathe a sigh, trying to clear the stab of hostility I suddenly feel towards Emily's coworkers. "Em, I don't understand how you work at Hot Topic, dress twenty-first century Gothic, and are attracted to guys who look like Reid."

"Opposites attract?"

"Not usually," I say, and she shrugs.

"So, the fan pages are speculating that you and Reid are having hot sex all over Austin."

"*What*? God. Well, we're not." I cover my face and Hector meows in complaint until I begin stroking him again. "I still don't know what kind of relationship he wants. Or, you know, *if*. He's used to girls throwing themselves at him. I'm sure I'm confusing the crap out of him."

"Hmm." He stares at us from the back of her door. "Official dilemma."

"Seriously." Hector rolls over, flopping between us on the bed, legs in the air, begging for a tummy rub. "Um, is

Hector on drugs or something?"

"Maybe one of Mom's plants is a cat narcotic. God knows he chews on them enough—every plant in the house has teeth marks. Drives Mom insane."

"Grandma tried putting Tabasco sauce on the leaves. Worked pretty well."

We laugh, imagining the effects of this on an unsuspecting Hector. "Your grandma was an evil genius."

I remember her so much more clearly than I remember Mom. "Yeah, she was." I stare at the ceiling. "Right before you picked me up, my father asked if I wanted to go for a run tomorrow morning, 'like old times.' I was standing there in that revolting yellow room with that flowery duvet and furniture that looks like an animal has gnawed on it, and I was thinking *'old times'—like when I was what, five*?"

She's silent for a couple of minutes. "Are you afraid if you talked to him, you might actually tell him how angry you are?"

It's true. This is not standard annoyance. I'm livid. "Maybe. Why now? Why *now* do I give a crap?"

"You've always given a crap, Emma. You just pushed it inside. Acted like a miniature grownup. What else could you do? Of course you're angry."

I suddenly burst into tears like one of those geysers in Yellowstone erupts—pop, pop, *gush*, and she sits up and grabs me, pulls me close and stretches her arms around me.

"What am I supposed to do now?" I hiccup, sniffling.

She sighs. "Maybe it's not the best timing, right in the middle of filming the biggest movie of your career so far, but emotional self-awareness doesn't always sit around waiting for the perfect time to reveal itself." She hands me the tissue box. "You'll wash your face so you don't scare my parents, then we'll eat the pasta and sausage meatballs they're making, watch some bad television or a good DVD, and munch something calorific. And after that, we'll figure this shit out."

I take a shuddering breath and lean my head into her lap. She strokes my hair, pulling it from my wet face and tucking it behind my ear, which makes me ache for my mother. I can't recall her face, exactly, but I remember vividly the feel of her fingers threading through my hair. People are right about time healing wounds. But the scars are always there, waiting for something to poke them. I close my eyes and just let myself miss her.

Chapter 30

REID

I'm geared up for another hour or so of awkward silence on the drive back to LA—even more awkward now that we've seen Mom, now that her damage is out there, undeniable, visible to us both. The therapy session was like being cut in a hundred tiny invisible ways, and it's inexplicable to me how that kind of opening up is helpful.

I pull out my phone to text John, but before I get far, Dad says, "I made reservations for dinner tonight." My first thought is *why are you telling me?* Then I realize he means reservations for *us*. Oh, hell no.

"I've already made plans with John—"

His jaw tightens. "Push them back. Our reservations are early. Seven."

My jaw mimics his and I fight to relax it. "Fine. I'm staying over with John. Probably tomorrow night, too."

He nods curtly and I send John the text telling him to pick me up at ten. A late party is better than no party.

"Have you thought about what's next, after *School Pride* wraps?"

What's this? Interest in my career? "George sent a few scripts for me to look over."

"I guess there's no more cold auditioning for you, is there? You've arrived, as they say."

I shrug.

The waiter fills our water glasses from a Perrier bottle and leaves it to the side. "Would you gentlemen like to peruse the wine list, or have a cocktail before dinner?"

"I would," I say.

Dad shakes his head. "No thank you. We'll be ready to order in a few minutes."

"Yes, sir." The waiter snaps the wine list closed and removes the wine glasses with one hand, crossing them like Marcie crossed her legs earlier today. Thinking about her doesn't help my already fed up state of mind.

"What the hell, Dad?"

He fixes me with one of the stares he's perfected after years of cross-examining hapless witnesses. I wait him out. "I'm aware that you drink, despite the fact that you're considerably underage. You've been out from under my direct control for a while now, so I know there's little to no hope of me influencing that behavior. But you're not doing it in my presence, out in public. I have a reputation to maintain. So do you, not that you spare any concern for it."

Wow. This trip is just one joy-infused moment after another. I should have stayed in Austin. "Why, exactly, did you decide we needed to have dinner together?"

He exhales through his nose, his patience as close to snapping as mine, though I can't imagine why. He could have saved himself the agony by simply leaving me to my own devices for the evening. "I thought you might have questions about your mother's rehabilitation process. Also I wanted…" he exhales again, his mouth a thin line, "…wanted to thank you for coming this morning. If nothing else, I know you care about her, and I appreciate the effort."

If nothing else? What the hell kind of backhanded

accolade is that? "I didn't come for *you*, so you don't need to thank me."

"Nevertheless, I'm thanking you."

"Awesome. Well, you're so very welcome. Will that be all?" I sit up, put my napkin on the table.

"Why are you so hostile?"

"Why are *you*?"

"Look, I'm doing the best I can—"

"*This* is the best you can do, Dad?"

"Dammit, Reid. Let's not do this here."

"I concur, counselor. Let's not do it at all." I sit back, fix an unnatural smile on my face and try to appear relaxed. "I don't have any questions concerning Mom's rehab at this time. I'll let you or *Marcie* know if I do." Marcie had given each of us her card and told us to call or email any time. Riiiight, *that* was going to happen. "Also, George and I are considering an action flick for my next project. They want someone older, bigger and more buff to do the part, but George is selling them on the idea that I can be each of those things. I'll have to train like hell to get the role, but if they give it to me, I'm doing it."

"Hmph," he says, but it's an impressed *hmph*. I haven't gotten one of those in a while. I hate how good it feels—it totally pisses me off.

Emma

"Have you told Emma about Derek?" Emily's mom asks as we sit down to dinner.

"*Abercrombie* boy." Jason, Emily's twenty-something brother, moved back home three weeks ago, temporarily between jobs. Again. He makes a hobby of torturing his little sister.

Emily jerks the basket of rolls out of his reach. He's

already eaten two and was going for a third. "At least Derek *has* a job."

Mr. Watson starts to laugh and tries to turn it into a cough as his wife gives him a tight-lipped look. Mrs. Watson believes that in order to succeed, young people need emotional support and encouragement. She's the queen of cheerleading her kids, which worked well with Grant, the oldest, but appears to be backfiring in Jason. Em migrated to her dad's way of thinking (that sometimes a person needs a swift emotional kick in the pants) when Jason moved back in for the third time.

"I've *had* jobs." Jason scowls and digs into his pasta.

"That's true," Emily answers, "but *keeping* one seems to elude you. And really? The getting is easy; the *keeping* is the important part."

"Like you know anyth—"

"Children!" Mrs. Watson says, and I wonder how that one word doesn't make Jason go job-hunting immediately, and stay out until he finds one. "Emily, have you asked Emma's opinion on the homecoming dance?" Uh-oh. I know this is a loaded question before Emily sets her jaw, because when Mrs. Watson invokes my view on something, she's grasping for already rejected straws.

"Mom, seriously. You've gotta stop with the dance thing. We aren't *going*."

"So Abercrombie boy didn't ask you?" Jason snatches a roll from the edge of Emily's bowl. "What, he didn't want to waste the money to see you wear a new shade of *black*?"

"Bite me, mister perpetually unemployed." Emily takes a roll from the basket to replace the one he'd stolen. "You can't afford to take someone to the Mini-Mart."

"Enough! We have a guest!" Mrs. Watson says.

"Emma's not a *guest*," Jason scoffs. Which is kind of true. I've slept over at Emily's house hundreds of times in my life.

"Jason, do you want dessert tonight or do you want to just

go to your room?" his mother asks, no differently than she would have asked (make that *did* ask) when he was twelve.

"What? Mom, are you serious?"

"Dead serious."

"I'm an adult! You can't send me to my room."

"The hell she can't." Mr. Watson glares at his son. I've watched them do this tag team maneuver on all three of their kids. Resistance is futile. You'd think Jason would know that by now, but I guess not.

"Dad, *Jesus*—"

"That's it! To your room." Mr. Watson points as though Jason needs directions. I bite the inside of my cheek and sneak a look at Emily. Her lips were pressed so tightly together that they're losing color. On the counter is some sort of berry cobbler, and a big scoop of that stuff has our names on it, so we're not getting ourselves sent *anywhere*.

"This *sucks*." Jason pushes away from the table, taking his roll. "I need my own place."

As soon as Jason is out of earshot, Mr. Watson mumbles, "Now *there's* a notion."

Emily turns to her mother. "Mom, *no one* goes to that incredibly sucktastic dance. Everyone just goes to the game. Things have changed since you went to high school."

"See there, Vera, it's how they roll nowadays," her dad says, and I swear it's all Emily and I can do not to lose it. Emily's parents bought a book called *Decode Your Teen!* when Grant was in high school, and are oblivious to the fact that adolescent lingo changes daily.

Hours later, we lie in Emily's bed, stuffed with raspberry cobbler and fresh whipped cream.

"So what's the deal with Abercrombie boy?"

Emily sits up and hits me in the face with her pillow, and I squeal. "Your brother is a bad influence!"

"My brother is a tool." She stuffs the pillow back behind her head.

"So, what's the deal with *Derek*, then?"

She throws an arm across her face. "It's hopeless."

"Hopeless how?" I turn on my side, watching her.

"We're complete opposites. He's super prep boy. He wears *khaki chinos*. He's never even heard of most of my favorite bands, and I've spent years making fun of his. I have purple stripes in my hair. Piercings in places I had to have parental permission to get. My favorite nail polish is called *Vampire State Building*. All of his friends think I'm a freak."

"Did he tell you that?" I ask, and she turns on her side to face me.

"He didn't have to tell me. I can see it on their stupid faces."

I sweep her purple-accented hair out of her eyes. "Who cares what they think?"

"Oh come on, all that 'If they're your real friends, they'll accept whoever you love' is a load of crap. I can't expect a guy to stand up to that kind of pressure. And I like me the way I am. I don't want to change!"

"Has he asked you to change?"

"No," she says, sounding almost disappointed.

"So how much do you like this guy?"

"Oh my God. So much." She turns into me and buries her face under my chin, her voice desolate, as though she's confessing to murder instead of attraction.

"Sounds like a bungee-jumping sorta moment."

She nods her head.

"Emma?" My name is muffled by the comforter. "I think I already fell."

"I guess all you can do is wait to see if the cord holds."

Funny how I can in no way apply this wisdom to myself, no matter how sensible it sounds when I say it to Emily.

Chapter 31

REID

I have every intention of taking a break from hookups while I'm pursuing Emma, but this party is full of hot girls who are flying so high they don't know which end is up. The invitation to ditch my temporary abstinence plan is powerful. Plus, Emma and I aren't actually *together* yet. She's taking her own sweet time about that, though I think we're getting there. I came home to LA this weekend certain I could be patient… but every moment that goes by is draining that resolve.

The exclusivity factor of this little gathering is high. I've recognized several film colleagues and a couple of John's friends—trust fund babies who live for rubbing elbows (and other body parts) with movie stars and music idols. Highly unlikely that anything would turn up on the Internet. Non-celebrities who get invited to these events understand that outing any of us puts them on the other side of that door in the future. That's why you seldom see photos of famous people misbehaving in private settings. Figuring out who narked amongst a restricted set of people is far too easy.

I'm both buzzed and high, lounging in a chair and watching the curls of smoke rise from half a dozen joints. John has his tongue down the throat of an aspiring runway model as they paw each other in the space cleared for people pretending to dance. Really they're all just committing foreplay in front of anyone watching. John *really* digs models. The foreign ones, especially. This one looks and sounds, I don't know, Swedish? I'm not the best judge at this point.

Tonight, I'm a voyeur. I can rein this in and wait.

And then some girl a few feet from John is dancing with another girl and the two of them are taking each other's clothes off. Slowly. Once they have my attention, they're both flicking glances my way at regular intervals, to make sure I'm still watching. No problem there—I'm riveted.

Damn. I'm not getting through the next half an hour without tossing my short-lived celibacy out the window, let alone the rest of the night, and I know it.

John's model is in the shower. He's too soft. My two were sent home in a taxi while it was still dark out. Now, he and I are sprawled on the sofa in our usual Sunday morning state: hungover. "What are we doing tonight, man?" John blows a few rings of smoke from the cigarette between his fingers, like a cartoon smokestack from a train. One of those people who smokes irregularly, he's curiously gifted with the stuff he can do with a cigarette, especially considering how infrequently he picks one up. He's made an art of it. "Do you want to go out?"

I watch the smoke rings dissipate, lay my head back against the cushion. The shower goes off. "I don't know. Sure. Nothing high-profile, though."

The bathroom door snaps open. "John?" His name in her mouth sounds more like *Jonah*—two syllables.

His eyebrows kick up once before he rolls off the sofa. "Yeah?"

She asks for a towel. He slips into the bathroom to show her where they're kept, and stays in. The sound of giggling pushes through the door, and I pick up the remote and click on the television. My voyeuristic tendencies have explicit limits, and listening to John screw some chick in the bathroom is definitely outside that perimeter. On the screen a correspondent reports on a politician who got caught cheating on his wife with their kid's nanny... who's in the country illegally.

My first thought is *what a moron*, and then they show a photo of the hot Guatemalan nanny. Damn—that poor bastard was doomed from the start.

Emma

"I'm just not sure this is such a great idea." I sit in Emily's vintage Sentra, staring at the house. "Talking to my father about how I feel is always an exercise in frustration, Em. There's no way I can tell him all the stuff we talked about."

"Then start with the college thing. Tell him you want to go."

"Do I?"

She sighs. "You said you did last night."

"I felt safe talking to *you* about it. It's different, bringing it up to him. He'll probably just say no, anyway, even if I manage to argue my point adequately, which is doubtful if he starts objecting right off. Plus I'm half scared to death that if he actually lets me do it, it might be a huge mistake." I hear the panic building in my voice. "I could flunk out. I could ruin the career I have. Emily, if that happens, what else do I have?"

She grabs my hand. "Emma, what the hell. A few hours ago, you were way more certain of yourself. It's like the sight of this place scares the confidence right out of you."

"He doesn't *know* me. He only thinks he does. I've just followed along my whole life, no big rebellion, barely any disagreement. I always thought that at least he understands my need to be an actor. But what if that isn't him understanding me at all, what if that's just what *he* wants, and what he really understands is *nothing*."

"He's your *dad*, Emma," she says, still holding my hand.

"Em, sometimes you and your parents argue. Yell at each other even. But you know they're trying. You know they love you." My throat feels tight. "It's not the same with me and them. It never has been. You know that as well as anybody."

She pulls me in for a hug. "If you don't want to talk to him, then don't. But I think you should go in there and say what you need to say. For your own sake. Because yeah, you're almost eighteen, and *it's your life*, and maybe this is the first step to just telling someone besides *me* what you *want* out of it."

"I don't know how to start, what to say." I'm stalling, and we both know it.

"Yes you do. Go in there. Just say it." Emily has this way about her when she knows she's right. Compassionate, but persistent. I take a deep breath, and go inside.

My father's sitting in his reading chair with a business magazine spread across his lap. He reads them all, in paper form and online. I fear the usual smallness of my voice. "I need to talk to you," I say, too loudly, because I have to force it out. He startles and the magazine jerks in his hands.

He exhales. "Okay. What's up?" Looking at my face, he reads something there that changes his expression from interest to wariness. "Um, Chloe will be home in an hour or so, if this is something important …"

I ignore that, clear my throat and sit, my hands clenching each other on my knees. No *way* am I waiting for Chloe to return. "I, uh… I want to go to college." Sitting on the sofa across the room from him, I wait while the silence lengthens between us. I think maybe he's in shock, and I wait for him to snap out of it.

He frowns, puzzled. "You do? You've never mentioned this before…"

"I've just been thinking lately, with high school almost done, you know… What's next? I've been talking to other cast members who are planning to go, and I started considering the idea. And I decided I want to go."

"Okay…" he says after a moment. "Do you have a university in mind? A course of study?" I look at him, searching for potential disparagement. I don't see any. Not that this means there isn't any. But I don't see it.

I swallow the lump in my throat, the half-dozen arguments Emily and I formulated last night jumbling together in my head, like I stopped short in the middle of the path and they all ran into me. And then I realize he's not saying no. "Theatre, I think. I don't know where, yet. I can start checking out places online, looking at requirements and stuff. I need to take the SAT…" My eyes slide to the floor. "Um, how will I pay the tuition?"

"Oh, you've got that covered with your Coogan account. After *School Pride* wraps up, you'll have more than enough, if you're sure that's what you want to use it for."

"I'm sure." I'm more sure about this than I've ever been about anything.

"Is there… anything else?"

I look at him, and I can't say any more. As high as this one thing leaves me, as giddy with truth-telling as I feel, I'm not ready to bare my soul just yet.

"Um, no."

He smiles, relieved. "Okay then. Well, you should probably go get ready for dinner. I think Chloe's planned a fun night out for your last night home."

Doubtful. But I'm not in the mood to dissent, so I nod and walk to my room in a sort of daze, shower and get ready to go out. Tomorrow I'm going back to Austin. And maybe I'll try a little of this honesty business on Reid when I get there.

Or not.

As I wait for the boarding announcement, I try to get some reading done for English, but give up after attempting to reread the same page of *A Room of One's Own* for the third time. I can't concentrate on the words in front of me. Bookmarking the page, I stuff the book in my bag and pull my iPod from a side pocket, pondering the changes that one conversation with my father could set in motion, in both my immediate future and long-term.

As far as I can tell, he hasn't told Chloe a thing. The only time he alluded to my college plans at all was over coffee this morning, when Chloe was still asleep.

"I'm going to sign you up for the SAT," he said, his voice low. "In Austin, next month."

"Oh. Okay." I stood at the counter, gripping the mug. The abstract idea of college was turning more concrete by the minute. Something in my expression must have let him know that the reality of what I was about to do to my life was flooding in.

"This is what you want, right?" He stared directly into my eyes, concerned. "Are you sure, Emma?"

"Yes, it's perfect." I sat down at the table with my coffee.

He nodded once, satisfied, smoothing out the pages of the Wall Street Journal. As he scanned the front page, he said, "I suppose you'll need to decide where you're going to apply."

I swallowed. "Yeah, I have a lot to think about."

"You have time. Once filming wraps up, we'll get those applications in, and there will probably be auditions of some sort, assuming you want to start next fall." My stomach dropped at the realization of what I'd done. I was going to be in class. With other people. In some cases, *lots* of other people. I can handle being on stage in front of an audience and filming in front of a production crew, but the thought of interacting with a classroom full of people in an academic setting scares the crap out of me. It's almost humorous.

I scroll through my library of music, barely focusing on the titles and unable to settle on anything. When my phone vibrates, I pull the earbuds out, giving up on both reading and music in a three-minute span of time.

Graham: Hey, heading back? Wanna run tomorrow morning?
Me: Sure. At the airport now.
Graham: Me too.
Me: I talked to my dad about college.
Graham: What did he say??
Me: He's signing me up to take the sat in austin in a month. Ugh.
Graham: Don't worry. You'll do fine.
Me: Thanks :)
Graham: NP. I'm about to board. See you in austin.

Chapter 32

REID

Monday evening, everyone hangs out in my hotel room, sprawled across the bed, sofa and floor space. We order room service while we watch (and mercilessly ridicule) an atrocious eighties movie. Tadd brought his guitar back with him from LA, and he and Graham trade subdued sets while we all discuss our weekends away. There are moments Emma is paying closer attention to them than to the conversations around us. I vaguely remember George telling me a few years back that I should learn to play an instrument. Another of his suggestions that I didn't follow.

Emma and I are sitting on the bed, and I'm having a hard time being aware of anything beyond her. I recognize the scent she wears now—sweet and subtle. If I could make everyone in the room disappear with the snap of my fingers, I wouldn't hesitate. She sits cross-legged and barefoot, her shoulder brushing mine, her toenails painted a purple so dark it's almost black. When I look up from her toes, she's smiling at me, and the girls from Saturday night are a hollow memory, nothing worthwhile to retain.

Quinton's ex is making an all-out play to get him back. We were on the same flight back from LA so I know the scoop and already gave him advice he won't heed. I listen distractedly as he shares his predicament with everyone else.

"I wasn't home thirty minutes before my ex shows up at the door. My little sister lets her in, almost like *someone* told her when I'd be home." He arches an eyebrow.

Jenna laughs. "Almost, huh?"

Tadd's fingers freeze on the strings. "Dude, my ex had sisters. If she decides to butt into your love life, you are so *screwed*."

"Yeah, what a coincidence, right? So I shut myself in my room, took a nap and then a shower, thinking I'd come out and she'd be gone. But when I opened my bedroom door, the whole damned house smelled like chocolate chip cookies." He shakes his head. "Kimber *knows* I can't resist those things. They're like little dollops of heaven."

Brooke holds both hands up. "Did you just say *little dollops of heaven*? I'm taking away your man card if you ever say that again."

"Oh, Quinton. What did you do?" MiShaun asks.

"You guys don't understand! This girl, we've known each other since we were five. She knows every weakness I've got!"

"You *got back together* with her?" Brooke asks. Quinton runs a hand over his face and nods, and the room erupts with opinions.

Graham continues to finger chords softly, and then he's glancing at Emma with half a smile, rolling his eyes. I feel her shoulders vibrate faintly with her silent laughter. Oh, hell no.

I turn my head and she looks at me. I want to kiss her, but that's too conspicuous on the jealousy scale—she wasn't thrilled the last time I did that. Instead, I lean my forehead to hers and speak just above a whisper, ignoring Graham's existence, asking her silently to do the same. "I missed you.

A *lot*."

"I missed you, too."

Something Quinton says sends the rest of the room into hysterical laughter, breaking our connection. Emma glances at her cell phone. "Wow, it's late," she says, unfolding her legs. "I need to get up early to run. I'd better get to bed."

"Running the first day back? Dedicated."

She smiles at me. "It only works if I'm ruthless about it." She tells everyone goodnight as I get up to walk her to her door, and I take her hand as we leave my room.

"I've just never thought of you as the ruthless type. It's kinda hot. In a scary sort of way."

She unlocks her door and turns to me, pushing the lever down and allowing me to press her to the door and shuffle her backwards until the handle hits the wall with a light thump. Bracing a hand against the hard surface on either side of her face, I watch her breath quicken, her chest rise and fall. Her hands are behind her, palms flat to the door. I lean in, kissing her gently, my tongue tracing her lips, opening them to deepen the kiss, my hands moving to her waist.

She tears her mouth from mine, and we're both breathing heavily. "Come back to my room," I tell her. "I'll go kick everyone out right now. They'll be gone in five minutes."

"Reid…" she says, and I feel as though we're sparring, bargaining for position along an unseen border. She's driving me crazy.

I back away, my hands up like she's about to read me my rights and toss me in the back of a patrol car. "Stopping. I just… haven't seen you in four days."

Her brow creases. "I'm sorry. I'm not trying to frustrate you, I promise."

"I can't help that I want you, you know. I just hope you'll start trusting me at some point." She's outright frowning now, and I tell myself to cut it out before I mess this up completely.

"Reid, what do you mean? I wouldn't be with someone I

didn't trust."

"Are we actually 'with' each other, though?"

Shit, I can't even listen to good advice from *myself.*

A door opens down the hall—my room, from the sound of it. Guess the party is breaking up. Graham and Brooke come around the corner. His eyes sweep over us and Brooke arches an eyebrow at me as if to say she expected as much. "Goodnight, you two." Her voice purrs with condescension. I fight to keep from responding.

They disappear into Graham's room, and I know I have to let this go for tonight. "Just, you know, forget what I said—hell, I've already forgotten what I said. It's been a long day. We have a hard week ahead of us. I'll see you tomorrow." I kiss her one more time, fight down the wave of wanting her, and turn to go back to my room.

I don't know if I have any virtues, or the potential for any, but I know one thing. Patience sure as hell isn't one of them.

Emma

I slip into my room and let the door close, change out of my jeans and t-shirt and into an oversized t-shirt and boxers. I can't forget what Reid said, just because he told me to. So, if we aren't sleeping together, we aren't a couple? Is that what he means?

His question feels too important, like a clue. He thinks I don't trust him because I'm not ready to have sex. Maybe in some way, that's true. Maybe I don't trust him to want any more of me than that, and just sleeping with Reid Alexander isn't good enough for me. Or maybe I don't know what I want, and he's suffering my indecision.

Unpacking as I brush my teeth, I force my thoughts elsewhere, wondering what's going on two doors down in Graham's room. I probably don't want to know. A lifetime has passed since Graham and I sat on my balcony, eating chocolate cake and talking about parts of our lives that are long gone. Brooke and Reid have made their desires known concerning each of us, and Graham and I are playing along, even if I'm not capitulating as fully or as rapidly as Reid would like.

I rinse my mouth of toothpaste and stride across the room to the balcony, pull the door open and go outside into the warm darkness. He's there on his balcony, alone, staring at the sky, and I exhale in relief without knowing why. The sight of him is comforting. The fact that he's alone, almost as much so, though there's no good reason for me to feel that way.

"Emma," he says, turning. I half expect to see a cigarette in his hand, but he stands with his hands hooked in the pockets of his jeans. "Are you okay?" he asks, concern in his voice.

"Yeah, I'm, uh, I'm fine." And I'm trying in vain to come up with any explanation for why I rushed onto my balcony to spy on him. Like it's my business if a twenty-year-old single guy, who doesn't at all belong to me, hooks up with a beautiful girl. "Er, I was just getting some air." Wow. Lame.

"Oh-kay," he says, unconvinced.

"Well. I've gotten some. Air, that is. So I guess I'll go in now."

I spin around to escape back inside, feeling like an idiot. "Emma?"

I attempt to compose my expression as I turn back. "Yes?"

"We're… running in the morning, right?"

"Oh, yeah, sure."

"Six o'clock, then?" he asks, and I nod. We both stand there for a moment, the silence lengthening and feeling significant, until his cell rings from inside his room. "See you in the morning," he says, going inside. I hear him say, "Hello?" before he shuts the balcony door.

Since I got back from Sacramento, Graham and I have been discussing college applications and essays, schools and programs available during our morning runs. He's enthusiastic about it, and it's contagious. He's texting me names of schools to check out: Julliard and NYU, I recognize, and other smaller schools I don't. Some have smaller populations than Emily's high school. I think I might like that.

When I ask him why so many of the schools he suggests are in New York, he shrugs and says, "That's where I live, so I know more about the area, since I wanted to go to school close to home. Do you want to stay closer to home yourself? We could look for schools you might like in California."

Staying near my parents is the last thing I want. A school on the opposite coast from Chloe is exactly what I need. "No, moving across the country sounds *lovely*." He laughs while I tell myself this has nothing to do with Graham living in New York. Nothing at all.

I start googling information on anything he suggests that's located east of Ohio.

The Bingley house would send Chloe into raptures of envy. Set into the side of a hill, it's several thousand feet of limestone, wrought iron and tile exterior, with soaring ceilings and marble floors throughout. No amenities were omitted, from a kitchen outfitted so spectacularly that it would make Emily's mom drool to the infinity pool that would cause Chloe to break into song. I feel an urge to cross myself at that thought.

The first two days of the week are spent filming what will be a three-minute scene with Meredith under the hood of the broken down Civic, in *front* of this beautiful house. Outside. In the billion degree heat.

Production hired an auto mechanic expert to help me look like I know the difference between a fuel pump and a spark plug while under the hood of a car, because for some reason not explained to me, present-day Lizbeth is familiar with the basics of auto maintenance. First I have to learn how to get the hood of the car up, which is *not* as easy as you'd think. Stan the mechanic is gallingly superior about it, rolling his eyes while my fingers slide back and forth where the stupid latch release is supposedly located. I'm forced to squat down and look for it.

"Ah-ha!" I release the latch as Stan stands with his burly, tattooed arms crossed over his chest, unimpressed. I narrow my eyes at him. "Okay, so I know *nothing* about cars. Can you make yourself cry on command? Go ahead. I'll wait."

He sighs and shows me again where to find the latch release. Once I can find it without looking, he drops the hood and has me find and unlatch it at least fifty times, until I can do it blindfolded. Ah, the useful yet trivial things I learn for my job.

Given the heat and humidity, our makeup people want to pull their hair out, and ours. Meredith and I ride back to the hotel at the end of the second day in exhausted silence, in love with the guy who invented air conditioning. The cityscape flows by as I dissect the reasons for my caution with Reid. I'm not immune to the way I feel when he touches me. The truth is, physically, I *do* want him—I'm just not quite ready emotionally. The more he pushes, the more wary I feel, and the more I want to push back.

Then there's Graham, who hasn't mentioned my weird behavior on the balcony Monday night, thank God. For a fleeting moment, I wonder if he was on his balcony for the same reason I was, hoping I would come out by myself, or just hoping I wasn't in bed with Reid.

Abruptly, I come to my senses. How preposterous, that Graham is absorbed with or even thinking about whatever transpires, or doesn't, between Reid and me. He has his own thing with Brooke to sort out.

Not that his relationship with her has any relevance to me.

Chapter 33

REID

I filmed with Tadd and Brooke today—indoor scenes that will be woven into the outdoor scenes Emma and Meredith did yesterday. I wasn't feeling well last night, so I went to bed early. I woke up with a hell of a hangover that wasn't a hangover. I can't describe it, really. I didn't think I drank that much last night, but I can't remember.

I got through filming, didn't have a single conflict with Brooke, which is *really* bizarre. All I know is I feel like shit and I don't want to be awake. I should just go to bed and sleep it off—whatever this is. I should probably text Emma, but I can do that when I wake up.

Emma

I haven't heard from Reid today. No calls, no texts, no knocks on my door. After a leisurely morning with Meredith, discussing the novels we've chosen for our senior theses, we had French class with Jenna and made plans for dinner which I assume includes everyone. I walk past Reid's door, annoyed. The silent treatment must be some form of male pouting.

Emily's previous boyfriend, Vic, pushed her to have sex. At first, she told me that they *had* been together for several months and maybe she should give it up, even if she wasn't particularly moved to do so yet. And then he began saying things like, "If I'd known you were going to be such a tease…" and, "I'm a guy. You have to admit I've been patient." The last straw occurred in the school cafeteria, where they were sitting with his friends.

"Hey Vic, how can you tell if a girl is frigid?" His friend paused for effect. "When you open her legs, a light goes on."

"Ding," Vic said, glancing at Emily as his friends laughed.

"That's not funny," she said, knowing then that he'd told his friends what was going on between them. Or more accurately, what wasn't going on.

"Ding!" echoed Vic's most obnoxious friend, a guy Emily tolerated only because she cared for Vic.

She got up and left the table to a chorus of dings, and Vic did nothing but laugh and call after her, "Come on, baby—it's just a joke!"

She found out a week after they broke up that he'd been sleeping with a sophomore from his art class for at least a month, maybe longer. He'd been telling Emily that the girl had a crush on him but he was keeping it strictly platonic.

"Since when is platonic synonymous with *screwing around*?" she asked him during their last fight, which occurred right after she found out.

"Newsflash, Emily—you and me are broken up, so technically, you have no jurisdiction over me anymore. But let me give you a parting tip—it's a stretch to call it screwing around on your girlfriend when she won't screw around with you in the first place."

She and I heaped curses on Vic's big stupid head for this preposterous excuse, but I'll be damned if it didn't seep into my brain just enough for Reid's pushing to make me wonder if there was any legitimacy to it.

I'm tired of Reid's moping. I want to let him know he can't manipulate me, but I also want to see it coming if he's going to use the Vic justification. Unsure exactly what I intend to say but determined to say it, I turn back and knock on his door. A minute later he hasn't answered, but just as I start to turn away, the door opens.

The last thing I expect to see is Reid bowed over, an arm across his abdomen. His usually perfect hair is plastered to his forehead and he looks pale.

"Reid? Are you okay?"

"Yeah. No. I don't know. I don't feel so hot, Emma. I've been sleeping since I got back."

"Do you need me to get someone? A doctor?"

He blinks slowly. "I'm just going to go back to bed."

"Why don't I bring you something—soup maybe—from the café? I'll be back in twenty minutes. Give me your room key, so you won't have to get up again."

He backs into the room, pointing to the dresser. "It's on my wallet." As I grab the room key, he collapses onto the bed with a moan.

"Reid, are you sure you don't need a doctor?" He shakes his head, and I'm unsure what to do except go get him something that I'm pretty sure he isn't going to eat.

By the time I return, he's gone from pale to flushed. I've brought chicken noodle soup and Sprite, but he doesn't take more than a sip of either. His knees are drawn up, both hands on his stomach, eyes closed. Placing my hand on his forehead, I know something is really wrong because he's burning up. "Are you nauseous?"

"I don't know," he answers after a minute. "You should probably leave. I don't know if I'm contagious. Tell Richter I might not feel like filming tomorrow."

"Sure." He's probably right, the best thing for me to do is leave, but I can't abandon him like that.

My phone buzzes from my bag—a text from Graham.

Graham:	Hey, you coming? We're about to grab some taxis.
Me:	I'm in reid's room. I think he's sick.
Graham:	Sick how?
Me:	I don't know. Fever. He's clutching his stomach but no throwing up...yet.
Graham:	Be up in a minute.
Me:	K, thx

I wet a washcloth under the cold tap, pull Reid's damp hair off of his forehead, and press the cloth to his head. He sighs but never opens his eyes.

Graham's knock is soft. I open the door to admit him, saying, "I hope I'm not exposing you to something."

"S'okay." He takes a disposable thermometer from a small paper bag and smiles. "Gift shop." Reid barely registers him coming into the room.

A few minutes later, I don't feel so reactionary. "One hundred three," Graham says. "We need to get a doctor up here."

I call the PA, who calls Reid's personal assistant for the film, Andrew, who locates a doctor willing to make hotel calls. Andrew is one of dozens of usually invisible film crew personnel. His celebrity assistant skills, until tonight, were primarily utilized for caramel macchiato runs and dry cleaning supervision. Tonight, he's in Reid's room, pacing back and forth in the sitting area, calling Reid's parents, manager and agent. Graham calls room service and orders sandwiches, charged to his room. When I try to object, he tells me I have to eat.

"Oh—you were supposed to go to dinner with everyone!" I say.

He shakes his head. "It's no problem. I told them to go

ahead."

When the doctor arrives, Andrew, Graham and I are banished to the hallway while she examines Reid. There's one anguished cry from the room, freezing Andrew and me in place, wide-eyed. Graham takes my shoulders and stares into my eyes. "He's going to be fine."

The doctor opens the door to let us back into the room. "We need to do a scan to check for appendicitis." She's already called the front desk to get an ambulance to the hotel. "Does he have family nearby?" she asks, and Andrew starts dialing like a man possessed.

Graham and I follow the ambulance in a taxi. He holds my hand all the way there, and in the waiting room, where we spend the evening. "He's going to be fine," he repeats, after we're told Reid is going into surgery; the doctor was correct in her initial diagnosis. "What if you hadn't checked on him, or if you'd listened when he tried to just go back to sleep?"

Andrew talks and texts non-stop, pacing by the windows and occasionally outside, where I suspect he's looking for somewhere to light up. Hospitals don't exactly cater to smokers. I lean my head on Graham's shoulder, thankful he showed up with a thermometer, that he knew what to do. My eyes drift closed, and I realize I've been asleep when I sit up and my neck feels stiff. He shifts, his hand massaging the tight muscles, pressing me back to his chest, his heartbeat in my ear.

Pacing a metaphorical groove into the floor in an effort to obtain and relay news about the surgery, Andrew buzzes between the waiting area and the nurses' station. The nurses, at first star-struck, quickly become pissed. "He's. Still. In. Surgery," one of them says, teeth gritted.

"Hmph!" Andrew responds, and Graham laughs quietly as I giggle into his shirt.

Minutes later, Andrew walks over and holds out his cell. "Richter wants to talk to you."

I take the phone. "Hello?"

"Hey, kiddo, I appreciate you being observant enough to realize Reid needed help. If this had gone overnight, he could have been in big trouble."

"It was more Graham than me." My eyes flick to him and he squeezes my shoulder.

"Well, you two possibly saved his life. You don't need to stay, though. I'm sure Andrew can take care of whatever needs to be done tonight." Andrew, jittery, does look prepared to jump on whatever task needs doing.

"We'll be back as soon as he gets out of surgery."

"All right. Give me Andrew so I can make sure he knows how to reach everyone." I hand over the phone and Andrew strides for the exit, talking. Time for another cigarette break.

I turn to Graham. "How are those patches working?"

"Pretty well, actually. I still have issues with my hands sometimes, though, because I'm used to holding a cigarette. Not sure what to do with them." He flexes his fingers and turns his hands palm up, staring down at them as though they belong to someone else. I take the one nearest me without looking at him, and we sit, silently holding hands, until the doctor comes to tell us that Reid is in recovery.

The filming schedule is modified to substitute the few remaining scenes that don't include Reid; he'll be out a solid week, possibly two. Since he's one of the two main characters, we do some scenes partially—a stand-in representing Reid's side of a conversation, or one of us filming a one-sided conversation, his portion to be filmed later, with everything spliced together in the final cut.

Production arranges for us to use the Bennet house again ahead of schedule, and Meredith and I do an emotional scene where her character, Jane, realizes that the guy she loves is gone with no plans to come back. I know from her concentration just before we begin filming that she's mining her recent breakup for emotional effect. She tells me that she wishes she could use something else, but she knows her leftover feelings for her ex are the nearest thing to a shared experience with her character.

"I talked to Robby last night," she says as we wait for the set to be readied.

"Oh?" I study her face, and even with the expertly applied makeup, I can tell she had a rough night. Red-rimmed eyes, dark circles still visible under the delicate skin.

"He says he misses me. I'm not an idiot… but it's so tempting. I know him. He knows me. I'm just afraid that what I'm feeling for him will never be over. Like if I let him go, I'll just die alone and miserable."

"Meredith." I grab her arm, wait until she looks at me. "Please tell me you know better than that. Or else I'm going to have to argue with you about not being an idiot."

"I know better," she mumbles. I lower my chin and stare at her. "I *do*. I don't *want* to love him," she says miserably.

"Mere, what kind of person expects someone he loves to give up what she wants to be, what she needs to do? That's not love."

"Yeah." She's listening but not hearing, and I want to shake her. "You know what, Emma?" She sighs. "Love freaking *sucks*."

Chapter 34

REID

I wake up in a hospital room, and George is sitting on the small sofa. A few seconds pass while I process what happened yesterday. Difficult, because my brain feels numb from what is undoubtedly some sort of analgesic. My manager glances up when I stir. “Reid. Going to stay awake for a few minutes this time?” He comes to stand next to the bed. “They’re keeping you a little sedated, so you won’t move around.”

I look at the IV in my arm. “What happened?” God, my throat feels like I swallowed sand.

“Your appendix decided it didn’t care for Austin so much.”

“You’re kidding.”

“Nope.”

“Dammit, I was supposed to film today.”

Chuckling, George says, “Don’t worry, directors tend to let people off to recuperate from emergency surgery. Everything’s taken care of—private room, of course, and your medical care is being filed and paid, so you needn’t worry about that. Your bodyguard is outside the door, and Andrew will be by in a little while to run errands for whatever you'd like."

I look down at the worn, mint-colored hospital gown. "Tell him not to even bother coming unless he brings me something else to wear. Shorts, t-shirts… I'm *not* wearing this." I pick at one of the stupid ties at the side of the gown. "So I guess Dad couldn't make it, huh? Sent you as his parental doppelganger?"

"What, you aren't happy to see me?" George looks slighted. He should win a mini-Oscar.

"I'm complaining about the absence, not the substitution. Of course I appreciate you coming. Why it would surprise me that he's not here, I have no idea. I mean hell, it's just major surgery. No big deal." My eyes are heavy; I'm sleepy already.

George grimaces, one hand on my arm. "Go back to sleep, get healed up. We'll work on your daddy issues another time."

"Ha, ha. Funny guy, George. That's why I like you."

Late afternoon the next day, Emma walks in, carrying a vase of Asian lilies. Maybe it's the drugs, but her face above the flowers makes me imagine her as a faery. "Hey you," she says. Tadd and Quinton are with her.

I mute the reality show blaring from the way-too-small television bolted to the wall. "Thank God, I'm bored out of my mind."

She smiles at me. "We figured as much." She places the flowers on the built-in veneer dresser and Quinton hands me gaming magazines.

"Dude, you look like ass," Tadd says.

I shake my head, try not to laugh because it hurts. "Tact. Ever heard of it?"

"Tact is overrated," Tadd says, eyeing the television. "Hey, I bet I could get a game console and a couple of controllers hooked up to that."

"Thanks, but I think I'm getting out of here tomorrow. If I promise to be good, I can convalesce at the hotel. The doc says I'll still be in bed for four to five more days, and not in a good way." I wink at Emma and she blushes the slightest pink. "I feel like I'm in prison here."

"The guard dog is at the door." Quinton refers to Bob, who's sitting on a chair in the hall, blocking fan and paparazzi intrusions.

"Yeah, we had an incident with a hospital *volunteer* earlier." I laugh and god*damn*, it's like someone stabbed me. I push a call button.

"Yes, Mr. Alexander?" Young, with a little bit of a Southern lilt. Nurse Monica.

"I could use some pain meds, please ma'am." Tadd quirks an eyebrow at my *please ma'am*, and I pretend not to notice.

"I'll be right in."

"What kind of volunteer?" Emma asks.

"The doing-her-community-service-for-prep-school-credit type. Allegedly, she took some photographic liberties with my sedated body and a strategically unbuttoned candy-striper outfit."

"Whoa! Was she at least hot?" Quinton says, then turns to Emma. "No offense."

She blinks at him. "Um, none taken?"

"No idea. I was drugged out. Bob let her in since she was dressed in hospital threads and had ID, but he had a weird feeling so he checked, and there I was, being violated by an underage candy-striper."

Nurse Monica comes in with a syringe, which she injects into my IV line. Tendrils of her copper hair escape from the twist at her nape, and Quinton is staring, not that I can blame him.

"There ya go. You should feel that real soon." She lays her fingers on the bare skin of my forearm, blinking when

Tadd stifles a laugh, abruptly jerking her hand away. Clearing her throat, she straightens the bedding. "Do you need anything else?"

"No, thanks. I'm good." She blushes and hurries from the room.

"Sure you don't need your pillow fluffed, or maybe a sponge bath?" Tadd mocks.

"So did your juvie stalker sext anything before Bob intervened?" Quinton asks. "Cause that could get ugly. In a legal sort of way."

"Nah, Bob came in, grabbed her phone, walkied for hospital security, and scrolled through her messages. She hadn't sent anything yet. She attacked him when he started deleting photos—"

"She attacked *Bob*?" Emma asks. "Bob's the size of a tank!"

"I know, right? But yeah. He held her by the wrists with one hand while deleting photos with the other until hospital security busted in. Tragically, during all the madness, her phone was accidentally crushed under his ginormous foot and the memory card went AWOL."

Emma smirks. "Sounds like Bob is worth his weight in gold."

"In Bob's case, that's *really* saying something," Tadd agrees.

Emma

After the guys leave, I stay to keep Reid company for the rest of visiting hours, like I did last night. He's alert today, though still a little groggy from the painkillers the nurse just gave him; last night he was drugged to the hilt, in and out of awareness—mostly out, and I was glad I brought something to read.

He's wearing a baby blue t-shirt and black jersey shorts today, rather than the hospital gown. "So is this authorized hospital-wear?"

He ducks his chin, peering roguishly through a few strands of blond hair—clean, which makes me wonder who'd washed it for him—the ginger-headed nurse? "Not exactly, but I tend to get my way about stuff, or haven't you noticed?" Only he could deliver such a line and have it come out charming and not insufferable. "Did you say they moved filming to the Bennet house? I seriously can't remember what we talked about last night, sorry."

"You were pretty out of it."

He scoots over in the bed to make room for me, grimacing slightly. "Come here. You're too far away." I leave the small sofa and climb up next to him, careful not to jostle him or mash his IV line. He takes my hand and kisses the palm. "I hear I owe you a debt of gratitude."

"Well, you were obviously unwell, anyone could have seen that."

His mouth turns up on one side. "The point is, *you* were that anyone. Though, was Graham there, too? I'm fuzzy on that whole night."

"Um, yeah, I told him you weren't feeling well, so he came up. He was actually the one who knew you needed a doctor."

"But you were the one who checked on me in the first place. Besides, no offense to Graham, but I'd rather thank *you*." His eyes are warm, staring into mine, and I brush his hair out of his eyes, feeling guilty, because I didn't go to Reid's door to check on him. I went to his door to tell him off.

Not that he needs to know that.

He leans closer and kisses me, withdrawing with a grimace and leaning back against the mound of pillows. He must have commandeered every pillow on this floor.

"Are you okay?"

"I'm fine as long as I don't move at *all*." He takes my hand and pulls me closer, so that I'm kissing him. "Mmm, better." His blue eyes open and he lifts a hand to my face, fingers coaxing me forward, into another kiss. "Much better."

Chapter 35

REID

I move back to the hotel to recuperate while everyone else continues filming around the scenes I'm supposed to be in, leaving me bored as hell. I've never had to sit out before—no illnesses, no injuries. Dad would be shocked to know I'm losing it over not being able to work.

Everyone drops in occasionally to hang out, and Emma keeps me company whenever she's free, which isn't often on filming and class days. Having her near naturally results in us getting physical, but there's only so far I can go without pain. For days now, we've been kissing and touching for one or two hours straight. Emma is leaving my room more breathless after these restrained makeouts than she ever has.

Today I went on location to watch her film a scene. My leaving the hotel room caused Andrew so much stress that we thought his head would explode. He threatened to call my doctor, my father and George. I glared at him and suggested a cigarette break. He spun on his heel and stomped from the room.

Emma has been anxious about this scene, which includes

Leslie and Tim, both Oscar contenders, as well as Jenna, the perpetually self-confident fifteen-year-old. The majority of primary dialogue is Emma's, though, and the timing has to be perfect for all of them. They get the scene done in only two takes plus some set-ups. Richter, ecstatic, lets all of them go for the day, leaving Emma feeling a little smug. Of course I've witnessed her acting ability firsthand, but observing from the sidelines is different. Filming a scene, you pay the most attention to your own performance; everyone else's performance is secondary. Today, I had nothing to do but watch her.

In the car back to the hotel, I raise the privacy glass between us and the driver, settle her legs across my lap carefully, stroke my fingers over her knee, teasing under the edge of her skirt. Her eyes are heavy as she waits for what I'll do next. "You're a natural, you know," I say. Her brows rise and she colors deeply. I laugh, squeezing her leg lightly and kissing along her jaw. "A natural at that, too, and I'll convince you of it soon. But I mean—you're a natural on film."

She scowls and I run my finger over the spot between her eyebrows. "Don't do that, you'll get a frown crease."

"What do you mean—'natural on film'?"

Why this observation would insult her is beyond me. "Your stepmother told me you'd wanted to do theatre at one time, not film. I can relate—I did some community theatre when I was a preteen. It was fun. But we're both naturals on film, that's all I'm saying." The scowl increases at mention of her stepmother. I'll have to remember not to bring her up again.

"I did want to do theatre; I *do* want to do theatre. But if it has to be film, I'd prefer something more serious than, you know, what we're doing now."

"Serious, like, limited run, indie stuff?"

"Yes, exactly."

Except in extremely rare cases, independent films make

little to no money, and hardly anyone sees them. They're the film version of literary fiction. "Why would you want that, when you can do something that will be wide-released into hundreds of theaters across the country and across the world, will make you crazy famous, sell a ton of DVDs in a few months, and when all is said and done will earn you a ton of money?"

"So, crazy famous and disgustingly rich is worth more than doing something that might have a social impact or garner critical acclaim."

"Hell, yeah. It's not like we're doing porn." She blanches and I laugh. Oops. "God, you should see your face."

"Yep, I'm a riot."

"Look, I get what you're saying, I'm just happy doing what I'm doing, that's all." I pull her closer and kiss her. She hesitates for a moment and then sighs, kissing me back. My hand inches up her thigh under the skirt until my fingers graze her hip.

The car comes to a stop in front of the hotel and Emma scrambles to pull herself out of my arms before the door opens. Bob and Jeff are waiting, as are a few photographers and fans. I wave and smile, giving her the chance to smooth her skirt back over her legs. I tuck her arm through mine as we walk into the hotel, people calling, "Reid! Emma! We love you!"

Independent films my ass. Who wouldn't want this?

Emma

I've sort of neglected studying for the SAT until tonight, when Emily mentions it right after she tells me the latest rumors—about myself.

We agreed a couple of weeks ago that Emily will check fansites and inform me on a need-to-know basis only. Before she took over researching the dirt about me, I occasionally read through it. *Bad. Idea.* For instance, some fansite declared that I'm the most unattractive star in Hollywood and I have no right dating someone as "hot and delicious" as Reid.

Definitely *not* need-to-know. Emily is my first line of defense.

"There's a photo of you and Graham running… And several sites are arguing whether or not he's coming between you and Reid. One suggested that you guys go for runs right after you roll out of bed… *together*."

"Wow, great. So now I'm sleeping with two guys. What, they couldn't get a photo of me and Quinton? Or hey, how about me and Brooke? I mean who cares what's true or not."

"Did you get that SAT prep book I suggested?"

I'm thrown by the sudden change of subject. "I got it, but I really haven't had time to go through it."

"Emma, I know in your world the SAT doesn't seem like a major deal, but it can determine where you go to college. You should already be halfway through the guide by now."

"I know it's important, but I've been really busy…" (*My* world? What does *that* mean?)

"Busy making out with Reid Alexander, hanging out all day and every night with all the other *celebrities*, you mean?"

"Emily, really?" I think I'll wait to tell her about the increased makeouts… and the fact that I think I'm almost ready to sleep with him.

"You're always complaining about being busy, but you're all over Austin—shopping here, drinking and partying there, visiting Reid a dozen times while he was in the hospital—"

"I visited him *twice*, not including that first night, besides which, what is your deal?"

"What is my deal? We haven't talked about *my* problems with Derek at all, and you aren't here to help me find a dress for homecoming, which by the way is like four days away and I'm royally stressing over it; all we ever talk about is you and your issues with *this* hot guy and *that* hot guy and it's like I don't have a best friend at all."

"Emily, if you want to talk about something just talk about it, and it's not like I can just drop my life because you need a *dress*—"

"I haven't even *bought* a dress since I was ten or twelve—"

"You got one for Grant's graduation from Penn State! That was like two years ago!"

"Whatever!" she huffs, cutting me off. "That's not even important!"

"What the hell *is* important? Emily, I can't believe you'd do this to me right now."

"You can't believe *I'd* do this to *you*? Classic. Because *you're* the one who needs the attention, right? And I'm the one who *gives* the attention. You're the one with the spotlight, and I'm the one to the side. And who gives a shit about my problems? Clearly *not you*. You know what? Nevermind. I don't need your help or your support, I have Mom." Thc linc clicks, and shc's gonc.

I sit on the bed in my hotel room, staring at the phone in my hand, my breath coming thin and shallow, tears welling up and spilling over. There are too many things to feel at once, and all of them are bad. I'm an attention whore, and she doesn't need me? She has a mom, and I don't? Is that what she actually meant to say? I feel my heart pounding, hard and fast, hear it echoing in my ears. My face feels hot and I think I might be sick.

And then all I can think is: did Emily just break up with me?

Several sleepless hours later, I don't mention my fight with Emily to Graham during our run, though he notices something is wrong not long after we start out.

"You okay, Em?" This is the only time he's ever called

me by the nickname Emily and I have called each other since we were five, and it's all the push my emotions need. My eyes water and I dash tears away, mumbling some excuse about pollen counts and allergic reactions.

I've never had allergies a day in my life, but this week I appear to have the worst case ever. I don't think he's buying it, and after a couple of days, I text him that I should probably avoid the pollen and take a break from running. He texts back, asking if there is anything he can do. All I can say is no. Which is utterly true.

I alternate between wanting Emily to see nothing but pictures of me smiling and having a good time plastered all over her damned browser, and not wanting her to see photos of me at all because it would justify what she said. While everyone else goes out to unwind after long days of filming, I stay in and order room service, study the prep book, work the practice tests, and blame the SAT and fictitious allergies for my reclusive behavior and constant sniffling. Brooke offers her prescription allergy meds while Meredith pushes the holistic cures her homeopathic doctor recommends.

Emily's homecoming comes and goes, and she never calls.

I don't know if she found a dress, or if Derek convinced her he doesn't want her to change who she is, or if she misses me at all.

I'm spending an hour every morning pressing ice cold rags to my eyes, trying to get the swelling down from crying myself to sleep.

I'm equal parts broken and furious.

Chapter 36

REID

I'm supposed to start filming tomorrow, though my doctor and production are only allowing a few hours per day. I'm ready to get back to it, and it's beyond frustrating. "Half a day is better than no day," Richter tells me. "I'm happy I can use you at all."

Emma sits next to me, translating a passage from a French novel. Or I think she is, until she says, "Eww. Did you just… kill that thing… with a *skillet*?"

I bury an ax in the shoulder of the next zombie and lop off an arm. "Damned… undead." I meant to nail him in the head. "Technically, you know…" I sever the next zombie's head from its body with the ax and she makes another disgusted sound, "…it was a frying pan." I glance at her again, laughing at the revolted look on her face—one side of her upper lip raised like a sneer. Pausing the game, I lean into her line of vision. "I have to be ready to protect you, since you suck so bad at killing zombies."

She rolls her eyes and I kiss her, pushing her book off of her lap and ignoring her feeble protests. I slide an arm around her. "Makeout break." That's all the warning she gets.

I press her back into the pillows, following her carefully, because stretching at the wrong angle still hurts like hell. "Are you sure you're okay to… you know…" she says.

Leaning above her, I smile. "To what? Kiss and touch you until you throw me down and have your way with me? Yes, I'm plenty up to that."

She sighs and laughs, and I figure at this point we don't need to talk anymore.

One thing that doesn't happen often is finding myself alone with Graham Douglas. Most people are fairly uncomplicated, once you know their motivations. I was certain one of his was Brooke. But even though he stays near her, he watches Emma as well. I'd be stupid not to notice. And I'm not stupid.

At the moment, he and I are standing next to each other, waiting to film the only scene featuring just the two of us in the entire movie. I'm wondering if he's doing Brooke, if he has plans to try with Emma as well.

"How's it going?" His expression is relaxed, but tension runs between us like a taut wire. I wonder whether plucking it would disclose where we stand more clearly.

"Good." I nod. "Emma says I should thank you for summoning the doctor the other night. I was too out of it to be aware of anything."

He half-shrugs. "Yeah, I noticed. Glad I could help."

I'm trying to find the condescension I expect from someone who hangs out with Brooke and might have plans to bang the girl I intend to hook up with, but I can't find it. Either he's *really* good at hiding it, or it's not there. The PA calls us to our places.

"Yeah, well, thanks."

"No problem," he says.

Emma

I'm running with Graham this morning for the first time in a week, and he hasn't mentioned my allergy Armageddon. We've discussed auditions at Julliard and studio placement at NYU, but there's something unsaid under the college talk, and I wait for him to sort out whatever's weighing on his mind. He pretends not to notice the one time I say "huh," which seems like a clue. Like he's afraid to upset me.

"So, is everything okay with you and Reid?" he finally asks as we hit our turnaround point.

"Yeah. He's definitely feeling better."

He's quiet for a moment. "Um… I mean between the two of you… is everything okay."

I blink up at him and realize from the way he *isn't* looking at me that he's uncomfortable asking this question, that this is the thing he's been withholding for twenty minutes. I think about what Reid and I have been doing lately and feel a trace of guilt, even though what Reid and I do is no more his business than what he and Brooke do is mine. "Um, yeah, it's fine. It's great."

"Oh. Okay. Good. I'm not trying to pry—I just wanted to make sure. You know, that you're okay. And you know you can talk to me, if you need to talk, vent, whatever."

"Okay," I say. "Thanks." I can't imagine talking to Graham about Reid.

Our kiss on my bed has never been mentioned, or repeated, or even nearly repeated. It's as though it never happened at all. I wish I could forget it as easily as he's been able to, and most of the time the memory of it is neatly filed away—zip, zip, gone—but every so often I think about it and *God*.

We've also never talked about Reid kissing me in front of hidden-camera-wielding, photo-uploading Reid Alexander fans. So I have no idea if the reason Graham withdrew was because I kissed Reid the next day, or because of Brooke, or because kissing me simply didn't do anything for him. I guess in the end it doesn't matter which reason it was.

I consider asking for his advice concerning my fight with Emily, but just thinking about her makes me tear up, and I'm determined not to start crying again while I'm out in public. So I don't say anything. And after a few minutes, he mentions something about filming tomorrow and the moment is past.

Today is the one week anniversary of our fight. Emily and I have never gone more than three days without talking or texting each other, usually not twenty-four hours. I've begun texts and emails to her at least fifty times, I've clicked her speed dial number and *almost* hit talk, but I don't know what to say.

How do you apologize for living your life?

Reid started short stints of filming this week, though his doctor limited him to three hours per day max. The problem is, there are a lot more hours remaining in his day, and not a lot to fill them. I have several hours of filming daily, plus class work, plus studying for the SAT. By Sunday afternoon, I'm playing catch-up before beginning another week of filming.

"Tell me again why you're taking the SAT?" He stretches, pauses the game and reaches for me.

"College?" I shove the math prep book off of my lap as he kisses me. We're sitting in the middle of his bed, remnants of our room-service lunches on trays at the foot of the bed, game controllers and study implements surrounding us.

He takes the pencil from my hand and tosses it onto his bedside table, his brow furrowed. "Yeah, but, why?"

Meredith and Brooke asked the same question, with the same perplexed look. Our kind tends not to pursue higher education. What reason is there, when our career paths are right in front of us, and time off would result in forfeited film roles and lost momentum? Both of them dismissed Jenna as some sort of oddity because of her academic family.

Is it enough to say that it's what normal people do? (Probably not, because all of them would ask me why I'd want to be *normal*.)

"I don't know, Reid. I just want to go, all right?"

"Okay, I'm just curious. Seems like a lot of work." He pulls me onto his lap.

"Be careful," I say, uneasy, but he only shrugs.

"I'm fine. My doctor said I'll be able to start some light workouts with my trainer next week." He tips my chin back to kiss my neck. One arm supports me as the other unbuttons the top buttons of my shirt, his mouth following his fingers. Nudging the fabric aside, he runs his tongue over the upper curve of my breast, and I close my eyes and try to breathe.

Fifteen minutes later, his shirt is off, mine is completely unbuttoned and I'm straddling him. He runs his hands up and down my back before nudging the straps of my bra off of my shoulders. "Emma, you're so hot. I can't take this anymore." His kisses my shoulder, moving towards my throat. "Do you want me to beg? I'm begging. My God, you're killing me with wanting you."

"But your incision," I say, gasping at what his mouth is doing—soft little sucking bites along the curve of my neck.

"Screw the incision, I'd gladly go back in and have it sewn up again. I want you, and I don't care about anything else." He pulls me tight and kisses me, almost too fiercely.

"But…" I'm caving—oh, boy am I caving. My brain casts around for an excuse. "I'm supposed to meet Meredith in half an hour to do econ homework, and after that everyone is going out..."

"Tonight, then." His tone is resolute, his hands gripping my hips. "After we come back from whatever we're doing, and everyone is safe in their rooms, I want you, back here, in my bed." He stares into my eyes. "Say yes, Emma. Please."

I tell myself that I'm only scared because I've never done it. Maybe once it's over it won't feel like such a big deal. "Yes," I answer in the smallest possible voice.

"That's my girl," he says, kissing my now-bruised lips more softly, and a thrill runs through me at his words. And then I want to run to my room and hide in the closet. I knew this was coming, we were getting closer every day, but suddenly it's here and I'm petrified.

He laughs softly. "I can wait. What's another—" he looks at his watch "—four or five hours."

Every time I think about tonight I break out in a cold sweat, so any distraction is good, even homework. Meredith and I spend an hour on economics ("I fail to see why I will *ever* need to know this stuff," she says) before we give up and decide that supply and demand can wait. We have to dress for a cast field trip to a new dance club.

"Reid's looking restored to almost full health." She gathers her hair up at the crown and lets it fall, draws it up and lets it fall again. "What do you think—up or down?"

"I like up. It's different for you." I don't reply to her comment about Reid, though thanks to that my hands are shaking just enough to make applying mascara dangerous.

"I agree. Up. Robby likes it down, so whenever we go out I don't get to put it up."

I stand there watching her in the mirror, holding the mascara wand aloft like I'm about to conduct with it. "Robby *likes* it down?"

"Yeah… um, we got back together last night." She smiles mischievously, examining her own reflection. "He's coming down this weekend."

I barely manage to keep from blurting *What the hell are you thinking?* "So he's going to be less possessive, and stop accusing you of stuff you aren't doing?"

"He promises to trust me more." She begins to pin locks of her hair up. "He knows he was being jealous for no reason before. He's going to change."

"Hasn't he said that before?" Somehow she missed my cynical tone.

"I really think he means it this time," she says, utterly blissful and trusting.

"Huh."

"Let's put yours up, too. Turn around."

I turn away from her, away from the mirror. It's better for both of us if she doesn't see the incredulity on my face.

Chapter 37

REID

John: theres some shit going around about that emma chick, that shes doing both you and that graham guy

Me: Meh. Those sites are jacked up.

John: yeah ok but there are photos of them together. not just one or two but it looks like they run together all the time did you know about that?

Me: wtf – when???

John: this one site has hotel employees saying that they come downstairs together pretty much every morning. like theyre screwing then running. i don't know man i just thought youd wanna know.

Me: k thx

I usually avoid the tabloid sites like a disease. All of us do, as much as we can. Most of the time, it's fabricated by some imitation "journalist" who just wants to sell a story and couldn't care less if it's true.

The hitch is when there's photographic evidence. Not that this can't be deceptive, too; photo alteration software can be a horrific tool in the wrong hands. But there's nothing fake about the multiple photos of Graham and Emma running, stretching, talking, laughing. Their clothing varies, so it wasn't a one-time thing. This is something they've been doing or were doing regularly.

Bob manages one of his bait-and-switch routines tonight to prevent paparazzi obstruction, sending one of his less beefy cohorts—wearing one of my caps—out the front door with the others, while Emma and I escape straight into a waiting SUV out back.

As we're pulling away from the hotel, I ask, "So, how long have you been running with Graham?" My tone is as nonchalant as I can manage. I am *not* used to this jealousy crap. It's not that I'm trusting. It's that usually, I don't give a shit.

"Huh?" she says, caught off guard.

"Running. With Graham. How long?" I repeat the question one phrase at a time, my fingers stroking the back of her neck.

"Um, sort of on and off since we've been here."

"Since we've been here in Austin?" I tip my head to the side. "Were you two already acquainted?"

The expression on her face changes. She knows where this is coming from now. She knows about the photos online. She's unused to everything she does being scrutinized so closely. She clears her throat and swallows. "No."

"So, you just started running together when we got to Austin, even though you've never met before, and don't know each other at all." I'm trying to sound merely curious. *Fail.*

"We both run early, and we ran into each other one time that first week, and the time goes more quickly to go with someone else..." she trails off.

"He's a good-looking guy," I say, watching her reaction.

"Graham? Uh, I guess so." Her tone says, *Oh really? I hadn't noticed.* Her eyes, widening slightly, says she definitely has.

I smile. Might as well lay it all out there. "What's weird is that some of the fansites are posting pictures of you guys together. Saying you're sleeping together."

"*What*?" She's good. I almost can't tell that she already knows this.

"Weird, yeah?"

"That's insane. We're just exercising together, and that's *all*." I can hear both truth and lie in her words, and I'm not sure what to make of it.

"Okay. I was just checking." I tug her closer and leave off the cross-examination, stroke my fingers along the side of her neck and kiss her. I'm not letting anything screw up tonight.

Emma

Reid seems to forget what he brought up in the car, but I can't look at Graham without recalling every word. It's true, I haven't been forthcoming about running with Graham every morning, but I didn't think I needed to account for every waking moment. Reid never struck me as that type, and frankly that sort of expectation would alarm me, especially after the Meredith/Robby drama.

The kiss Graham and I shared was weeks ago. I shouldn't feel guilty, but I do. There can only be one reason for that. I still feel it. It still means something to me, even if it shouldn't. Walking into the club with Reid holding my hand, I'm determined to forget it. I can't take that kiss, and these feelings, into what Reid and I will do tonight.

Production wants nothing happening to Reid that could cause a relapse. The bodyguards are sticking close, keeping him separated from non-cast people. The fans and photogs are forced to content themselves with drooling over him from afar. Every now and then someone talks her way past security and is escorted close enough to salivate over him at close range.

He dances with me a couple of times, pulling me full against him, swaying so slowly that we're hardly moving. Mostly, though, he leans against the bar drinking, talking with other cast members and the occasional favored fan, and watching me dance. Every time our eyes meet, his look is pure fire, reminding me of our later plans.

I'm dancing with Tadd when I glance up to see Reid talking to Graham, who's spent most of the evening at the bar in conversation with Brooke. At first, I don't think anything about it, but then Reid gestures towards the dance floor, and though he doesn't look towards me, my instincts say this exchange has something to do with me. Uh-oh. As the song ends and another starts up, I see that Brooke is at Graham's side and all three of them are talking, and while they all appear under control, the antagonism between them is visible.

I wonder what's being said, and how it will affect my relationships with either of them. Something is about to change, I can feel it, and I realize with blinding certainty that despite what I was thinking when we entered this place, I do not want to lose Graham's friendship. I don't want Reid to do anything to end it. Oh, my God.

I have no idea what to do. As I've done for more than half my life in times like this, I reach for my phone and start to dial Emily's number, faltering when I recognize what my mental autopilot is making me do. Suddenly I'm overwhelmed with indecision and grief. As a new song begins, I leave Tadd talking to one of the extras and bolt for the bathroom. Bob points me towards a secluded VIP lounge.

I'm alone for the space of about fifteen seconds.

"Reid is following me," Brooke says as she enters. "If you're trying to avoid him, you'd better hide."

Darting into one of three stalls, I click the stainless steel door shut behind me, put the toilet lid down, sit and pull my feet up. Before I can ask myself what I'm doing skulking around a bathroom stall like I'm in a bad spy movie, Reid enters. "Anyone else in here?"

"No," she answers. "What, you wanna check the stalls? Be my guest." I hold my breath, but she knows him well and he takes her challenge as confirmation.

"Just answer one question. Tell me the truth, if you can. Does Graham know?"

Through the quarter-inch strip of space between the door and the frame, I watch her remove her lip gloss from her bag and apply it carefully. After a cursory glance over the door behind which I sit motionless and mute, she studies him in the mirror before answering. "Yes, he knows."

He makes a sound of irritation. "God, I *knew* it. Why would you tell him. *Why*?"

She throws the tube of lip gloss back into the bag and turns to face him. "Graham was in the movie I had to break contract on because I was *pregnant*. When you didn't give a shit and my parents and my agent were pressuring me about 'the right thing to do,' he knocked on my trailer door and found me sobbing. So I told him. And he told me to do what was best for *me*. He was the only person I knew, and I barely knew him at all, who cared about what *I* needed."

My blood is pumping so violently that I can barely hear.

"No one forced you to have that baby, Brooke."

"'That baby,'" she says, her voice breaking, "was *your* baby, you asshole. When I told you, I thought—" she stops. "Well. No one cares what I thought. All that matters are the facts. You wanted nothing from me but sex. You said whatever you had to say to get it. I was a naïve little girl, and I got stuck with the consequences."

I'm not breathing, and it's just as well because it feels as though there's no air left in the room. "You have no idea what I wanted," he says, so quietly I could barely hear him. "If you'd had an abortion like your parents wanted you to, there wouldn't have *been* consequences. It was your choice. Your choice to derail your career, your choice to screw up both of our lives if the public ever finds out."

She stares at him. "How *dare* you act like it was oh-so-simple. Flip a coin. Throw a dart. It wasn't that goddamned *easy*. You know what, Reid? My decision *did* sidetrack up my career, but I made the right decision for *me*. And I'll take my life over your miserable egocentric *I am God* existence any day."

"Miserable? Hardly. Egocentric? Okay. *I* can live with *that*."

"Get. *Out*."

"Going. No problem." The bathroom door wooshes open and shut behind him.

I can't move.

"He's gone," she says, and I unwind my legs and open the door.

"I don't know what to say."

She shrugs, blotting excess gloss from her lips. "Join the club. What is there to say, anyway."

"Whcn did it happen?"

"Three years ago. I was sixteen. Three years ago today, in fact, which was also the last time I saw him." She grabs a paper towel and presses it into the corner of each eye. "Reid doesn't even know his birth date. He never asked. God *dammit*. I was fine all day. I thought I could handle it this year. Guess *that* was wrong."

Our eyes meet in the mirror, and I think of how young she is, how much more so she was three years ago. How scared she must have been. "Is there anything I can do?"

"Just ask Bob to get me a car? I just want to get out of here. I'll be fine tomorrow."

"Sure. No problem." I start for the door.

"Emma…" I stop, turn with my hand on the door handle. "Don't go in blind. Whatever he's saying to you, he's saying to get what he wants. If that's all you want, too, then more power to you. Just don't fall in love with him."

I find Bob, who assures me he'll get Brooke back to the hotel. Her request accomplished, my head is crammed with impulses and empty of solutions. Sneaking along the wall, I merge into the crowd, reluctant to confront Reid, who absolved himself of responsibility or even emotion over getting someone pregnant.

I want Emily. My eyes fill with tears and I head for the exit, missing her, needing her advice, the way she centers me. For as long as I can remember, I've thought of her as permanent, but she wasn't. She's detached herself from me, and she's gone, just like everyone else I've ever loved.

Chapter 38

REID

I cannot *believe* this night.

First, the text from John—the rumors online concerning Emma, Graham and myself. Since I don't usually do exclusive relationships, the speculation about Emma has been crazed since it became apparent that I was more interested in her than my usual catch-and-release pattern. If the tabloids can't get confirmation of a relationship, they invent it. And then they try to dig up any evidence of infidelity they can find.

I do *not* let this shit get to me. I don't. But this is the first time since Brooke that I've been in this position—in a relationship of sorts with someone who might be screwing around.

I'd just danced with Emma and turned her over to Tadd, who's in better shape to dance at the moment. Chatting distractedly with some of the minor characters and a few of the extras who found out where we were going tonight, I watched her dance, the way she moved, the way she looked over every few minutes to see if I was still watching her. Her shy smile when she saw that I was. Everything was on track for this night to be mind-blowing.

Brooke was a bit wasted, sitting at the bar a few feet away, with Graham. I ignored her. Until.

"Excuse me—Mr. Alexander?" the bartender said behind me.

I turned. "Yeah?" He handed me a screwdriver, which I definitely hadn't ordered. "What's this?"

He pointed at Brooke, who blew me a kiss. Undeniably wasted. I picked up the drink, walked the few steps to her. "Um, thanks? But I think you'd enjoy this more than I would."

Her expression turned almost pouty. "You liked them at one time."

I narrowed my eyes, wondering at her game. Graham sat silently on the other side of her, staring into his drink, his lips pursed. "Oh? When was that?"

"I shouldn't be surprised that you don't remember."

Oh, I remember all right. Not long before our breakup, Brooke smuggled a bottle of vodka into my house in her bag. "Let's get some OJ and make screwdrivers," she whispered. I made a show of making popcorn in the microwave while she grabbed two large plastic cups and half-filled them with orange juice and ice cubes, and we told my parents we were going to watch a movie in the media room as we disappeared into my wing of the house.

An hour later, we were completely hammered, giggling and all over each other. We'd been aware of little but each other that night, and we were reckless in every possible way. Why she'd want to remind me of that night—with Graham right next to her—was incomprehensible.

"Is there some *reason* you expect me to remember drinking screwdrivers with you, Brooke?"

She stared, while under the surface, both of us popped and snapped with tension. She was a live wire, dangerous and unstable, and some presentiment pushed forward, telling me to beware. In a flash of idiocy, I discounted it. "Only because of what came from it," she answered.

That's the point my eyes flicked over to catch Graham closing his eyes, breathing out a sigh. He turned, his hand on her forearm. "Brooke. Let's go back to the hotel."

"I want him to remember. Just tonight. Just *once*." That was when I knew she'd told him.

I leaned towards her. "So you're saying you know exactly when? Please. I doubt you really even know exactly *who*."

She slipped off the barstool, fists clenched, livid and not as sloppy drunk as I'd assumed. "You *bastard*—"

Graham stepped in front of her. "That's uncalled for," he said to me, his hand on her, keeping her just behind him, as though I'd hurt her if I was too close.

All of us spoke quietly, hyper aware of the fact that we were in public. Even still, I was pissed at the condescension in his tone. "This is none of your goddamned business."

"As her friend, I'm making it my business. Just back off."

"*Friend*? Right. Does Brooke know you've been running in the mornings with Emma, and who knows what else? That you're trying to have your cake and eat it, too?" The way I said this left no doubt as to my meaning. "At least I'm only after *one* girl." I gestured towards the dance floor.

Graham glanced in that direction. "I will kick your ass if you hurt Emma. Don't think for one second that I won't."

Okay. Confusing, right in front of Brooke. "My relationship with Emma is *definitely* none of your business."

At that, Brooke took off for the lounge. I threw back the tequila shot the bartender had lined up at my spot and went after her. Graham followed me, but I didn't give a shit. I had to know if she'd told him, though I *knew* she had. Our conversation in the bathroom confirmed it. When I shoved the door open minutes later, he was standing just outside the door, his jaw clenched. I saluted him and walked straight back to the bar, scanning the floor for Emma.

Emma

I have no idea how I manage to get out of the club and hail a taxi without being stopped by anyone, but I do. As I reach for the door handle, Graham is there, opening the door for me.

"Emma? Are you okay?"

I shake my head, wiping the tears off of my face.

"Get in," he says gruffly, and I obey, folding myself into the back seat and scooting across when it becomes clear he's getting in with me. My face hurts from trying to prevent myself from sobbing, and I turn towards the window as he gives the driver the hotel name.

We don't say another word during the drive back, though he takes my hand, pulls me into his arms while I cry. My mind is pure chaos. I've just left Reid with no explanation, not even a goodbye, and I can't imagine what I'm going to say to him. Can I do what Brooke suggested, and just use him the way she thinks he wants to use me? Hardly. I picture Emily telling me that using Reid Alexander to lose my virginity would be the most mind-blowing way I could possibly lose it.

At least I'm not in love with him. My disillusionment over the not-so-perfect Reid Alexander is the finishing touch to a miserable week. Disappointed and shocked? Definitely. Broken-hearted? No.

The loss of him can't compare to how much it hurts to have lost my best friend. I close my eyes as fresh tears course down my face and drip from my chin. I can't bear the way I miss her. Like a missing limb. Like the quiet voice of conscience. Like hunger.

"Emma," Graham says as we pull up to the curb and he pays the driver. "Stay close." I wonder about his directive for two seconds, and then the flashes start. He draws me close and swiftly heads for the door as a couple of security people rush out to usher us inside. The stories tomorrow should be fascinating. Luckily, I don't care.

When we get upstairs, he glances at Brooke's door as we pass it, and I know that's where he wants to be. I hope she realizes what she's got. He's nothing like Reid. I can't believe I ever thought to compare them.

Shoving the key card into the door, I say, "Thank you. Go… take care of her. I'm fine."

"Are you sure?" His concern is so sweet it almost hurts.

I nod, and he takes my chin in his hand and examines my face. I close my eyes, knowing I must be a total mess. "You're going to be okay, Emma. You're stronger than you know." His voice is soft but sure, and I nod again. He kisses my forehead gently and turns away.

My phone buzzes as soon as I get into my room. When I check the screen, there are two missed calls and four messages, all from Reid. I slump onto the bed and scroll through them.

Reid: Where are you? Are you still here somewhere?
Reid: missed call
Reid: missed call
Reid: Seriously, you disappear and then don't answer? I'm worried, call me back.
Reid: Jenna said she saw you talking to brooke. Gonna ask my side or just listen to her?
Reid: K. I get it. Call me back in 5 or i have to assume we're over.

It's been two minutes since the last text. I lie on the bed and watch the clock tick away the final three minutes of his ultimatum, and then turn onto my back.

I don't care if it's absurd to reject what might be a fantasy for every other girl in the world—losing my virginity with someone like Reid Alexander. I don't care if it's old-fashioned to hold out for losing it with someone who matters. Maybe once that someone breaks my heart, I won't give a crap who I sleep with. Maybe I'll look back on this moment and think I was the biggest moron in the state of Texas.

My God, Emily *would* kill me.

Chapter 39

REID

No answer. Un. Believable.

I feel as though I could electrocute someone with a single high-voltage touch. For me, anger is something I release in short bursts, to lessen it before the rest is swallowed. I learned that living with my patronizing father. I never let myself get this furious, because I can't hide it. If I can't hide it, I'm vulnerable.

I throw back another tequila shot at the bar—the bartender quirks an eyebrow because the stuff I'm throwing back is old and expensive and meant to be sipped, respected. It might as well be shots of the cheapest shit available for how I'm ingesting it. Just then, a hand falls on my shoulder and I turn, too quickly, and nearly knock a girl down.

"Oh!" she says, stumbling back on her stilettos.

I grab her before she falls, one arm encircling her waist and the other catching her wrist. "Oh," she says again, hands on my chest. She's pretty, in that dark hair, big eyes, trying a little too hard with the makeup sort of way. I recognize her from the set.

"You're one of the extras."

"Yes." She's breathless, her eyes dilated—though from alcohol, club drugs or the fact that my arm is wrapped around her, I can't tell.

"What's your name?"

"Blossom?" She says her name like a question, as though if it isn't good enough for me, she's willing to change it. I press my lips together. Smile down at her.

"Would you like to dance, Blossom? I can't do anything strenuous, since I'm still recovering from surgery…"

"Oh, yes. Slow works for me." Her breath is coming in little gasps. After trying to seduce Emma for the past several weeks, I forgot how easy it usually is.

"Does it now," I say.

She smiles a wicked little smile as I lead her onto the floor, and it isn't long before I'm whispering in her ear, drawing out her acquiescence to go back to the hotel, as effortless as it ever was.

Emma

After a restless night, I send Graham a text saying I'm not running this morning. He's probably still with Brooke anyway. I ignore the prickly twinge that thought causes.

I know I can't avoid filming, though I seriously consider faking laryngitis. Or a killer migraine. Or a heart attack. The whole day—the rest of the week—will be full of scenes with Reid. I wonder what his explanation will be. I wonder if I'll accept it, if I can believe that what happened between him and Brooke was immaturity and not callousness.

"Emma, what *happened* last night?" Meredith asks in the car on the way to the Bingley house location. The others have already left, so it's just the two of us. "I looked up and you were gone, Brooke was gone, Graham was gone… and then when Reid came back to the hotel with one of the extras. I thought you guys were going out, or hooking up?" I feel my mouth hanging open, but I can't seem to snap it closed. "Oh God," she says. "You didn't know. Oh *shit*."

"No," I say, blinking. He brought a girl back to his room? *Last night*? "No, we, uh, it's okay. We're… over."

"Wow. That was quick."

She could say that again.

"Jeez, they don't waste any time. Look at this," she says, holding out her phone. One of the fansites is on the screen, and suddenly here in my hand are surprisingly clear photos of Reid and some girl getting cozy at the club, climbing into a taxi together, exiting at the hotel, his arm slung around her shoulder, his mouth near her ear. There are also photos of Graham and me going into the hotel, my face hidden by his arm.

The theories are all over the place, from almost rational: Reid and I had a fight over Graham, or over Reid's New Girl, to mind-boggling: the whole thing is a ploy to throw the public off the truth—that I'm actually pregnant with Reid's baby, or is it Graham's?—cue the close-up of my supposed baby bump (my tummy in this photo looks as though I may have eaten half a slice of bread or missed *one freaking day* of crunches last week).

I hand it back. There's no way I'm reading any more, certainly not the fan comments. I'm enough of an emotional wreck, thanks. "What a load. We just decided… that we didn't match up so well."

"That's so weird; I thought things were going well the last time we talked. Are you okay? You've seemed kind of depressed lately."

"Yeah, I'm fine," I lie.

While I'm in makeup, I'm doing what I can to get into my character zone so I can face Reid. I'm unsure whether the antagonism of these scenes between Lizbeth and Will is going to be to our benefit or the reverse; how Reid will play it is the only indeterminate factor. Unfortunatcly, it's a freaking important factor. We don't even make eye contact on set until Richter calls, "Action."

INT. Bingley house - Night
Bingley party. CHARLOTTE and LIZBETH observe the other guests. WILL approaches them.

CHARLOTTE
(aside to LIZBETH)
Don't look now, Will is coming this way.

WILL
(to LIZBETH)
Wanna dance?

(He's either perfectly in character or he's angry over my desertion last night. I might have listened, if he'd have explained, given me a chance to understand. No chance of that now.)

LIZBETH
(glancing at CHARLOTTE)
Sure.

Cut to:
CHARLOTTE shrugs at LIZBETH as WILL leads her to the open space where people are dancing.

Reid takes my hand and presses into the crowd of minor characters and extras, pulling me behind him. They make room for us as we pass, and we settle into the middle of the floor, Reid's arms encircling me, holding me as close as he had when we danced last night. When Richter calls, "Cut," his arms drop and he turns from me without a word.

Someone from makeup runs up to push a lock of my hair behind my ear and spray it in place. Over her shoulder I see Graham in his goofy Bill-wear, which makes him look like an unfashionable dad. He glances up, sees my bemused look and smiles, adjusting his glasses and waggling his eyebrows, coaxing a reluctant smile from me.

"Places everyone," the assistant director calls, and I turn back to Reid, who's whispering in the ear of the girl from the paparazzi photos. She scampers back to her scene partner; as I'm watching her, he's watching me.

His arms go around me again and mine return to his shoulders. "Good morning, Emma," he says, his expression glacial. "Did you sleep well?"

Before I can answer, Richter readies us and calls action. We dance in silence for five minutes as close-ups are shot of the two of us avoiding each other's eyes. This will undoubtedly be the easiest five minutes of filming with Reid today.

During the break, Brooke takes my elbow and we move apart from everyone else. "Graham told me you came back to the hotel last night without talking to Reid." She looks uncomfortable. "I didn't expect… I mean, your relationship with him isn't my business." She's hesitant and concerned, and I'm struck by the fact that I have no idea who she really is. One thing is clear: the Brooke I thought I knew is a facade. "I know I said not to fall for him. But… maybe that's just how he was with me. Maybe he'd be different with you."

"I don't think so," I say, glancing at him talking to the extra, Blossom. "But it doesn't matter, now."

"I'm sorry," she says, her gaze direct.

I shrug and glance away. "Don't be."

The dialogue of the next scene is too close to reality in reverse, the proximity and eye contact made more awkward by the words.

"Action."

WILL and LIZBETH dance.

LIZBETH

A few days ago, you told me that your opinions about people can't be changed.

WILL

(curious)

Yes.

LIZBETH

I hope you're careful when you make up your mind about people, then? That you're never so close-minded that you're prejudiced from the start.

WILL

I hope not. Why?

LIZBETH

I'm just trying to figure you out.

WILL

And?

LIZBETH

I haven't.

This is the point where the song on the soundtrack will end, and we stand looking at each other for ten seconds. His eyes are cold, and the chill between us twists in the pit of my stomach. It's all I can do to keep from shivering. Ten seconds can be a very long time. It feels like an hour before Richter calls, "Cut!" and we turn and walk in opposite directions.

Filming breaks are like coming up for air after being under water for a few seconds too long, but breaks are their own sort of misery. Everything we do is being scrutinized by everyone on set. They all know that last night, whatever was going on between us ended. Unpleasantly. Speculations fly, buzzing near but never landing; no one knows exactly what happened, only that something did, and they probe for clues to what.

This goddamned day is never going to end.

Chapter 40

REID

The scenes with Emma are the hardest I've ever had to film. Would it make any difference if I got her alone, begged her forgiveness and told her that Blossom meant nothing? Does it make any difference that it's true? I needed a distraction last night to numb the emotion boiling under the surface after the confrontation with Brooke, after Emma disappeared and wouldn't answer my calls or texts. Now there's a glacier between us, cold and mountainous and lethal. When I see her talking with Brooke, staring at Blossom, glancing at me and away, I know crossing it won't be possible.

It's a good thing Will Darcy is sort of a dick, or I'd never be able to pull this off.

I bristle at the idea that I should feel sorry for what happened almost four *years* ago, when it likely wasn't even mine to feel sorry for. I haven't thought about this shit in years. Even seeing Brooke when filming started—sure, I remembered the relationship, but I sought long ago to purge the ending from my brain. The way she was hooking up with another guy, maybe several, while telling me she loved me, while getting me to say it back, *feel* it back. I adored her, and she betrayed me. So what if that kid might have been mine? Why should I have cared?

Emma probably doesn't see it that way; she's a girl. She views my actions as desertion. And maybe it was.

I don't need this shit. I have enough to deal with—an alcoholic mom and a career to keep on track and build. I'm done. I'm *so* done.

Emma

"Emma, what's going on?"

My father's question hangs in the several hundred mile space between us. I'm sitting on my bed after this hell of a day, in the middle of taking an SAT practice test online. I'll have to start over if this conversation doesn't end quickly.

"Um, what do you mean, exactly?" I stall, unsure if he's referring to the rumors that I'm sleeping with Reid, and/or Graham, or breaking up with one or both of them, or the report of my baby bump… or something else altogether.

"Is there anything you need to talk to me about?" This is a characteristically evasive question that I'm both grateful for (because I don't have to answer to anything specific) and annoyed by (does he even care?).

"No."

He's quiet for a moment, and I begin to relax. He never presses about anything like this. Sometimes he asks, because he thinks he should. But he doesn't really want to deal with it. So I'm taken by surprise when he doesn't drop the subject, but instead asks a question that blows my nice predictable view of my father apart.

"Emma, you know how much credibility I give to celebrity gossip, but I can't pretend it's all crap, I can't ignore it if… if you need my help. Because, *dammit*, I'm your father, and that's my job. So I need to know," I actually hear him gulp, "are you pregnant?" If this isn't a nightmare moment, I don't know what is.

My mouth works as though I'm speaking, or chewing something, nothing but little clucks coming out until finally I say, "No. *No*."

He exhales, and I imagine his hand at his forehead, his eyes closed. This time, his moment of silence doesn't fool me. I'm on high alert, not that it helps. "I know we've never really discussed, uh, sex, before," he charges on, "but as your father, I have to make sure you have the tools you need to be safe."

"Huh," I say, my face flaming.

"So, you know that uh, condoms are necessary to protect yourself against not only unwanted uh, pregnancy, but also STDs—er, sexually transmitted diseases…" He's explaining this stuff as though I've never heard it before, as though I haven't known it since Grandma and I talked years ago. I'm thinking *late much?* and trying to contain my hysteria while he morphs into one giant sex ed TMI, "…herpes and chlamydia. Um, I think those are the major half-dozen, though there are more, but you don't need to know them all…"

"*Dad*." The word feels strange, like someone else is saying it, because I don't think of him as *Dad*. He's *my father*, formal and impassive. Like our relationship has been since Mom died. "I… I know all of this."

"Oh? Did Chloe—?"

"*No*," I say, too harshly. "No—Grandma, and Emily's mom." And then because I said Emily's name, I'm crying.

"Emma, what is it?"

"I had a fight with Emily!" It bursts from me, unable to be contained any longer. "She's not talking to me and I don't know what I did or what I can do or should do."

He goes quiet again, and just as I start to berate myself for blurting this out to *him* of all people, he asks, "Have you tried calling her?"

"Sort of. Not really. I don't know what to say." I sniffle. "She thinks I was ignoring her, and maybe I was, but I didn't mean to…"

"Then that's what you say, sweetheart." He hasn't called me that in so long. Not like that—like a caress, like a hug. "You and Emily have been like sisters for almost your whole life; she'll listen."

"What if she hangs up on me? What if she hates me?"

"Emma, do you really believe that's possible? Think how long you two have been attached at the hip. Now you're both about to be adults, have separate lives. Maybe she's scared of losing you."

"Then why is she pushing me away?" I sob.

He's quiet for a moment. "Because that's what people do sometimes, when they're scared, and they're just being reactive. Maybe you need to be the brave one."

"But I'm not brave," I say, my voice small.

"Oh, honey, I don't know anyone braver than you." *What?* "Let's make a deal, you and me. You call Emily tonight. And I'll tell Chloe that you're going to college next fall. SAT a week from Saturday, right?"

"Yes." I shake my head, saying, "You haven't told her?"

"Time for me to be brave, too," he says, not thrilled. I start laughing and he joins in.

"Are you going to tell her about your lunches at McDonald's?" I ask, teasing. I try to be rational and suppress the hope that this is for real, but hope has a way of closing its eyes to reason and it just keeps growing.

"Let's not go crazy, now," he says, all pretend-serious. "In some cases, what she doesn't know… well, you know Chloe."

"Yeah, I do." I take a shuddering breath. "Thanks, Dad," I say, liking the sound of it, afraid that this image of him is a mirage, that if I look away and look back, it'll be gone. I think about what he said. That I'm brave. If that's true, maybe I won't let him go so easily this time. Maybe I'll remind him, if he forgets again.

"Goodnight, sweetheart," he says, and I let that one word envelope me and shove the doubt away, at least for tonight.

"Night, Dad."

Me: I'm sorry. I was selfish, but i didn't mean to be. I'll do whatever it takes to make you believe me. To make you forgive me. I miss you so much.

As I hit send, I tell myself that a sliver of bravery is better than a load of cowardice. It will hurt less to have her ignore a text than it will if I call and she doesn't answer and I get her voicemail, or worse, if she answers and tells me that she meant everything she said.

I survive an agonizing five minutes, during which I rock in the middle of my bed, my arms around my knees, staring at the phone in my hand as though I can't trust sound alone to tell me if she texts back. When it rings, I startle and drop it onto the bed, then grab it up. "Hello?"

Her voice is so soft I can barely hear her. So unlike Emily. "I'm sorry, too," she says, and we both start crying and talking at the same time. "I didn't mean it—"

"Emily I'm so sorry—"

And then we're laughing and crying, and she says, "Let me start. First, don't ever let me do this again, even if you have to send Chloe over to bitch-slap some sense into me."

"I could never."

"Yeah, well, seriously. Second, for a long time I've congratulated myself on what a great friend I am—with you being on television, then getting this movie and getting *famous*, and me not being a bit jealous. Then all of a sudden you're having this fantasy romance while I'm scared to death that I'm about to have the worst case of pathetic unrequited love ever with a guy who works at the freaking *Abercrombie*. So it turns out that I'm a *horrible* friend—" she hiccups.

"Emily, no you're not, *I* am—" I object, but she plows on

as though I haven't spoken.

"—and your fantasy romance has gone to the shitter and it's clearly all my fault for deserting you when you needed me!" Now she's bawling, and I butt in while I can.

"Emily, I'm okay, and you're *not* a horrible friend, you're the best friend ever."

"Psshh!"

Before she can object more, I say, "Honest, I'm okay. I've been more upset thinking I was losing *you* than anything else going on. I'm sorry for making you feel like I always got your attention when you never got mine, for making you feel like I didn't care about your problems."

"Em, that's not even true. I was just jealous. Forget what I said."

"No. You needed me, and I was obsessing over Reid and Graham, and I should have been listening to what *you* needed, instead of expecting you to always be the one listening. When I lost *you*, I didn't care much about anything else."

She sighs. "Even if I felt ignored, I knew better. You've never not been there for me—and *oh my God*, I just used a double negative. Clearly I'm traumatized! Please, just forgive me."

"If you forgive me."

"*Fine*. I forgive you. Happy?"

"Yeah," I sniffle.

"Okay. Now what the crap is going on down there? Mom is off her freaking noodle—she called your father and ripped him a new one. She even used a couple of actual curse words! Not any really good ones, but still."

"I guess that explains that..."

"What?"

"He called earlier… do you think he only did it because she told him—?"

"I don't think so. At first, yeah, she was all over him, but then they started talking, and from her answers, he was asking the right questions. I think he had no idea how badly he was doing. Until, you know, she *told* him, in that way that only Mom can do."

"Oh."

"Now. What's going on with this baby bump crap."

"Emily, I'm not—"

"Oh, I know that. I also know how conflicted you were over Reid and Graham. And it looks like everything just blew to hell. So what happened."

"How long do you have?" I ask, lying back on the bed.

"All night, baby. I even called Derek before I called you, and I told him, 'Don't call me; I'll call you,' so we have as long as you need."

"I'm doing it again, we should talk about Derek—"

"Everything is fine with Derek; he can wait, we'll talk about him soon enough, don't you worry. So quit stalling and start talking."

I tell her everything. And the first thing she says after is, "Wow. I had no idea how much I missed knowing more than the freaking *National Enquirer*."

"Huh."

"Em," she says then, "have you ever noticed that you say 'huh' whenever you can't think of anything else to say?"

Chapter 41

REID

I almost feel sorry for Blossom. I couldn't tolerate her for even a full twenty-four hours. Turns out there actually *is* such a thing as too much flattery and adoration. Next up was a girl playing a Netherfield High cheerleader (I asked her to leave the costume mostly on), followed by a woman billed as one of the teachers.

I've avoided any social interaction with cast mates—except Tadd and Quinton—until tonight, when everyone is gathering in Brooke's room to celebrate Jenna's birthday. I've stupidly brought last night's girl along. Vivian was hot and inventive in bed; out of it she's rude and grating. Even still, I need a buffer between myself and Emma, or I'm going to end up doing something rash like getting on my knees and pleading for mercy.

Tadd is opening a bottle of Riesling, sort of. He's actually mangling the crap out of the cork as Emma looks on, laughing as they pour the wine into glasses and then fish bits of cork out of each one, using straws, spoons, napkins and toothpicks.

"Did you *chew* the cork off, Thaddeus?" I say.

"Piss off, man," Tadd says as he traps the last piece.

Vivian slides up to me and asks, "What're you doing?" while fixing Emma with a defiant stare. Christ. I do *not* need this.

"Getting you something to drink, babe." I grab a glass and hand it to her with a smile, wondering if alcohol will make her mellow or more belligerent. She stands on her tiptoes and rubs my nose with hers, marking territory. You have *got* to be kidding me.

Emma, sharing a look with Tadd, sticks a finger in her mouth, her tongue out, and he chuckles. Unfortunately, Vivian catches the pantomime. She narrows her eyes at Emma and snaps, "Got a problem?"

"Hey now," I steer her to the opposite side of the room, "nobody's got a problem."

Why couldn't my appendix have died *tonight*? It's a toss-up which was more painful, that night or this one.

Emma

For almost two weeks, I've had a freaking front row seat as Reid cuts a trail through the cast of female extras. *Step right up. Reid Alexander is accepting applications for one-night internships.* On one hand, I don't care, and on the other, it's borderline humiliating and I feel like a total dumbass for thinking I could be some sort of exception for the way he is with girls.

I've avoided talking to or looking at him or tonight's plaything, but I could feel her eyes on me from the moment they came in the room. With the SAT tomorrow, I'm avoiding alcohol, but I assisted Tadd with uncorking the Riesling bottle. We managed to disintegrate the cork with the corkscrew, and while we were fishing chunks of cork out of the glasses, Reid appeared at my side with his date, who attached herself to him like a barnacle to a ship.

She was trying to start something before he dragged her away. I *don't* want him to think I'm jealous. You'd think being an actress would help in situations like this, but we're human, with emotions like everyone else, and sometimes they just won't stay submerged. I escaped onto the balcony to pull it together.

I close my eyes and breathe until Graham comes outside and stands next to me, hands in his pockets; I know he's there when I inhale the familiar spicy scent of him. We scan the view as the sky darkens and the streetlamps flicker on. He doesn't speak for several minutes, and I consider the fact that he and I spend a lot of our time together not talking, comfortable in each other's company despite long silences. This is probably the result of running together, the exertion not always conducive to conversation.

"SAT tomorrow, right?" I love the texture of his voice, the husky timbre that triggers reverberations somewhere inside me. Too bad for me that he belongs to Brooke.

"Yeah. I guess I've got my excuse to bail early tonight."

"Hmm. Are you doing okay, with—?" He indicates the indoors, and Reid.

"Yeah, I'm good."

Brooke joins us then. "Hey, are you okay? Because trust me, I'd *love* to tell him to take his skank and get out."

"I'm fine," I lie.

"Well just say the word and they're out on their asses." She gives my shoulder a squeeze and goes back inside.

My world has done a 180: I want Reid to disappear, and somehow Brooke and I have become BFFs. What. The. Hell.

An hour later I'm in my room, bitching to Emily. "...and Reid's piece of ass for the night was getting territorial. Like I'm competition. *As if.*"

"God, how many does that make?"

"Four—that I know of."

"Jeez, what a man whore."

I sigh, throwing myself against the pillows. "If he's going to start bringing them around when we all hang out, I don't think I can handle it. It's hard enough just sitting in the same room with him."

"Em, maybe you're more hurt about this than you're letting on," she suggests.

"I'm just pissed, that's all."

"If you say so…"

She doesn't believe me, but I need to forget Reid for a moment, forget where I am and everything I'm feeling. "I do. And in other news—how's Derek?"

"Derek's good," she says, and if there's such a thing as being able to hear a smile, I'm hearing her smiling through the phone.

Chapter 42

REID

Production rented out the thirtieth floor of an office building in freaking *Dallas* for Rosings Corp headquarters. Which means three days (and two nights) on location in Dallas with Graham, Emma and MiShaun. I'm not exactly a favorite of any of them at the moment.

I head for the elevator Monday morning, a travel bag slung over my shoulder, my arm around last night's entertainment. She's giggling and wearing my shirt (dammit, I'll probably never see *that* again, and it's one of my favorites). She's cute, but after a night of her, I'm desperately craving *silence*.

As we round the corner, Emma has just pulled the door to her room shut and stands in the hallway, grasping the handle on her rolling carry-on bag. She turns back to the door as soon as she sees me, but it's too late—it's clicked closed and automatically locked; we're all stuck in the hallway together.

As we pass her, I say, "Good morning, Emma."

Lips pursed, she raises her eyes to mine before sweeping them away as she turns towards the elevator. "Good morning," she murmurs.

Pointlessly, the girl in my shirt giggles. I angle her shoulders towards her room and swat her ass, resisting the urge to *shove* her in that direction. "Get some sleep, young lady."

Ow!" she says, followed by more giggling. Jesus.

Following Emma to the elevator, I can't help but inventory everything I ever found physically attractive about her—how her hair flows over her shoulders, the way she holds herself as she walks, the curve of her hip and the line of muscle down the side of her legs below the hem of her white shorts, the wrist of stacked bracelets on her left arm, and on her right hand, the silver band with the story I'll never learn. We enter the elevator and ride to the ground floor in silence, her pale shoulder against the opposite wall. I hum to myself as we take what feels like the slowest descent in the history of motorized, pulley-operated boxes. I find myself thinking *Is this goddamned thing even moving? I could* crawl *down the stairs faster*, when not long ago, the two of us appreciated the elevator's lethargic pace.

Graham and MiShaun are in the lobby, along with Bob, who walkies that he's bringing us out. Luckily, the early hour yields just a couple of paparazzi photogs. MiShaun takes Emma's arm, talking nonsense on the way to the car. She sits next to Emma and Graham takes the seat across from her. They've joined forces to make sure I'm as far from her as possible.

Awesome.

Emma

"You never told me how the SAT went." Graham loads his tortilla with some of everything from the fajita platter we're sharing, including the sour cream, cheese and guacamole that I avoid lest I be accused of another baby bump. The two of us found a Tex-Mex place for our last meal out in Dallas. MiShaun's computer guy is in town on some consulting project, so she's with him, and Reid is probably hooking up with one of the new extras or a local groupie. Filming was hell, but it's done.

"The exam was protracted and arduous." I tap my foot to the rhythm of the music in the background as I select lean pieces of grilled chicken and veggies. Graham smiles, and I notice a bit of sour cream at the corner of his mouth. I wonder what he'd do if I reached out a finger and cleaned it off. Maybe with a napkin. Maybe I should just say something. Maybe just ignore it.

"Sounds traumatic," he says. Huh? Oh, the SAT.

I shrug, take a sip of iced tea and glance back at his mouth. Sour cream still there. I have a vision of leaning across the table and licking it off, and I blurt, "You have a little…" and point to the corner of my mouth. He pulls the napkin off his lap and swabs at the corner.

"Gone?"

"Yeah." Must stop staring at his mouth. I lean back into the soft leather booth and force myself to look away from him. If Graham and Brooke are together, or trying to be, then I have no business contemplating… licking him.

"Fans, three o'clock."

"Huh?" I say, and he raises an eyebrow. "Okay, that doesn't count. That was basically a *question*, not a *huh*."

"All right," he smiles. "I'll spot you that one."

I try to be covert in looking over my shoulder, but covert doesn't matter—an entire table of sorority girls is staring back. My glancing at them ignites all of them to begin talking to each other excitedly, and then the cell phones emerge.

"Crap. Can we leave?"

"I haven't paid yet." He looks for our server, motions her over. "Restaurants sorta frown on customers who leave without paying. Even famous ones." The server arrives with the check and Graham hands her a credit card. "You know, we talked about this a while back. It's going to happen even more, once the movie's released." He laughs softly as I scowl at my lap. "Emma," he says, prompting me to look at him. He's leaning up, his forearms folded in front of him on the table, his eyes dark and direct. "You're the lead female role in a major studio film. This is about to be your normality."

He's right, of course. I lean up on my forearms, too. "Emily told me the fan pages are going crazy wondering why Reid's being seen with everyone *but* me." I could get so lost in his eyes. I must stop gazing into them like I *want* to get lost there. "You know what this will do, me being photographed at what will no doubt be described as an intimate dinner, with you."

He smiles, signing the receipt and stowing his card away. "I can take it. Now put on a little attitude, and let's get out of here." He calls our driver to meet us out front and takes my hand as we exit, and despite the people staring, pointing cell phones, or just plain pointing, I feel calm with my hand in his.

Chapter 43

REID

The last weeks of filming are moving in a blur.

According to the fan pages, Emma and Graham continue their morning runs and are rumored to be making out all over town—despite no photographic evidence beyond the hand-holding incident in Dallas. In private, they're no different near each other than they've ever been. Easy familiarity, but no staring across the room as though they can hardly wait to get each other alone and no touching that I've witnessed or heard about. Graham continues to appoint himself as Brooke's protector—which at least I get now. I still think they're involved.

Emma was chosen to play Lizbeth because of the chemistry between us, which refuses to ebb just because we want it to. And oh, how I want it to. Delivering Will Darcy's declarations of love to Lizbeth is torture. Touching her is torture. Kissing her is torture.

When possible, I bow out of any group social activities in which Emma might be involved. Tadd, of course, is the one who notices my discomfort. Or maybe he's just the only one who gives a shit or doesn't automatically think I deserve to reap what I've sown. "Almost over, dude."

"What?" We're on set, waiting to see if Richter wants any more takes on the argument between Will and Charlie, when Charlie figures out that his best friend sabotaged his relationship with Jane. I sense Tadd isn't referring to today's filming, though. The chemistry between us on film is as easy as our relationship has always been, so we're probably good.

Swinging his hair out of his eyes, he levels a look on me, his mouth in that sarcastic twist I know so well. "I've never seen you so whipped, man. Why don't you just give up and beg her forgiveness?"

My mouth drops open. "In one sentence you're calling me whipped and in the next you're suggesting I plead for mercy? What the hell, man. That makes no sense."

He sighs noisily, crossing his arms over his chest. "Yeah, it kinda does. You managed to be a dickwad to someone you were falling for. You could try apologizing. God knows you've given *screwing* her out of your head your best shot." He chuckles softly. "*So* not working, by the way."

I stare at the object of this discussion across the room where she sips from a water bottle and laughs at something Meredith just said, and my jaw clenches. "I'm *not* falling on my face at her feet so she can kick me more easily. The effort would be futile, not to mention degrading."

"More degrading than it is for her to watch you bed every girl in the cast?"

I love the guy, but *God*, Tadd is a know-it-all sometimes. "She listened to Brooke's side and didn't even ask mine," I hiss. "Where's *her* apology to *me*?" When the production assistant looks over, I know this discussion has gone too far. I don't want to debate whether or not I should apologize to Emma for some perceived thing I did to *Brooke*.

Tadd turns to me, his clear blue eyes unnaturally serious. "Dude, you're miserable—"

"No. I'm *pissed*. But like you said, it's almost over."

"Good job, gentlemen," Richter says then. "No more retakes, you can vamoose."

As we turn, Tadd nods once, clamping his mouth shut and containing whatever he was going to say. I'm deaf once I've made up my mind, and I've always been good at shutting my emotions off. I'm getting better.

Emma

I'm home.

The last weeks of filming were challenging, not because of the scenes themselves as much as what happened between them. When Reid and I filmed intimate scenes, staring into each other's eyes and reciting the play of words between Will and Lizbeth as they fell in love despite all intentions otherwise, he was utterly convincing. But Richter's "Cut!" shut off the passion and devotion in his eyes like a thrown switch.

I was afraid kissing him would be unbearable, but with preparation, once my eyes were closed, I became Lizbeth Bennet kissing Will Darcy, and Reid Alexander wasn't there anymore. There were a couple of times I wasn't prepared, and the trace of his mouth on mine constricted my breath. Both times, I could have sworn he was affected as well, until the inevitable end to the scene, when he blinked and the connection was gone.

On the last day of filming, the celebratory mood was shaded with the bittersweet grief of ending. Simultaneous laughter and tears, hugs and promises of keeping in touch were passed between all of us. Reid's lips grazed my temple, briefly, before he turned away to do the boy-hug thing with Quinton. He and Richter left the hotel that night. The rest of us checked out the next day.

Graham and I took a taxi to the airport together; our

flights were at the crack of dawn, departing within ten minutes of each other. We got through security more quickly than we'd expected, and decided to hang out at the cramped coffee bar. We sat watching the other travelers: some bleary-eyed, some lost, some type-A frustrated with all the others.

Graham tore off a hunk of the cinnamon roll we were sharing. "Have you applied anywhere yet?" he asked, consuming his sticky portion in one bite.

"Doing that when I get home. We've got everything organized—which schools want an essay, which have extensive applications, which require recommendation letters."

He smiled. "That's great."

"What about you—after graduation?" I nibbled at a much smaller segment of our joint breakfast, licking my fingers reflexively. And then Graham was staring at my fingers and mouth, suffusing me with an unexpected warmth so strong it felt visible. As he lowered his gaze to the last bit of roll, I wiped my fingers on the napkin in my lap while struggling to stop imagining his mouth sucking the sticky sweetness from each one, slowly and thoroughly. "You can, um, have the rest." I strove to sound impassive and heedless of the electricity zipping through my body.

He cleared his throat. "My agent called yesterday—I've got another indie film lined up for mid-summer, to be filmed in New York." After looking at me for another long moment, he said, "If you decide on a university there, I'll probably be around when you start next fall." He clicked his phone, checking the time. "We'd better get to our gates."

We stood at the same time and faced each other; our gates were in opposite directions. He reached for me and I walked into his arms. I pressed my face to his chest, breathed in his scent. He was going to walk away, and I was going to let him go without ever asking him why he'd kissed me. "I'll miss you, Emma," he said. Under my ear, his chest resonated faintly with my name.

"I'll miss you, too."

Relaxing his hold, he took my face in his hands and kissed my temple softly. "I'll miss you more," he whispered before turning to gather his bags. When he was fifteen or twenty feet away, he looked back, tipped his chin, and smiled at me. I gave a little wave and took a deep breath, memorizing his familiar gait. The way he paid no attention to the girls who turned to watch him pass. The way I felt the loss of him already, when he was still within my sight.

"So… I think he took that well," Dad says after the phone call to Dan to tell him I would be taking a hiatus from blockbuster roles so I could go to college. Dad rubs the back of his neck with one hand while he stares at the phone in the other.

"You aren't a very good liar, Dad."

"Well, he's *received* the news. I guess how he likes it is his problem."

"Hmph," Chloe says from the kitchen table, where she's grading exams. She's still disgruntled that I'm giving up my film career, possibly for good. Her dreams of being the mother of a huge star, jet-setting all over the world, rubbing elbows with celebrities, have been dashed. She didn't speak to either of us for days, but she's almost resigned herself to the idea now. I think.

Dad winks at me, leaning over her shoulder and telling her, "I thought you and I could use a weekend getaway. Visit a winery or two… stay at a B-and-B?"

"Really?" She brightens, and then her expression falls. "But what about—" she gestures towards me as I pour a glass of orange juice.

"Emma's an adult now, Chloe. She can handle a weekend at home alone." When he mentioned the idea last week, I assured him I was *more* than fine with it.

"Sure," I say. "You kids go, have fun."

I scroll through my texts as I walk to my room. There's a

thread with Graham from last night that I want to reread.

Graham: Hey, birthday girl
Me: You remembered
Graham: Of course. Doing anything special to celebrate being 18?
Me: Like what, voting?
Graham: HA
Me: Just going to dinner with dad and chloe
Graham: How is that going btw
Me: Really well, actually
Graham: Good. I just registered for my last semester. Heading upstate with my sisters for some r&r this weekend.
Me: Jealous. I always wanted sisters.
Graham: Trust me, it was the opposite of awesome for the first 15 years, until i was cool enough for them to know me in public.
Me: Lol. Enjoy your weekend.
Graham: Thx, you too

I move the text into permanent storage on my phone. I haven't seen anyone from *School Pride* in the weeks since we wrapped the film. The new version of my old life has reabsorbed me. These few lines and a few weeks of memories—countless conversations and one unforgettable kiss—are all I have left of Graham.

The day I met Derek, he and Emily had both just gotten off work. Each was dressed to sell an image to their respective customers—most of whom wouldn't be caught dead in each other's social circles. From the violet stripes in her dark hair and her black-tipped fingernails to her biker boots with buckles running ankle to mid-calf, she couldn't have appeared more incompatible with him—tan and lanky with short blond hair, dressed in a button-down shirt, untucked, skinny chinos and Sperrys. As I watched them from my bedroom, I couldn't help the thought that they were doomed. And then, taking her hand, he pulled her to a stop and smiled down at her like she was everything in the world that made him happy. As he framed her face with careful hands and kissed her, she melted into him.

Emily confessed that they're applying to the same colleges, mostly her choice. Derek's aspirations include earning an English degree while writing a novel—and he says any decent academic environment will do. I've never seen her like this. My best friend, independent and uncompromising our entire lives, has fallen in love. *Hard.*

I'm still stuck on living in New York, though I no longer feel the need to escape my home state. Once the prospect of moving there lodged itself in my mind, everything else seemed inferior by comparison. Dad and Emily have resigned themselves to losing me to the east coast, at least for a while.

I did some community theatre over the holidays—a starring role in a low-budget production of *It's a Wonderful Life*. Dad didn't miss a single show. The thought of leaving him next fall stings, though I've been coming and going for years. But it's good. The sting tells me I'll miss him and the way he looks at me now—like he hasn't seen me in years, like he can't get enough now that I'm here.

Chapter 44

REID

It's March, five months since we wrapped up *School Pride*. I've hung out with Tadd several times since then and Quinton twice. I haven't seen or heard from anyone else. Now, the main cast is in Austin for a couple of days to do a photo spread for *Vanity Fair*. My flight arrived late, and no one's up and about when I check into the hotel. Disoriented to be back in Austin, I fall asleep thinking of Emma. My dreams are vivid and unsettling, receding to the edges of my consciousness when I wake, yielding no clear details and leaving me anything but rested. Coffee and breakfast from room service delays the prospect of seeing any of them until the concierge calls to let me know the limo has arrived.

When I exit my room and turn the corner, she's standing in front of the elevator. "Emma," I say softly, not wanting to startle her. Her shoulders tense slightly, but she turns with a pleasant, if artificial, expression.

"Hi, Reid."

"You're looking good," I say, and she does.

"Thanks. You, too."

The elevator doors part and we enter and stand a foot apart, staring at the descending numbers. Memories swirl around us, sharp and silent—how I would back her against a wall as soon as the elevator doors shut behind us, pinning her against the cold stainless steel panel while my hands skimmed her waist and my mouth moved over hers until neither of us could think straight. I wonder if she's forgotten.

"Okay, Emma, lie back with your head in Reid's lap. That's good. Reid, one hand on her stomach." The *VF* photographer is Virgil, one of those artists so well-known that a surname is unnecessary. He's known for sensual, romantic photo spreads. Arranging Emma's hair to cascade over my knee and pool on the blanket they've spread over the rough boards of the dock, he says, "Emma, at me. Reid, at her… longing, desire on your face." No problem there.

Snap, snap, snap.

The next series has me perched on a stool while she sits on my lap, facing me, her legs locked around my hips. She's making a concerted effort to keep her eyes averted—quite a feat in this position. "These are waist-up shots, but I need you guys close," Virgil says. "Emma, arch into him." *Snap, snap, snap*. "Good, now lean your head back, chin up." *Snap, snap*.

"Back farther, eyes closed." I press my mouth against her throat, and Virgil is euphoric. "Stunning." *Snap, snap*. He crooks her arm, moving her hand to the back of my head, holding me in place over her heart, the beats echoing through me as we stare into the camera and Virgil snaps like there isn't enough film in the world to capture this moment.

We stand back to back, our hands joined at our sides, while I look out over the lake, spotlighting what's been termed my "archetypal male profile." Resting her head between my shoulder blades, Emma stares into the camera as Virgil snaps off shots. "Emma, gaze over my shoulder. Imagine you're far away, somewhere lovely and perfect..."

Off to the right, the others are gathered, talking and watching distractedly, waiting their turns. Quinton and Tadd stand behind the others, laughing. The girls sit in a semi-circle, Jenna reading, the others talking. Graham reclines just apart from them, legs out in front, ankles crossed, leaning back on his elbows, watching Emma. His mouth turns up on one side and I know she's returning his gaze. His chin tips back, *hey*, and Virgil murmurs, "Perfect," firing off rapid snaps.

The group shots are full of clowning around, some of which will make it into the spread, most of which won't. Quinton, Tadd, Graham and I, holding Emma horizontally across our middles like a burlesque singer. A hands and knees pyramid, guys on bottom, then Brooke, MiShaun and Meredith, with Jenna and Emma on top. Tadd groans and pretends to crumple under the weight as tiny Jenna climbs atop Brooke and Meredith, and everyone screams and laughs as the whole thing nearly crashes to the mats covered in blankets and sand.

Tomorrow will be divided up, girls in the morning, guys in the afternoon. "No hangovers, dudes," Virgil says. "The camera isn't kind to dehydrated, red-eyed subjects." He chuckles as our eyes roll and we drag ourselves to the waiting cars.

I duck into a car with Emma, Meredith and Jenna. Touching Emma's shoulder, I draw her out of their conversation. She's as wary of me as she was in the elevator this morning. "Still going off to college in the fall? Have you chosen one yet?"

Her hands are clasped in her lap, and I maintain a small empty space between us. "I'm visiting a couple next month, making a final decision."

"Cool."

The four of us talk about upcoming projects, and Jenna grills Emma on the colleges she's chosen to visit next month and what she'll be studying. I shouldn't be surprised that they're both in New York—for theatre it makes sense—but I wonder what this has to do with Graham, and if it has everything to do with him. We arrive at the hotel and everyone decides on room service in my room, sans Meredith, who's staying in her room with Robby the Controlling Boyfriend.

"That guy is a total dick," Tadd tells Emma, using the shaker from my bar to make margaritas. "How can she *like* that?"

"No idea," she answers as he unscrews the shaker, pouring the mixture into three glasses, handing one to her, one to me.

"A friend of mine got into a *seriously* messed up relationship with a possessive guy," he continues after taking a sip. "He checked his phone messages, separated him from his friends, hacked into his computer. It was a fucking nightmare. Actually, he said *that* part was pretty good, and the rest was a nightmare."

Emma and I narrowly avoid spraying him with margarita.

"Getting everyone hammered already, are you, Tadd?" Brooke says as she joins us.

"Want one?" he asks. "They're magically delicious."

"Yes, please—one for Graham, too. He'll be here in a sec. He's on a call."

I'm looking at Emma when Brooke mentions Graham, and I can't unsee the split second of joy that crosses her face. The apprehension that follows it. After filming was over, speculation about the two of them fell off completely. According to the media, she and I managed to hook up a couple of times—rather unreasonable given the fact that we haven't been in the same *city* since filming ended.

There won't be any drinking games tonight in light of Virgil's edict against hangovers. Everyone is relaxed and nostalgic, knowing that after this one night, there will be a few high profile premieres in May and that will be it. Even if any of us work together in the future, it will never be this group again.

Graham comes in, folding his legs and settling on the floor between Brooke and Emma. “Hey, Emma,” he says.

“Hi.” She returns the smile and looks away, listening to the discussion between the others. Nothing else passes between them that I see.

“Maybe they’ll want a sequel,” MiShaun says. “Will and Lizbeth get married and settle down to a life of brooding, bookishness and boredom.”

“That’s the way to ruin the idyllic dream of Darcy and Elizabeth for all time,” Tadd agrees. “Show what it was really like once they got married.” He turns to Quinton. “You’re a gloomy twat!” he says in a falsetto voice.

“And you’re just like your mother!” Quinton barks.

As everyone leaves a couple of hours later, I take Emma’s arm, gently. “Emma, hold up a moment. I want to ask you something.” She’s guarded, but nods her assent.

Emma

“Come sit.” Reid takes my hand and leads me to the sofa.

“Um, we have to get up early—well, I have to get up early, I guess you don’t have to be there until later…” The excuses tumble through my brain disjointedly.

“It’s not that late,” he says, and I decide to just hear him out. We sit. “You looked gorgeous today.” He’s still holding my hand. “I couldn’t take my eyes off of you.”

He’s as beautiful as ever, dark blue eyes sweeping over my face, his blondish hair a bit darker, a bit longer, still perfectly disordered. I blink, his words settling around me. “Reid, what are you—? I mean, I don’t…”

“Emma, I made a mistake. A *huge* mistake. I was upset when you disappeared that night, but I should have never given you an ultimatum; it was thoughtless and juvenile. I should've waited for you to talk to me. I could have explained. You're reasonable and fair, and I'm sure you'd have listened."

My heart slams out a rhythm in my chest, pulses it through my body. "But… you *didn't* wait. You *didn't* explain. You just went off with the first girl, and then the second, third, fourth. I just stopped counting after that—"

"I was reactionary, just trying to make you jealous—"

"No, you were trying to show me how unimportant I was. And you succeeded."

This is the combat zone we sidestepped when he took up with Blossom and I just let him go. There'd been no confrontation, no breakup. My throat closes up now as I fight tears. I didn't think, at the time, that he'd actually injured me. I thought I was just pissed off at his attempts to humiliate me. An ambush of emotions takes over as I realize I sold the whole thing short. What he'd done had hurt. And apparently still did.

He wipes his thumbs under my eyes, carefully removing tears. "Emma, I'm an arrogant guy. I'm used to having things my way, every time, with every girl. You were different. That's why I can't get you out of my head." He leans up, cradling my face between his palms. "Forgive me. Please." His eyes are mesmerizing, dark blue, and I know there's more depth to him than he's allowed me to see, but it isn't enough.

"I forgive you," I say. "But I can't forget. And I can't trust you, Reid."

He takes both of my hands in his. "I could be different with you." He's so sincere that it takes everything in me to think logically. "You may be the only one who'll see through all my bullshit and help me try to be something more, something better."

I stare at our intertwined hands. "I don't want to help you try to be anything. I want someone who's *already* something more. On his own. With or without me."

He's quiet then, and I don't dare look at him yet. "*Is* there someone else?"

I think of Graham. Graham, who cannot be mine. "No, there isn't. But that's really not the point."

"Then what *is* the point?" He tips my chin up with his fingers, making me look into his eyes again.

My chin trembles, tears spilling over onto his hand. "The point is, I'm not going to settle for less than I want, less than I deserve. Brooke trusted you, and you abandoned her—and yes," I say before he can object, "maybe you were just too young to handle the situation at the time, but you never gave me a chance to find that out. You started screwing your way through the rest of the cast like my feelings didn't matter. I forgive you, because I'm past it. But that's the thing. I'm past it."

With the last bit of effort I can manage, I get up and leave his room, shaking from head to toe. He doesn't speak, doesn't follow, but I can't unclench my shoulders until I'm in my room, the door shut and bolted behind me. I flip on a light and fall onto the bed, crying and dialing.

"Emily," I say when she answers, feeling ten times better the moment I hear her voice.

Chapter 45

REID

It begins the same way it did last time, with a glass of wine during dinner. Within a week, it's a cocktail before dinner, and wine during. And then something before bed. When it moves into the daylight hours, it's all over.

Some people leap off of the wagon and some people fall. My mother simply climbs down, calmly and with the same resolve under which she's checked herself into rehab three times. The first time she tried to get help was when she'd discovered she was pregnant, but she lost the baby during that first cut-short stint of rehab. When she came home and sank into depression, numbing herself regularly because otherwise she did nothing but cry, no one blamed her—not her ten-year-old son, not her husband, not her mother, who lived with us.

My grandmother tried to get her to go back and get the help and counseling she needed to deal with her grief, but Mom wouldn't go back. Her refusals are never loud and messy. Her dissent is genius, really. She never constructs an argument or has an ugly outburst. She merely nods agreement to whatever is proposed, and then doesn't follow through.

Whether from the grief of losing her mother, or guilt of never living up her to own expectations of being the perfect daughter, Mom tried rehab for the second time a few months after Grandmother died. I returned from being on location—the movie where I met Brooke—to find her gone. Dad was happy. He thought she would kick her addiction and all would be well with the world and the Alexander family.

Clearly that was a stretch.

I don't remember when she began drinking again, just that I had already started by then. I felt better that she was, too, for some irrational reason.

Brooke and I had broken up—exploded, more like, after multiple allegations that she was cheating on me surfaced. When she told me she was pregnant, I told her, "What's it to me? Sounds like your problem." I was utterly convinced it wasn't mine. I'm not sure now, not that it matters anymore.

Mom knows I drink. Somehow, though, she managed to be stunned when I went out with John on my nineteenth birthday—a couple of weeks ago—and got so loaded that I'm not exactly sure what we did after some point. That's the first and only time I've ever actually blacked out. I woke up in agony at John's place, my hand swollen double and throbbing with no idea why.

According to him, we and some other guys pulled an SUV under a fire escape, climbed to the top of a building, screwed around (particularly horrifying considering I was drunk enough not to remember *any* of this) and then attempted to descend without falling. I failed right at the end and fell on top of the SUV, but seemed fine, John said—offering as evidence the fact that I was laughing the whole time. I'd broken my left hand. The hand surgeon had to operate to remove stray bone fragments, set it correctly, and insert a metal rod in my thumb, which is a bitch. I go in to have the rod removed in a few weeks, and then I have to go—I kid you not—to *hand therapy* twice a week for I don't know how long.

Days after that little mishap was the first time I came home to Mom with a drink in her hand. She'd even made it through the holidays this time, but she couldn't make it past my thwarted fire escape stunt. Dad had been coming home a bit earlier sometimes, making it to dinner here and there, making weekend appearances. Once the relapse occurred, those changes came to a screeching halt.

Way to be supportive, Dad. Everything back to normal, whatever the hell that is.

Emma

While Dad orders coffee drinks, I fantasize about mittens and campfires and down-filled blankets. My fingers are numb from the unexpected cold that is April in NYC, and I crave the latte as much for the digit-thawing warmth of the cup as for the caffeine the double shot of espresso promises. New York will take some getting used to after a lifetime in California; very little resembles my suburban hometown—the local dialects, the crowds, the weather. I remind myself that *different* was sort of the original idea.

As I glance around looking for an open table, I see a tiny girl wearing a man's jacket over a lime green leotard and tights with a pink tulle tutu. The jacket hangs past her knees, and her small arms are no match for the sleeve length. Protruding from the arm of the jacket as though she has no hand at all is a wooden stick with a glitter-covered star and streamers attached to the end of it. She skips around her table twice, sits down, and is up again five seconds later, skipping in the opposite direction, her short hair bouncing up and down with every step.

My eyes move to the man whose jacket she's wearing. I

blink, because the man is Graham. He tips his chin back, and the girl turns to look at me. They have the same dark eyes, same shape of mouth, but her hair is straight and strawberry blond, where his is wavy and dark, though I remember that in the sun it would be reddish. I remember, too, that Graham has two older sisters. This must be a niece.

I haven't seen him since last month, but I've thought about him often since then. I smile, thinking *what are the odds*? I feel an uncharacteristic shyness with him, this guy I ran with nearly every morning while I was in Austin, shared aspects of my life that only Emily had been privy to before him. And then it was over.

I'm struck then by the fact that I still don't know why he ever kissed me, or why he pulled away from me after. I assume he withdrew because of a relationship with Brooke, because of my very public kiss with Reid. Yet we became friends, apart from the two of them. Apart from that kiss in my room.

"Here's your latte," Dad says. He's balancing a slice of cheesecake on top of his coffee, taking advantage of being several thousand miles from Chloe's latest nutritional regimen. Spying the vacant table next to Graham, he makes a beeline for it.

"Hey," Graham says when we sit.

"Hi. Dad, you remember Graham Douglas?" Graham's niece stops circling the table and presses her face into his side.

"Mr. Pierce," Graham says, reaching to shake Dad's hand while circling his opposite arm around the girl, who is now appraising me openly.

"Graham, of course." Dad stirs sugar into his coffee. *Sugar*. Chloe would have a cow. "According to Emma, you were the most talented actor in the *School Pride* cast. And she doesn't impress easily."

"That's interesting," Graham says with a smile. "*I* thought *she* was the most talented." I could track the flush that spreads across my face.

Dad smiles at the girl as she spins the wand streamers in a blur of color. "And who do we have here?"

"This is Cara."

My father leans his elbows on his knees. "Are you a princess, Cara?"

"I'm a fairy godmother. See?" She shucks off Graham's jacket to reveal flattened wings. "Oh, no! My wings are effed up!" People at nearby tables turn and I bite my lip.

"Um, that's the closest to not cursing my sister can seem to get in front of her." Graham shrugs, his lips twitching. "Less shocking coming out of a four-year-old than the alternative."

"Would you like me to fix them?" I ask, and she stares at me for a long moment, contemplating how trustworthy I appear to be, I think, before scooting closer and turning around. I pull the translucent wings away from her tiny shoulder blades, reshaping the wire supports and admiring the silver glittered feathering. "Your wings are beautiful."

She nods. "They're magic."

I smile at her. "Is that so?"

"Yes!" She grabs her wand from the table. "Close your eyes." I obey. "Now make a wish." Into the emptiness of my mind, which hasn't made a genuine wish in a long time, comes one unambiguous thought. *I want to see Graham again. Alone.*

She touches the wand to my forehead; the ribbons tickle my nose. "Okay. Your wish is granted."

I open my eyes, hear her asking Dad if he wants a wish, too. Graham watches me. "Whatever it was, don't doubt her. Cara's wish-granting abilities are legendary."

I smile into my cup, swirling the remnants of foam and espresso.

A minute later, Cara peers into my face, her small hands on my knees. "What did you wish?" She smells like chocolate, the evidence of which rims her upper lip.

"I thought I wasn't supposed to tell."

She considers this for a moment. "Then how can I make it come true?"

I can't help but be struck by her logic. "You're a very astute fairy godmother, Cara."

"Yes, I am." She goes on a figure-eight trek around the two tables, stopping in front of me again. She chews her lower lip. "What's asoot?"

"Astute. It means you're very smart."

"Yes, I am," she says again, without a hint of smugness. And then she turns to Graham with a random question, prefaced by a not-so-random title. "Daddy, do I have to like broccoli?"

Graham gazes at me over her head, absorbing my reaction, and there is nothing I can do to conceal my astonishment. I couldn't be more wide-eyed and dumbfounded.

His eyes fall to her. "You don't *have* to like broccoli. There's lots of other green stuff to eat. But maybe you'll like it someday."

She wrinkles her nose. "I don't think so."

"Graham must be older than he looks, to have a daughter that age," Dad says once we're in the taxi. Though I know Graham's exact age, I can't respond. I'm still so in shock that I can barely focus. Graham never hinted at this. He returned home for that unspecified family emergency during filming, but that doesn't exactly say, *I've got a kid*, does it?

"Why don't I cancel that dinner with Ted." He takes my hand. "We'll go do something together. We're in New York! You shouldn't be sitting alone in a hotel room; that's just crazy."

I shake my head. "I'm going to be living here in a few months. I should start getting used to the idea of staying in occasionally, or I'll go bankrupt in a year. You never get to see Ted. Go out. I've got this alone-in-a-hotel-room stuff down."

He sighs, looking out the window. "Cara reminds me of you at that age. Full of energy and ready to question everything, classify everything, using magic to make the world perfect. Now look at you—in this city, visiting college campuses, redefining yourself. I'm proud of you, Emma."

I lean my head on his shoulder, much as Cara did to Graham. "Thanks, Dad."

Forgiving him is easier now, so close to separation. We've found each other again, and feeling bitter won't bring back the years we've wasted. The years I hadn't verbalized my pain to him. The years he hadn't seen it in my eyes. What's done is done, and all that matters is where we go from here.

Chapter 46

REID

The premiere of *School Pride* is next month, preceded by the inevitable red carpet events, talk show appearances and interviews. I've seen enough of the final product to know it's good. In the date night genre, in the hopeless romantics genre, this movie will be hot.

It's over with Emma. I *know* this, but my brain hasn't completely accepted the fact. I keep running through everything I did wrong, looking for a way to repair the total clusterfuck of decisions I made that night. I shouldn't have let her out of my sight. I shouldn't have baited Brooke like that. And I sure as shit shouldn't have taken that girl back to the hotel.

Is it possible that I was in love with Emma? I don't know. Am I even capable of that emotion? I don't know that, either.

What I told her last month wasn't just a line to get her into bed. I'd be lying if I said the companionship was more urgent than the attraction between us, but I enjoyed the afternoons she spent in my room after the surgery, when we hung out and watched movies or I played video games while she studied. I liked the comfort of just having her near. We didn't get a chance to discover what could have been, because in the end I treated her like every girl I've ever come across.

Most girls who want me want the Bad Boy. That persona isn't just an act, it's who I am. There was never any possibility of me being anyone other than who I've become, and maybe that's what Emma finally saw.

She said she wants someone who's already something better. Something better than me, obviously. She doesn't want to have to read between the lines to see who he is, or how he feels about her. As much as I wanted to be that guy, I don't have it in me. I am who I am.

Emma

Graham: I'd like to talk to you. Alone. If you're willing to talk to me. Can i come to your hotel, or can we meet somewhere?
Me: Whcn?
Graham: Now, if you want. Later tonight. Tomorrow.
Me: Now is good. Dad is out with a friend. I was going to order room service and watch movies.
Graham: Where are you?
Me: Soho grand
Graham: Be there in thirty minutes

"Hey," Graham says, for the second time today.

"Hi." As I pull the door open, it occurs to me that I'm getting the wish Cara granted me.

He walks into the room as the door shuts with a snap and we pause feet apart. An old Switchfoot video plays in the background, the refrain flowing through the room like a private soundtrack. "You and your music videos," he smiles, running his fingers over the information folders from college visits that we've left on top of the dresser. "Have you decided on a school?"

"I think so. It's between those two."

He nods. "Both have great programs. I guess you'll be moving to New York?"

"Yes. We'll go over everything when we get home. Make an informed decision." He nods again, but I know he didn't come to talk about my college plans, so I don't elaborate.

"So… I thought you might want an explanation. I'm not sure where to begin."

We're both quiet then. Everything about Graham, everything I thought I knew, all of it has tilted. My vision of him, my feelings for him, all still the same and yet nothing the same. His hands are balled into loose fists at his sides.

"You have a daughter." I have no right to the accusation in my voice. The last thing I want to do is make him feel interrogated, but he isn't talking, and the questions are crowding into my skull, knocking around, every one of them wanting an answer *right now*. "I thought we were friends… so why didn't you tell me?"

He spreads his hands, "I don't… tell people. Outside of my family, only Brooke knows, and a handful of friends from way back."

"Were you… are you… *married*?" The concept is so foreign that the word comes out like something distasteful.

"No. I'm not, I wasn't. Cara's mother… she's never been in the picture. Not since Cara was born."

I'm trying to process this. Failing. It's like the puzzle box has the wrong illustration on the front, and as the pieces fit together, the image generated is something completely different than what I was expecting. "How did you… end up with her?"

He walks across the small room and faces the window, silent. I give him time to gather his thoughts. Finally, he turns with his hands in his pockets. "My relationship with Cara's mother was over by the time she knew she was pregnant. She was considering her options, but she didn't want to keep her. And I just… I *wanted* her. The possibility of claiming her, of raising her, it gave me a purpose. I *had* to do it."

He takes a deep breath, runs a hand through his hair, staring at the carpet. "I talked to my family. I was sixteen at the time, so there was no going it alone." When he raises his eyes, they're ablaze with resolve, and it's easy to picture the face his family had seen then. "If they hadn't been supportive, I don't know what would have happened. But I'd made my decision, and they could see there was no changing it."

"So they agreed to help you?" He nods. "And then?"

"And then I had to convince my *ex*-girlfriend to carry her to term, and give her to me."

I sit down on the bed, in a semi-state of shock. "Wow. I don't know what to say."

He sits next to me. "Yeah. That's the usual response." His hands grasp each other and he stares at them. "The family emergency, when I disappeared during filming? Cara had an asthma attack, and was hospitalized. I've never been that scared."

He'd disappeared hours, maybe minutes, after he kissed me on my bed. He could have told me then, but he didn't trust me enough. "Wow, this is just… so awesome." I'm grasping for words, wincing at my falsely joyful voice, but it's like if I stop talking I might hyperventilate. "I mean, you're, you know, a father. Somebody calls you *daddy*. And that's just so…"

"Awesome?" He's disappointed, or hurt, but at the same time, unsurprised. He's used to this reaction. "Anyway, now you know everything." He stands up. "Listen, I've got to, um, do a couple of errands. We can talk later, okay?" I don't hear the likelihood of a later in his voice.

"Okay." I follow him to the door, realizing that he just shared this really *intimate* thing with me, and I freaked out. He's standing in my room, my wish in solid form. "Graham,"

I say gently. He turns, and I lay my hands on his chest, feel his heart hammering the same accelerated rhythm as my own. His dark eyes are sad, staring down at me.

My hand shaking, I reach up and push my fingers through the hair at his temple, pulling his head down to me. I kiss him, softly, carefully, and for a moment, he doesn't react at all, and I'm sure that I've read everything wrong… And then his mouth crushes into mine as his arms go all the way around me, pulling me to my toes.

I thought I'd idealized kissing him, but his lips against mine now make that first kiss a distant echo. His hands skim up my sides and lace through my hair, turning me until my back is pressed against the wall and his body is pressing into mine, his heartbeat pounding under my hand. Pulling him against me, my arms draw him closer still, fingers kneading the hard muscles of his back, up and over his shoulders, down his arms and back again. When we break for air we're gasping, our chests rising and falling in unison as he leans into me and I arch into him, every physical indicator declaring *I want you, I want you, I want you.*

When he pushes away, I'm confused. When I start to follow, blinking, he holds up a hand to stop me. "Emma, I can't. This isn't—I can't."

He turns and yanks the door open. Three seconds and he's gone. Lying back on the bed, I review every detail of what just happened, over and over, but it doesn't get any clearer. I almost call Emily, but don't. It's a rare night that she and Derek both have off, and I don't want to interrupt them with my problems. This is a riddle I need to figure out by myself. When Dad comes back later, clicking the television off and whispering my name as he pulls the comforter over me, I pretend to be asleep.

My puzzle is missing pieces. Not as many as it was missing earlier today, before we ran into Graham and Cara. But I know about her now; she's one less secret between us. What made him pull away? There must be someone else.

Brooke? They were obviously still close last month. By his earlier admission, she's one of the few people who know about Cara. She could be the reason he withdrew after he kissed me in Austin, and again tonight.

The light-blocking draperies cloak the room in darkness, but I've been half-reclining against the cushioned headboard and wide awake for two hours. My adjusted eyes distinguish the outlines of each piece of furniture, the mirror across the room, the shape of my shadowy reflection in it. I raise my hand and wave, and the ghostly mirror image waves back.

The drapes can't block the sounds of the city below. Unlike my periodic nights of insomnia in Sacramento, I'm not awake and *alone* here, in the city that never sleeps; I'm one of millions, like I already belong.

Dad snores softly in the other bed. I click the button on the side of my phone, the screen lighting up. 2:18 a.m. We're flying home in ten hours. I pull up Graham's number, click *send message*. The cursor blinks, waiting for me to type the message, and I sit there in the glow of the tiny screen. After thirty seconds, the display turns off. What do you say when the feelings don't fit into words? Finally, I type the message and hit send:

Me: I'm leaving today. I want to see you. I'll be in the lounge downstairs at 6 am.

There's no answer, and I feel discouraged and a little bit pathetic as the minutes tick by. As my eyes grow heavy, my grip on the phone loosens and I snuggle down under the covers, my phone under my pillow, the alarm set to 5:30 a.m.

Unsurprisingly, there are few people in the lounge this early on a Saturday. I request a booth in the back and wait, somehow sure he'll show, despite the fact that he never answered my text. Minutes later, he arrives, his hair falling over his forehead, still damp from a shower, a days' growth on his face and wearing jeans, boots I might see on a guy working the construction site down the street, and a faded t-shirt featuring another band I recognize from Emily raving about them.

He slides in across from me, his hands clenched on the table top. His gaze is direct, unlike yesterday—when his eyes seemed to land anywhere rather than connect with mine.

A waitress steps up when he sits, and he orders coffee. At my nod he says, "Two, please." He sighs, fingers splayed on the table. "Look. I'm sorry I never told you about Cara. I thought about telling you a hundred times, and the longer I didn't, the harder it got to bring it up. I meant what I said about not really telling people about her. I've led two lives for so long that it's habit, and until now I've escaped combining them."

The waitress arrives with the coffee and he falls silent until she moves away.

"I'm sorry for freaking out on you like that last night…" he says.

"I freaked out first." I stir a packet of sugar into my coffee as he pours cream into his.

"You had reason, I think." He grimaces into his coffee cup. "Cara is the most important thing in my life, a defining part of me. It was unfair of me, not telling you. When I took on the father gig, I didn't consider how it would affect future relationships. For years now, I've kept my family on one side, and… almost everyone else on the other."

"That sounds hard."

"Yeah…" He breathes out a sigh, rolling my empty sugar packet into a ball. "It is."

I breathe in, breathe out, clenching and unclenching my hands under the table. "Graham. I'll be living here in four months. Maybe we can meet up for a run now and then. Or take Cara to the park, or whatever. I could babysit, if, you know, your family's busy and you want to go out. I'd love to get to know her. Because… you mean a lot to me. And I've missed you." Staring at the table top, I run my fingers over tiny grooves in the glossy surface. "I miss our friendship."

"So you want to be friends?" he asks, and I look up at him. His hands are still, his expression serious. "Friends, and that's all?"

The kiss last night. "There's no reason we can't be friends. I was out of line last night. I understand how you feel about Brooke—"

"Wait. What about Brooke?" he interrupts.

I swallow, my throat tight. "Um. Your relationship with her."

"My relationship with—? Emma, Brooke is my friend. I know everything that happened with her... and *him*. She knows about Cara. We bonded years ago over parts of our lives that no one else we knew could relate to. She's a close friend. But a friend is all she's ever *been*, and all she'll ever *be*."

"So you aren't in love?"

He looks at me for a long moment. "I didn't say that. I said I don't love Brooke."

"Okay..." There must be someone here in NYC. Someone else he's never told me about. This is like being bitten by dozens of mosquitoes. Like a scratchy tag on the inside back of a shirt. Like bamboo shoots pushed under your fingernails.

Not that I know about that last one.

"Are you... over Reid?" he asks then. "That night at the club, you were so upset."

Reid? I close my eyes and attempt to refocus. "No. I mean, *yes*, I'm over him, but... that night, I was mostly messed up over a terrible fight I'd had with Emily a week or so before." I open my eyes, stare into his. Talking to him is so easy, even now. "We've been best friends since we were five, but we've never said things to each other like that. We weren't speaking, and after everything happened with Brooke and Reid, I needed her. I wanted to call her, and I couldn't. I was afraid I'd screwed up so bad that I'd lost her forever."

He considers this. "So the whole week before that—the 'allergies'?"

I knew he'd seen through that ruse. He must have thought I was upset over Reid. "Yeah. That was about Emily, too."

He scoots out of his booth and into mine, effectively blocking the two of us from view. His hand falls warm on my arm, and it's not fair that he has no idea what he's doing to me. His dark eyes draw me in. Friendship with Graham is not going to work. Not when he's this close.

I fight to keep my voice light and level. "The girl you love—is she someone I know?"

His expression is full of wonder. "Emma, you're the most imperceptive person ever, right behind *me*. Maybe both of us need straightforward facts. No ambiguity. Everything clear."

I nod. "Clear is good."

He traces one finger down the side of my face. "How's this for clear," his voice is low and hollow as his fingertips brush over my lips. "I haven't wanted anyone but you since the night we met. And as much as I value our friendship… being friends with you is *not* what I have in mind." Cupping my chin in his hand, he kisses me softly, the tip of his tongue skimming my lips, and when I open and kiss him back, it turns deep and possessive and full of promise and I forget where we are and I feel it to my toes and back.

"Huh," I say, my thoughts swirling as he smiles and rests his forehead against mine, staring into my eyes like he's trying to read what I'm thinking right through them.

"You know, I think I'd prefer you keep that particular habit after all," he says, before he kisses me again.

ACKNOWLEDGEMENTS

Heartfelt thanks to my critique partners Jody Sparks and Carrie Sullivan. Without your honesty, encouragement and line-item vetoes, these characters might have languished in my head forever. You guys are the best.

To my beta-readers—your optimism kept me writing and revising instead of pulling my hair out, and trust me, nobody wants that: A ginormous, extra-special thank you to Ami Keller for detailed, enthusiastic feedback and letting me know if the characters were staying on track or wandering off on their own. Thank you to Robin Deeslie and Hannah Webber for multiple read-throughs and superior discovery of grammatical goofs, to Kim Hart and Lori Norris for unwavering belief in me, and to MiShaun Jackson, Alyssa Crenshaw, Joy Graham, Zachary Webber and Keith Webber for providing plot feedback and character insights.

Thank you Paul, for putting up with my personality craziness, my sleep patterns, my ability to find and retain cats.

Finally, thanks Mom and Dad for loving the daughter you produced, even when you don't understand why I curse so much.

ABOUT THE AUTHOR

Reading was one of my first and earliest loves, and writing soon followed. My first book was about a lost bear, but my lack of ability as an illustrator convinced me to abandon that effort and concentrate on passing 3rd grade. I wrote sad romantic poetry in high school and penned my first half-novel when I was 19, for which I did lots of research on Vikings (the marauders, not the football team), and which was accidentally destroyed when I stuffed it into the shredder at work.

Addictions: coffee and Cherry Garcia frozen yogurt. Also carrots, but not with coffee or frozen yogurt, because that would be disgusting. I also love shopping for earrings, because they always fit - even if I occasionally "forget" to work out. I'm a hopeful romantic who adores novels with happy endings, because there are enough sad endings in real life.

facebook.com/TammaraWebberAuthor
TammaraWebber.blogspot.com
twitter.com/tammarawebber

Made in the USA
Lexington, KY
23 September 2012